Carmen Stefanescu

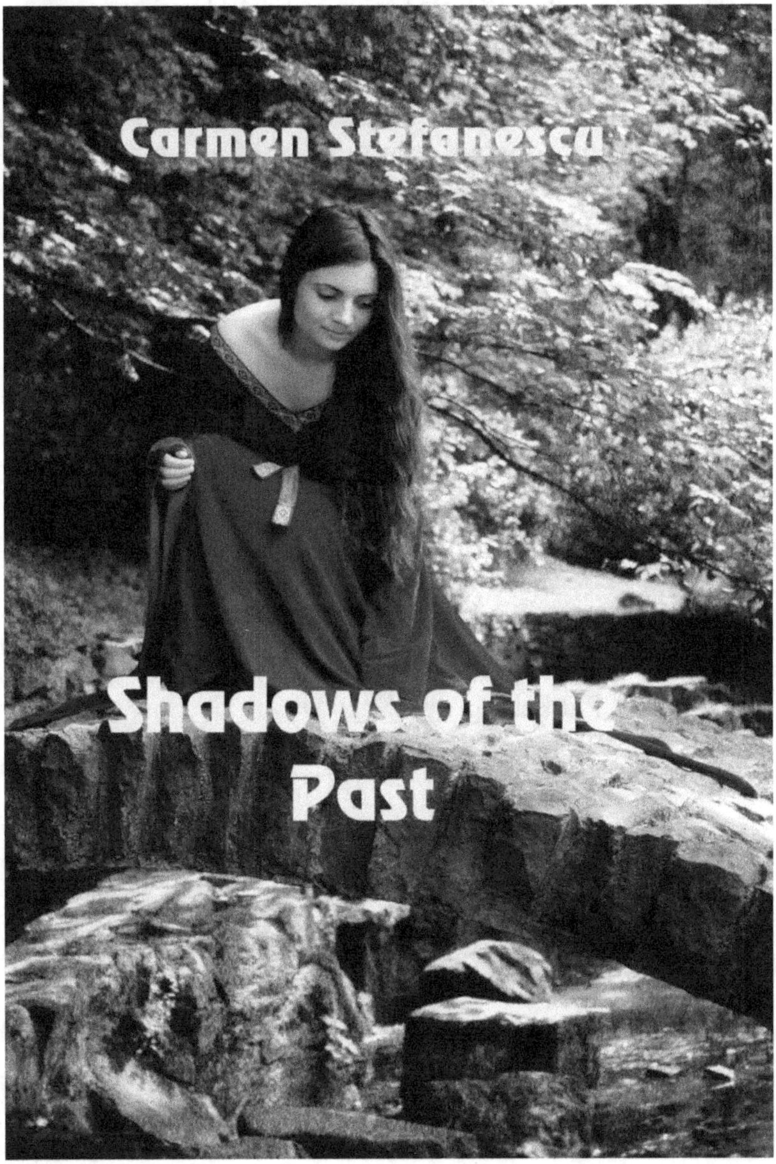

Shadows of the Past

Shadows of the Past

By

Carmen Stefanescu

In the quiet solitude of a small, remote convent,
Only prayers seem alive
On the lips of holy sisters.
Candles flicker in their hands
Like lost souls in search of light,
And the yellowish, faint glimmer
Makes a halo round their whispers.
(Eternity)

Prologue

England, October 1480

The peal of the church bells from the abbey tower startled Genevieve. The sound added to her mounting anxiety.

The massive abbey loomed over the stone paved path. All the nuns were at evening mass. With a bit of luck, her disappearance would go unnoticed for a few more hours. The Abbess would assume she was cleaning the toilets as ordered.

Fear skittered through Genevieve when she turned away from the abbey towards the path leading to town. Nothing stirred. She hesitated. Evil emanated from the forest surrounding the abbey. With a shiver, she leaned against the solid oak gates that flanked the abbey's main path. They had hidden her from detection for the past couple of hours, but how much longer would she be safe?

The mountain shadows grew thicker and closer.She moved her weight from one leg to the other. They ached from so much standing, but she lacked the strength to return to the gardener's cottage and wait for Andrew's arrival as planned. Genevieve closed her tired eyes. The image of old Ryan, slumped dead in his chair in his cubicle, caught life in her mind and made her whole body ripple with fear.

She'd rather wait for Andrew here, outside.

Had he forgotten his promise? What if something terrible befell him during the last three days, or he had changed his mind? Why should he risk all for an ordinary nun?

Had his folks talked him into giving her up, made him see reason? Helping her out of her predicament meant a huge risk for him losing his family, his friends and his position among his peers. His words echoed in her mind. "I will risk everything for you, even life, if necessary."

A gust of wind swirled the dust on the path and dried the beads of sweat covering her temples. She shivered and pressed her cool hands to her cheeks. Had she misunderstood Andrew? No. She remembered vividly what he'd told her when they talked in Ryan's cottage. Three days. The evening of the third day, she should wait at Ryan's.

Her gaze strayed again to the impassive building of the abbey, her home for such a long time. She blamed the increasing wind for the sudden trail of dampness on her face, for the unmistakable tears blurring her vision. She blinked several times to clear her view. This was no time for tears.

Genevieve's brow wrinkled, and her breath caught in her throat. Sister Francesca and Sister Benedicta smiled and waved at her from the abbey's entrance.

She shook her head and closed her eyes. Impossible. Both were dead. Genevieve wiped her tears and gazed at the abbey again. The image of the two Sisters, so dear to her, faded out.

Genevieve dared another peek along the path from the town.

Not a sound. Not a shadow.

Hopefully, Andrew hadn't decided to follow the direct route through the forest. Danger lurked there. He should know all the dark legends people told about the cursed forest.

"Dear God, protect Andrew from the evil forest," she prayed. Andrew's face came to her as she'd last seen it three days before.

His kind loving eyes. His soft encouraging words. His tender touch.

She recalled the turmoil of emotions she'd experienced when she first met Andrew. Everything made sense now, in the light of the latest events. The warm waves coming from him and engulfing her, searing her body and soul, and the anxiety following those waves. It had been love at first sight. A feeling neither of them wanted to admit to until recently.

Love. Love and sin.

The monotonous muffled sound of hoof beats came up the path. Her gaze snapped to the dusty road. Nightfall descended with shadows, and she trembled with apprehension. What if the rider wasn't Andrew but someone summoned by the Abbess to dispose of Ryan's lifeless body and grab her, too?

An eerie sensation of danger whispered in her ears, invaded her, and sent shivers down her spine. She should find shelter behind the bush of musk rose, and later, if everything proved safe, start down the path to town. She might meet Andrew along the road. If not...

She could no longer remain here. Once mass was over, any of the other nuns might discover her and bring the information to the hateful Abbess.

An overwhelming sense of relief washed over Genevieve when she saw that Andrew was the approaching rider. He came to the abbey riding his black mare and holding the reins of another horse. His eyebrows peaked with surprise. He inclined his head to his shoulder. The abbey's wide open gates, with nobody in sight, must have surprised him.

Genevieve understood his amazement. She'd told him three days ago about the Abbess' order to Ryan. Sister Clementa had asked the old gardener to keep the gates locked, even during the day.

Ryan said Clementa feared that one of the few nuns who disagreed with her behavior might leave the abbey unnoticed, at night. The Abbess didn't want any of them to take denouncing messages to the town's Archbishop.

No sooner had Andrew swung off his horse and tied the reins of both horses to a tree than Genevieve, managing to break out of her petrified state, hurried from behind the gates.

A warm smile brightened his face upon seeing her. His smile melted away. Something about her expression must have warned him all wasn't well. His gaze, worried and questioning, lingered on her face.

"What's wrong, my darling? Have you changed your mind? Why are you here by the gate? I thought I'd find you in the old man's house? Someone could have seen you and alerted the Abbess," he said.

He pulled an ivory wood anemone from his saddlebag and gave it to Genevieve. "I picked this along the way. It looks like you: pretty and delicate."

She heaved a sigh and accepted the flower. "Oh, Andrew, how sweet of you." She managed a smile.

"Come, we should leave at once," she said and glanced nervously over her shoulder. "Something terrible happened after you left for town. I think the Abbess found out about us. Our meeting in Uncle Ryan's cabin is no longer a secret. We have been overheard. For all I know someone spies on us even as we speak. I think the Abbess, or one of her 'friends,' is hovering somewhere nearby and listening to every word."

Andrew pulled her into his arms and tightened her in his embrace. "Calm down, please. Tell me what's wrong."

"No, please, let's leave. There's danger all around us. I know what I'm saying."

"Then you can tell me what happened along the way." Andrew took hold of her hand as if trying to instill courage and confidence in her. He untied the reins of the horse he'd brought for her. "Have no fear. This is Vinnie, a tame mare. I brought her for you. She'll not throw you down, trust me." Placing a tender kiss on her forehead, he helped Genevieve up and then swung himself into the saddle of his horse. He turned his head as if to hide the worried frown across his face. "A scorned woman is worse than an unleashed hurricane," he said under his breath. Then he addressed Genevieve, "We'll follow the most direct route through the forest."

Genevieve flinched.

The forest. The very cursed forest. The main reason for the tragedy in her family.

He nodded, saying, "Don't worry. We're together. Have faith, my love." He led the way into the forest.

Genevieve wrapped the dark mantle covering her shoulders more tightly around her and swallowed her fears as they began the cautious ride through the silent forest, through the silent night, enveloped by their own silent guilt.

Once St. Mary's Abbey was out of sight, Andrew turned in the saddle to Genevieve.

"I'm sorry I didn't bid farewell to good old Ryan. He'll understand, I'm sure."

Genevieve bent her head and in a trembling voice replied, "Ryan's dead. That same evening, after your departure," she said, "the Abbess summoned Sister Francesca to her room. Later, Francesca told me our Mother Superior asked her if she had complaints about her life at the abbey, and if she thought something should be done to improve the living conditions. She also asked Francesca a lot of questions about me."

Genevieve frowned and spoke in a wondering tone. "Whether any relatives of mine still lived, or if she knew of a place I might stay in case of unexpected circumstances."

Andrew raised his eyebrows. "Quite odd."

"Poor Francesca thought it odd, too," Genevieve continued. "Baffled by Sister Clementa's unusual interest in an ordinary nun's opinion, she pretended she was satisfied with her life here. She didn't dare express her real feelings. She admitted she didn't have any idea about my family. The Abbess then offered her a cup of wine and insisted Francesca should drink it all as a sign of friendship towards her."

"Did she drink it?" Andrew asked in a voice tinged by worry.

"She couldn't avoid drinking the wine in the end. Though she remembered Sister Letitia's death after a similar invitation, Francesca had to obey. Half an hour later, Francesca fell ill and called me to her room to tell me what happened. I wish there was something I could have done to save her."

Genevieve shivered. In a small voice, she went on, "The Abbess hated her for being my friend. Francesca passed away in my arms. In the morning, the evil woman told everyone the plague had caused Francesca's unexpected death, and nobody was allowed to enter her room. Two men came and buried Francesca's body, like a sack of rotten potatoes. No stone placed above, no prayer said. I don't know if the other nuns believed the Abbess' story. I don't doubt for a second my dear friend died because of some poison the Abbess gave her." She stifled another sigh before continuing.

"All these three long days, wherever I came across the horrible woman, a grin of satisfaction sat on her face and the ice cold waves coming from her hit me." A violent shudder shook Genevieve. No tears shadowed her vision.

"There's something else Francesca told me before dying," she continued, her words strained. She raised her shaking hand to her brow. "Francesca said she saw the three books -- The Gospel, The Leech Book and The Bestiary, the ones the Abbess took from me -- on a shelf in her room. She didn't destroy them as she'd threatened. She kept them for herself. And Francesca insisted she didn't have any doubt that Sister Clementa dealt with black magic."

"Black magic? The Abbess? Here under the monastery's roof? Even she couldn't dare such blasphemous behavior."

"Francesca also said there was a strange statuette on the table: a repulsive three-headed woman with serpents coiled round their necks. The Abbess hurried to hide it when she entered. Francesca added that an odd shiver passed over her at the sight of the strange object."

"I'm not sure what she saw," Andrew said. "It might have been a statuette of the Gorgons. Three hideous, winged demons with serpentine locks of hair and wide mouths showing powerful tusks of swine, named Medusa, Sthenno and Euryale." Andrew frowned. "In Greek mythology, Sthenno and Medusa are vicious female monsters. It doesn't sound good to me. Some say that the Gorgons' presence heralds misfortune and death."

Genevieve pressed her hand to her mouth. She shook her head and went on, "Earlier this evening, when I couldn't find Ryan in the garden, I went to his cottage. I intended to tell him about Francesca's pagan burial and wait there for you. I knocked at the door and, since I didn't get any answer, I entered and found him. I thought at first, seeing him heaped in his chair with his eyes closed, that he was sleeping. Touching him, I realized he was cold. Dead, I mean. Poisoned too."

"Poisoned? Dear God! Are you sure?"

"Yes. I learned about such things, poisons and their cures, from old Bertha and from the Leech Book that I inherited from her. The color of the foam on both Francesca's and Ryan's lips left no doubt. I couldn't find the gate key on the key ring Ryan kept in the cabin. I found it among his spares. If he hadn't showed me where he kept them, I couldn't have opened the gates and left the abbey."

"Poor old man. I liked his honesty and valued his knowledge. Before I left the abbey, I promised I would take him to my manor to be my gardener. Save him from this evil woman's claws, too. He was so glad at hearing it." Andrew shook his head. "I didn't want to believe all the rumors about the Abbess. Now, after all you're telling me, I think the woman may be a dangerous witch and murderess, on top of all her odd behavior."

Genevieve's hand fluttered to her throat. Large tears she couldn't suppress anymore gathered in her eyes.

"I'm the only one to blame for Francesca's and Ryan's deaths. If I hadn't talked to you, if I hadn't been Francesca's friend, they'd both be alive. It's God's punishment I must pay for the sin of falling in love with you." Genevieve bowed her head under the burden of her grief.

"Don't blame yourself, my love. She'll burn in her own hell, sooner or later. It tears my heart to pieces to see you tormenting yourself."

A thick fog covered the whole mountain in gray cool folds, making the path between the old trees almost invisible. On the other hand, clothed in the grey mist, they were less visible to the possible followers.

The hair on Genevieve's arms pricked when the distant barking of dogs, sounding more like howling, came through the forest. To her knowledge, no animals inhabited the old forest. Except, perhaps, the legendary heralds of evil, the ghost dogs. The howls rose again in the deepening dusk, and sent needles of ice along Genevieve's spine.

Andrew rubbed one hand across his forehead as if to brush away some unexplained fear troubling him.

What was he more afraid of: the dark, eerie forest with its bloodied past and lurking ghosts, or the two-legged beings that could become wilder and crueler than the wildest beast? She muffled a moan of grief.

Andrew turned in the saddle and looked at her. "Don't cry, please. I'll make sure that nothing bad will ever happen to you. I'll do my best and help you forget your troubled life. I promise."

"Yes," she said in a voice full of agony and bowed her head. Despite the darkness and mist, she feared he could see the silent tears sliding down her cheeks. "Yes, I believe you."

Andrew brought his mare to a sudden stop. Genevieve's horse almost collided with his. They were by the mossy banks of the stream. He reached across and touched her wet face. "Have faith, my love. I'll always love you and stand by you. These three days, I thought only about you and your future. Our future. Your face didn't leave my mind for one single moment. Nothing in the world matters to me more than you."

"I know, Andrew, I know. I feel the same."

"And... I intended to tell you something after reaching my mother's manor. I don't think I can postpone it until then." He caught Genevieve's hand and met her gaze. "Dear Genevieve, please, would you do me the greatest honor of agreeing to become my wife? I want to spend the rest of my life making you happy. I'll help you forget all your troubled past. Mother will soon move to my sister's castle. She wants to be close to her little grandsons, so don't worry about having a mother-in-law on your head."

Since she didn't utter a word, Andrew went on assuring her of his most honorable intentions. "The course of our lives depends on your answer. If you agree, we'll both have to leave our clerical life. God will forgive us. God's not spiteful or vengeful, and He doesn't punish those having a pure, honest heart. He can read deep in our souls and can see we still love Him. He's kind and forgiving, and will understand our love for each other is untainted... and He will approve of it."

Caressing Genevieve's hand he continued, "I'm not rushing you. Take your time, my delicate wood anemone. I'm willing to do everything in the world for you."

Genevieve nodded. Her heart drummed in her chest with happiness at his words. Tears of elation welled in her eyes. Despite her happiness, she shivered under the nagging feeling of close danger that gripped her body in its cold claws. An irrational fear clogged her heart.

"Oh, Andrew, I love you, too, and yes, I'll gladly become your wife, but what about your family?" Her voice trailed off. She raised her hand and touched his face as if to make sure he was real. "I'm so afraid."

Andrew brushed his lips across her hand. "No need to be afraid. I'm not hurrying you, my darling. There's no trouble with my family. We'll talk later after we safely reach my house." He took off a cross that he wore round his neck and held it out to her. "Here, wear this cross. The Abbess forced it on me last week. She said she'd be offended if I refused her present. I wanted to return the cross to her, three days ago, but the circumstances made me forget all about it."

Genevieve shook her head reluctantly. Andrew insisted gently. "It doesn't matter that she gave it to me. It can't harm you. It's a cross, after all. Take it, please, to protect you, my precious wood anemone," he whispered and held out a richly bejeweled cross she recognized at once. The cross the Abbess wore around her neck all the time, until a couple of weeks ago.

The hairs on the back of her neck stood on end at the sight of the cross Andrew presented her. Genevieve shrugged. "Everything touched by that evil woman bears her demonic seal."

"Nonsense. Please, take it." He punctuated his reassurance with a soft caress on her cheek.

She took the cross from Andrew. As soon as she touched the golden chain a chill pricked the tips of her fingers. The unpleasant coldness spread through her body, making her shudder. Dark feelings passed over her in a dizzy spell. She didn't say anything and slipped the cross around her neck. She trusted him and his judgment, and in view of what he said, the piece of jewelry represented her belief and his love, not something evil.

Andrew turned his horse and headed along the narrow path in silence.

Genevieve pressed a hand to her breast to calm her humming panic. Any other woman would have been thrilled by Andrew's proposal. In her, his words triggered contradictory feelings. On the one hand, it confirmed, once again, his deep love and honest intentions for her. On the other hand her mind returned to a day, years ago, when she talked to the former Abbess, the late and regretted Sister Dominica, about joining the order and Sister Dominica's slight hesitation.

The old woman read her like an open book. Dominica foresaw that Genevieve would be easy prey to her body's desires; she wasn't made for a life of piety.

"Was my father right when he claimed all his children were seeds of evil? Am I a seed of evil, too?" she bitterly whispered to herself.

Doubt swamped her. What was the right thing to do? It was difficult to decide when she'd just tasted the bittersweet savor of love.

What if time and life together turned her and Andrew into another couple resembling her parents? 'The happily ever after,' the blissful ending of the stories Genevieve's mother used to tell her, never came true for her parents, no matter how deep their love had been at first.

They'd also married, against the will of others, because they were madly in love. Their love turned sour over the years, quenched by a life of difficulties and want, ending in the tragedy that brought her to live at the abbey.

Thinking back over her life, starting with her childhood days, Genevieve concluded she brought only misfortune to the people around her, above all, to the ones she cared about: her family and her few friends, old Bertha, sister Benedicta, Francesca and Ryan. All dead.

Andrew was the first and only man she'd ever loved. For his own good she had to reject his proposal. She must tell him she changed her mind. He'd never know the way her skin tingled under the warm touch of his hand. How her heart quickened at hearing him call her "my wood anemone." He'd never know her love for him was the most beautiful thing to have ever happened to her.

If only everything hadn't been so complicated.

No, she couldn't risk his life, too. Her presence next to him and her feelings for him might become a curse bringing him an undeserved death. God would punish him because of her. For loving her. A knot tightened in her chest. If something bad happened to Andrew it would be solely her fault.

She wouldn't let it happen. If love meant sacrifice, she must do it. For Andrew's sake, she ought to accept even the bitter sacrifice of her one and only love.

When they reached the manor house, she would find a moment to talk to Andrew's mother and tell her she decided to join another abbey. It might upset and distress Andrew. He'd recover after a while, understand and forgive her, and in the end forget her. Genevieve didn't doubt that such a piece of news might bring Andrew's mother great relief. Her son wouldn't leave his clerical life, bringing shame and dishonor on all his kin, at what he intended to do -- leave his priesthood and marry a nun.

Genevieve shook her head in deep thought. Was she the Genevieve who years ago made up her mind never to love and trust a man? The Genevieve who took vows of celibacy? The one who considered God her bridegroom? Yes, she was probably all those Genevieve's, adding to them the Genevieve who discovered love, the special feeling enlightening the spirit. Something she, no doubt, didn't deserve.

Andrew's horse neighing nervously startled Genevieve back to reality. She followed Andrew's disconcerted gaze and waited.

He narrowed his eyes as if to guess the right way to follow. They'd been riding in darkness for about an hour, and Genevieve couldn't break free from the nagging sensation they had lost their way.

The mist had cleared a bit. Dismayed. she discovered they were back at the stream, a clear sign they'd moved in a circle. It meant they'd wasted precious time. The Abbess might have already noticed her disappearance. The thought that the nuns wouldn't leave the abbey to go down to the village and ask the villagers to start a search party until morning calmed Genevieve a little.

***

Andrew dismounted his horse and helped her climb down, too. He knelt by a hollowed oak tree, that stretched its branches over the water, and washed his face in the cool waters running between the grassy banks.

Genevieve moistened her lips and brow. The whisper of threat enveloping them became almost palpable, no matter how hard she banished the thought from her mind. She sighed, a barely audible sound of distress, still loud enough for him to turn a concerned look to her. A sickening sense of inevitability gripped her heart, warning her about the menacing stillness closing in on them. It had to do with the Abbess, no doubt.

Andrew pulled her to his chest. "Do you regret you've come with me?"

Passion smothered Genevieve's doubt and guilt. "Never," she answered, aware of her body's response to his touch, and she succumbed to his embrace.

The moonlight bathed his face in silver light. Andrew lowered her head covering - the rough cloth wimple - and his fingers threaded into her curls. She swayed, enveloped by the dizzy sensation of drowning in the tumultuous ocean of his gaze. The tenderness of his touch raised in her the wish they had lived in another time and been simple, ordinary people.

She longed to feel the warmth of his lips on hers. How much she'd have liked to live the rest of her life beside him and bear his children. A dream not likely to ever come true for her. Why not let the feeling lurking in the pit of her stomach take over and consume her whole being?

Aware of the track of her thoughts, she shifted uneasily, a hot flush warmed her cheeks. Drawing in a deep breath in spite of herself, calming the gnawing unease in her mind and the thought of Sister Dominica guessing she was the dough of a sinner, Genevieve repeated, "Never."

With her eyes closed and their bodies touching she became, for the very first time, simply a woman. She melted into his embrace in spite of the invisible vicious threat breathing around them. Aware they might never be alone again, she fought hard to silence the voice of conscience berating her.

"Oh, God. Please forgive me," Andrew muttered under his breath when he bowed his head to kiss her. Their lips met in a passionate first kiss.

Chapter One

England, 1990

Anne

Anne glanced at the odd-shaped shadows lengthening over the mountain's grassy peak. The summer sun slipped behind the rugged outline. Her gaze followed the last rays still lingering on the tall pines.

The very first sight of the forest brought a deep frown to her face, an anxiety she found hard to explain. Her forehead furrowed with the intensity of her concentration. A strained, cold mood sucked into her soul. The forest ahead didn't exactly appear hostile, just as if it didn't want them to find out its well- hidden secrets.

She said nothing.

Neither did Neil, for quite a while.

A green, dense, indomitable army of proud trees stood guard at the entrance of the large forest. The branches rustled, stirred by a slight breeze, and soothed her strained nerves. Refreshed by the small breath of the mountain, she turned her gaze toward Neil.

He was busy scanning the steep mountain road ahead. His impassive face was proof of his being unaware of the gorgeous scenery unfolding in front of him. Each step took them closer to the edge of the forest.

For a second, a tender feeling of long suppressed love filled her soul. His simple presence, a glance in his direction, the sound of his voice were always enough to unnerve her. The scent of his aftershave and the proximity of his hard, masculine form made her shockingly aware of the emotional response of her own body.

The memory of Neil's urgent embraces, of their lovemaking, of the happy moments they shared not so many years ago before their separation, turned her skin hot and made her restless. His nearness and her own desire dazed her. The bitter bite of doubt replaced the memory and craving for him.

The traveling gear weighed heavy on Anne's shoulders. After walking and climbing for far too long, the suspicion they'd lost their way added to the burden of her pack. They'd met no other soul for more than two hours.

Anne glanced around at the unforgiving landscape. Treacherous, loose boulders covered the steep vales. The narrow paths between the slippery rock wall on one side and the abyss's black mouth on the other were definitely no incentive for mountain lovers or casual hikers.

She searched the rocks and trees for signs directing tourists to a chalet, or a well-worn path. No such thing existed. She narrowed her eyes and cast her gaze ahead again in the vain hope of catching a glimpse of the chalet they should have reached more than two hours ago. With a bit of luck, the weather wouldn't turn bad.

The whine of insects and her rugged breathing were the only sounds that reached her ears.

With an impatient movement, Anne pushed back a few stubborn strands of hair that escaped her braids and drifted down to her eyes. Tired, she wiped the beads of sweat from her forehead and passed the tip of her tongue over parched lips. The rich, raw smell of grass filled her nostrils and throat.

She caught Neil's look and read guilt and regret in his glance. Still, he didn't say a word. Her heart turned over.

She cleared her dry scratchy throat and taking down her backpack, bent over to ease the cramps in her neck and back. Thirsty, she drained the last drop of water from the bottle and then tossed it into her rucksack.

"Yes, let's stop for a while. I knew it. I knew it. I told you to let me carry your rucksack up the slope. You wouldn't listen." Neil's mild reproach broke into her thoughts.

Anne pretended she didn't hear him and didn't answer.

Neil pulled a small map from his zippered side pocket.

Unfolding it, he used his index finger to trace their route. His frown cut deep lines on his forehead in a gesture that confirmed her suspicion that he too had no idea where they were. Great, being lost was just what she needed after a daylong hike.

Chewing at his lower lip, Neil folded the map and took in the green wall of trees. "Well, no doubt. We're lost. Our dream evening at Alpine Chalet's history."

Anne, already lifting her rucksack onto her back, caught him turning to face her while he continued to speak. He might have sensed the need to fill the tense silence, which stretched and stretched.

"We'll have to set our tents at the edge of the woods," he said. "It's getting dark. We can't go back and I don't want to enter the forest, either. I think it's safer to stay here in the open overnight. Let's continue up the mountain tomorrow. What do you think, Hon?"

Anne swallowed against the dryness in her throat and nodded without a word.

Neil shrugged, in what to Anne looked like resignation. He returned the map to one of the many pockets of his jacket and went up the craggy slope leading to the forest.

She followed, dragging exhausted feet. Too many questions dogged her weary mind, adding to her inner tumult and discomfort. This was supposed to be a comfortable and relaxing vacation, a holiday meant to seal their reconciliation. Instead, here they were lost and confused, and her legs burned from the miles of walking and climbing.

Ten more minutes of steep climbing in silence, with the oppressive afternoon heat weighing down on her, passed slowly. Anne sighed with relief when at last they reached a flat area covered by thick, fragrant grass near a cluster of pines and oaks. With no alternative left, she helped Neil set their tents for the night.

"Well." Neil nodded approvingly, rummaging through the few packs of food Anne had brought, just in case. "Luckily you thought to add some apples. Since the lavish meal planned at Alpine Chalet is impossible now, the apples will have to do. We'll keep the chocolate and crackers for emergencies."

She didn't reply.

When they finished their frugal meal, they tidied away the remains of their unplanned picnic in the same cold silence that had accompanied them along the road.

The sunlight leaving the landscape caught her attention. What a pleasant sensation to do nothing, except sit and admire the breathtaking view of the clouds framed golden by the setting sun. This feeling eased her regret that they would have to spend their first night together, after two years apart, in a tent somewhere in the wilderness, instead of inside the safe, comfortable room they'd booked at the chalet.

Though she loved mountaineering, a passion instilled in her by her Aunt Megan, Anne hadn't done much walking for quite a while. Although her muscles screamed, Anne was saddened over the loss of her dream of a special reunion.

Darkness settled around them. Anne closed her eyes. Silence. Peace. The slight breeze brushing their faces on their arrival had died out. The trees no longer swayed. No branch or leaf rustled.

She let the calmness spread over her. Through half-open eyelids, she watched the night's wings covering the mountain in soft folds.

Then, the twinkling of the stars stopped. Everything seemed petrified. The darkness solidified in front of her eyes.

Frozen... Waiting. Eerie silence enveloped the peak. Not a good sign.

Goosebumps rippled Anne's skin, accompanied by a chill engulfing her in icy claws. Her heart began to hammer as the night filled with the thick smell of danger. She frowned. Her unusual gift of premonition nudged her. Cold needles trickled down her spine, sending a shiver through her body.

The fresh, strong scent of the pine trees, wafting from the forest, triggered a strange apprehension in her soul. An onrush of sensations unfamiliar to her followed. Dizziness and a malevolent feeling of unreality suffocated her.

Her throat turned dry, and she gasped for air. Anne stood up and walked to the edge of the cliff. She stared into the darkness of the abyss at her feet. It echoed the shadows in her heart. She turned to face the dark forest ahead of them, and her stomach contracted. Worry? Fear?

Neil's whisper filtered into her worry. "Anne."

She glanced over her shoulder to find him watching her. The note of concern in his voice was hard to miss. No doubt, he sought to mend the broken bridge between them. He probably didn't know how.

Tears welled in her eyes, blurring her vision. She couldn't explain them, or the sudden sadness seeping into her heart. This should've been a moment of happiness or, at least, contentment. She was with Neil again, and the outcome of their trip together should, very likely, bring their reconciliation. Why then did she seem detached from where she stood?

Anne shivered. Why the deep feeling of having seen this place, this forest before? And why the eerie sensation of being present here only in the body, while her mind was far away? Away from the forest. Away from the sunset.

Away from Neil, the man who'd betrayed her trust and her love.

***

"Anne, Anne, wake up. Wake up, please," the insistent voice whispered next to her ear. The touch of a hand, on her shoulder, startled Anne.

She opened her eyes, still half between sleep and reality. Her gaze stopped on a stranger, a woman, by her side.

The moon's pale face, the only light, filtered through a small gap in the tent's entrance; yet the stranger's whole body emanated a kind of soft ray, a yellowish halo making her figure and face easy to discern.

A long, dark robe, similar to those worn by nuns in monasteries centuries ago, covered her body. No traditional headdress covered the woman's red hair, which fell loosely over her shoulders in long, heavy tendrils and continued down her chest and back.

Anne stood up and studied the intruder with open curiosity. The stranger's wax pale face looked corpse-like. Anne opened her mouth to ask her who she was. She looked Anne straight in the eyes, placed her forefinger on her lips and whispered, "Hush, come. Follow me."

Anne's eyes widened.

The woman, moving away from the sleeping bag, appeared to glide above the ground.

As if hypnotized, Anne followed the illuminated silhouette heading into the forest.

Chapter Two

England, 1468

Genevieve

"See what you can do with the young'uns, Genevieve. If luck smiles on us, I'll get some washing or some other work to do at the lord's manor. Then we'll have some turnips or pig's fat to spread on the bread crust and fill our bellies."

"Yes, mum," Genevieve answered. "I'll make sure they stay put and behave. Have no worry. You know I will," she added, but her mother had already left.

Genevieve grabbed the broom and swept the barren earth floor to take her mind away from the hunger crying loudly in her stomach. Her nine-year-old brain took in the situation very well. Five sisters and brothers, all younger than her had enriched the family over the years. Victoria and Elizabeth, seven and eight years old; then came James, who was six, and the twins Emma and David, five years old. They were the only twins in their village of Glennridge. Their parents added, it meant eight mouths to be fed. Not an easy task at all.

Poverty ruled their household. All lived on the little money Father earned doing odd jobs for other people; and those jobs had become scarce.

Genevieve's thoughts shifted back to the days when, in spite of the increasing need, their small house never lacked for warmth and love. She felt a tremble skitter through her body. Warmth and happiness had disappeared from their house three years ago.

"Gen."

She stared at the starved, lint white face of the little boy tugging at her skirt. Two trusting and innocent round blue eyes gazed up at her. She patted him on his head and whispered, "What is it, David?"

"I'm hungry, Gen."

She jerked her head towards the door. "Mother's just gone. She's sure to bring you something good to eat. Please, be a nice boy. Go and lie down on the bed. I'll come soon and tell you a story. You'll sleep and won't think about food. Go, go now"

Her glance followed David's walk to the bed, his steps slow, his head hung. The time was far behind them when they ate every day. Little boys needed to eat. They needed to play and laugh, not lie around in bed. She sighed, blinking back tears.

Genevieve rubbed her hand over her brow in a futile gesture to brush away the sad thoughts crowding her mind. What happened to her father on that unfortunate trip to the cursed forest? What turned him into a drunkard? Three long, hard, heart-breaking years had passed since the unfortunate day Father spent a night alone in the forest. Agonizing years blowing away their former, peaceful life. Genevieve still couldn't grasp the reason for his transformation. What led Father to turn into a bully? She, or her mother, or the younger children had done nothing wrong.

Genevieve shook her head. The monster who tormented them was no longer her father. Where did the formerly loving man vanish? Why don't happiness and laughter last for as long as people live? Who stole the joy from their house?

The cursed forest and the evil lurking there were to blame for her family's predicament. The forest and its unseen monsters fed on people's happiness and greedily sucked it from their souls. A monster breeding monsters, the same as it did to her father.

Since the day she grew old enough to understand her father's' moods, Genevieve never witnessed him swearing at or fighting with her mother. She never saw him drunk. Mother said her father often visited the alehouse like the other men, but true to his word, he would only drink one mug of beer. Never more than one. Up to that last trip into the forest when everything changed.

Starting the day he stepped from the trees, the civil and sunny John Mason, the kind, considerate father and husband, had stopped existing, and he'd turned into a quarrelsome, mean, and violent bully. They all feared him, because he often hit them without any reason, and he never regretted his bad behavior.

Mother had looked for work at the manor. No permanent job was available. Now and then, if one of the hired maids got ill, she worked in the kitchen or laundry. More often, the masters at the manor had nothing for her, and she came home empty handed, which meant long days of hunger for her family.

Sometimes the neighbors took pity on the little children and brought them something to eat. Genevieve's heart contracted seeing Mother's sunken eyes and withered face while she sliced, with great care, a piece of bread or meat the villagers brought into equal pieces for all of them, father included. Mother, frail and pale, pretended she wasn't hungry and fed the young ones her own morsels too.

Father never gave his share of food to any of his hungry children. Drunk out of his mind most of the time, he would gobble every single bite, ignoring the hungry looks of his children.

Everyone called him *the drunkard* behind his back. All the money he received for his work went to pay for his drinks. On peaceful evenings, he fell like a log onto the bed. On tremulous nights, the children cowered in their beds while he unleashed insane fury on their mother.

Twice during the last week, Genevieve's mother asked her to help carry her father home from the ditch half a mile down the road. He'd fallen asleep in his own mess and after the hard job of hauling him home, her poor mother cried herself to sleep.

Genevieve kept a distance from her father; he emanated cold waves towards her. She couldn't explain the feeling and didn't want to bother her already unhappy mother with such questions.

The deep sigh of one of the girls brought Genevieve back to reality. Her siblings lay huddled together; so hungry they'd no power left to play like other kids of their age.

All the children slept in an iron bed in the back room, the big luxury being a straw pallet and some long-worn straw pillows, while her mother and father slept in a bed set up between the wall and the table in the front room also used as the kitchen.

Sweeping finished, Genevieve dragged her feet to the bed. She lay alongside the other children and forced away the memory of the fateful day that flooded her mind. She dozed until Mother arrived, exhausted but radiant.

She'd received laundry to do and the cook had given her turnips and pig's fat enough for a feast for them all.

"I hope John comes home tonight sober enough to be able to taste all the good food we have," her mother said with a nod, addressing nobody in particular.

***

Late in the evening, Genevieve was the first to catch sight of her father swaying from one side to the other as he came up the road. She hurried, without a word, to the bed where the other children were already asleep. Clearly, it wasn't the right moment to be in his way. Through half-closed eyelids, she watched him as he entered the room.

In one stride, Father came to the bed where the children slept and he bent over them. His unshaven face was swollen with too much drinking, his eyes had turned into bleary slits and his tousled, unkempt hair made him ugly and repulsive.

David, one of the twins, woke up. The monstrous head above him must have scared the little boy because he yelled in a desperate voice, "Mommy, Mommy! Help me! The monster, the monster wants to gobble me up."

David's frightened words brought him a severe beating from his once loving father. Genevieve didn't dare to stir in her bed. She'd already learned, the hard way, that it was no use, at such a moment, to try to reason with her father.Nothing good would come out of it.

Alarmed, Mother rushed to free the poor little boy from Father's hands, but a rain of fists and obscenities fell on her too.

"You are to blame. You fogged the children's mind with frightening things. All your silly stories are as stupid as you," Father spitefully shouted while hitting her. "You turned them against me. You taught them to call me names behind my back. I'm a monster, he says. All because of you, bitch!" The veins in his forehead stuck out, and he turned an ugly red.

Genevieve could no longer watch. She covered her head and bit the sheets to muffle her desperate cries.

She hated that evil man so much. It was a pity she didn't have the power to change into one of the mighty wizards from her mother's stories and turn this ogre to stone.

Silence fell over the room. Genevieve peeked from under the thin blanket.

Her father stood unmoving, his head tilted as if he were listening to something, his gaze alert. He spun on his heels and, slamming the door, left the room and vanished into the night's thick, suffocating fog.

"Why don't we go to Grandmother's?" Genevieve, trembled, afraid her father might return with renewed fury. The younger children huddled together, trembling and casting frightened glances at the door. Their round, large eyes were mirrors of terror and despair.

Mother sat on the bed, her hands joined in prayer. Silent tears rained down her face, bruised and swollen from her husband's beating.

"Let's go to Grandma," Genevieve repeated, a lump in her throat choking her, almost sure her mother hadn't heard her. "I heard you talking to our neighbor and she told you the same thing. Leave Father for good and never return to him. You said Gran's still alive, somewhere around Berkhamsted."

"No, I can't go back to them. There's no place for me at my parents anymore."

"You are their only daughter" Genevieve replied, and she cupped her mother's bruised cheeks in her hands.

Mother didn't answer.

Genevieve swallowed hard, aware of the reason why Mother wouldn't return to her parents. Because of her parents' strong opposition to her father, she had eloped fourteen years before and followed her love and destiny to Glennridge.

"We are their grandchildren," Genevieve continued, in an attempt to elicit an answer from her mother. "Maybe Grandmother has more mercy in her soul than Grandfather. She can't throw you out. She must have a bit of heart left in her. Tell Father nothing. We must go away before he returns. I'll wake and dress the young ones. Victoria and Elisabeth can help me. We'll leave the house in the morning. I'm old enough to work, Mum. Everything's going to be all right, you'll see."

Mother nodded, but didn't move.

Genevieve realized her mother was too tired and depressed to keep going.

"Oh, John, why? Why?" her mother whispered at last, her voice full of grief and sorrow. The sole reply came in the sharp cry of a night bird. John was no longer there to answer her questions. Genevieve stayed awake next to her mother, holding her thin, work-worn hand in her own.

The moment the day's first rays touched the sky, Genevieve headed to the bed where the children slept and woke them up.

"Mother, come quickly. Something's wrong with David," she called, furrowing her brows. The boy twisted in his bed, bathed in sweat, his face as red as a fire's flames.

"The monster, the monster," he whined again and again through fever-cracked lips.

"Something's wrong, indeed," her mother cried, alarmed. "It's no wonder why after last night.. You take this cloth and try to cool his forehead," Mother urged Genevieve.

"Oh Mum, he's burning like the glowing wood in the stove," Genevieve whispered, her voice caught in her throat.

David's small chest struggled for each breath.

"Yes, I can see. Hurry and fetch some more water. We'll need it. I'll start a fire and cook a bit of broth to bring some strength into him."

Genevieve fretted with the pails of water along the road, telling herself Mother would surely find a way to ease David's suffering.

The soup ready, Mother tried to feed it to the little boy. Alas, the poor soul couldn't be forced to swallow even a few sips of the thin broth his mother cooked.

"The monster, the monster," he kept repeating in a fainter and fainter voice, his tears drying as soon as they reached his feverish cheeks.

Genevieve gazed, concerned, at the day growing old and the evening turning into night. A cold wind coming from the forest gathered ominous clouds over the village. Father didn't come home the whole day.

Geoffrey, the neighbor's husband, came to their house and let her mother know that her father had joined the other villagers at the alehouse for a short while after midday. He'd left, she said, and headed into the forest swaying on his legs. Geoffrey even expressed his wonder about how long the alehouse's owner would continue to offer her father drinks on a credit he couldn't pay.

Deep and distant, strong rumbles warned them a storm was under way.

David's condition worsened before Mother's and Genevieve's eyes. His cries turned into hoarse whispers, and his lips became a sickly violet.

The closest available doctor lived three villages away, and it took more than an hour on horseback to reach him.

Bertha, the old woman living at the other end of the village, came to Genevieve's mind. Bertha brewed and prepared potions from plants, healing almost anything: cold, Rheum,husbands' beatings, and sterility.

Some people considered her a witch, a good one, and they spoke her name in whispers. These villagers claimed they often saw her gathering herbs, wild flowers and strange twigs at various hours of the day and night.

Others said she was the devil's messenger on Earth, since they'd seen the strange woman dance around a steamy cauldron in her room at midnight while a horde of bats fluttered their wings around the house's chimney.

"These are lies," Mother told Genevieve once, waving her hand. "Foolish inventions of the people envious of the old, quiet woman who never asks for anything from others. She's a kind person who likes to keep to herself and not mingle with the rest of the villagers. She has her reasons to behave this way, no doubt."

"Mother, I shall go and fetch old Bertha. She must have something for David's illness." Without waiting for a reply from her distressed Mother, Genevieve grabbed her patched shawl and dashed out of the room. She walked fast, despite the strong wind that blew the road's thick dust in her face, making her wince and stagger.

Broken twigs and leaves hit her in her chest, and slapped against her bare legs. The gusts of wind tore at her hair, whipping it around her face, the tendrils turned into cruel, angry fingers striking her. She kept her eyes half shut to be able to see ahead.

By the time she arrived at old Bertha's house, the fearful storm had reached the village. Frightening flashes of lightning, followed by deafening thunderbolts split the sky. It was as if hell's evil master had come upon the earth to claim all the villagers' souls.

"Sweet God, who's there?" the old woman grumbled, reluctant, at first, to open the door. "Come inside quickly." She grabbed Genevieve's arm and dragged her into the room.

"What in the name of God brought you out of your house in such terrible weather? Or have you lost yourself around here? I can't remember seeing you around."

The odd way Bertha uttered her words, the quaint sound of her language, brought a smile to Genevieve's lips, despite the tragic circumstances that brought her to the old woman's door.

After hearing the reason why the girl had come to her, Bertha refused to leave the house. She shook her head several times, watching Genevieve with pity-filled eyes.

"From what you tell me, there's little I can do for your brother. Take my word, I see no use for us to be soaked to the skin or struck by lightning on our way to your house. It would be madness to venture outside while the storm's raging.

"What you told me about the great fever, profuse sweating and pains in the head makes me think that what ails David is the fatal sweating sickness. The beating you say he got from your father hastened it. Stay here and dry yourself by the fire." The woman gently pushed Genevieve to the chair in front of the fire's crackling glow.

"Drink the brew I've just made and if the storm calms down, we'll hurry to the poor lamb," Bertha continued in a commanding voice.

Genevieve didn't have any choice, but to obey the old woman's words.

She took a sip from the hot tea. She'd never drunk such a fragrant tea, strong and spicy. Each swallow brought new life into her. While she drank, Genevieve examined the pleasant room, warm and better furnished than their house. Two thick carpets lay on the floor and on one of the walls.

A green ribbon pinned up a curtain of the same color, separating the front room from the back. There, Genevieve caught sight of wooden shelves stacked with rows of earthenware containers. Meticulously tied bunches of dried herbs and flowers hung from the ceiling, giving the whole house a sweet, spicy fragrance. A few thick, leather covered old books near a finely chiseled wooden cross completed the picture.

Genevieve hid a shudder as she caught sight of a shiny skull next to the books. Large letters covered the skull from one temple to the other. Bertha read the words aloud in a language she called Latin and also told Genevieve their meaning,

"What I am now, one day thou'll be,
What thou are now, I was like thee."

A fat cat, as black as the night outside, sat on top of the highest shelf. Indifferent to the unleashed hell outside and to the presence of a stranger in the house, it continued to lick its paws and clean its ears and head.

Childish curiosity urged Genevieve to better study the room's darker corners. Yes, indeed. There it was. A broom with a long stick, leaning against the wall, near an empty bucket. Genevieve frowned, but didn't dare utter her thoughts.

Old Bertha, following her gaze, laughed in a gurgled, throaty way. She slapped her thighs several times in amusement.

"Oh, my child, no, I don't use the broom to fly in the night. Although, I can't deny it would be useful at my age. I do the same thing your mother does with a broom. I sweep the floor and the yard. Ha, ha... Old Bertha, 'the witch.' This is what they all say about me, don't they? Yes, I know, yet I don't care a bit." She shook her head.

Genevieve dipped her head and stared into the large cup. Yes. Bertha must be a witch if she read her mind, the very thought nagging her about the woman in front of her.

"Drink, my dear. Drink the tea. Why not tell me the rest? Take your time. By the way you look, David is not the only one who needs my help. Tell me how things started. The night's long and we must pass it in some way, waiting for the storm to subside. Speak, my child. People find old Bertha whenever they are in big, big trouble," Bertha continued in a kind voice and nodded several times.

Genevieve cleared her throat. She frowned, shrugged and threw Bertha an undecided glance.

"Have no worry. No need to be shy. Your folks won't get upset with you for revealing their problems to me. No word you utter here leaves my house."

At long last, Genevieve took a deep breath and then exhaled, shuddering. She told Bertha how, not so many years ago, while waiting for father to return from work, she and her younger sisters, Victoria and Elisabeth, used to huddle together in the large bed. All three asked mother to tell them a story.

"Among other beautiful stories about fairies and wizards and dragons, Mother told us the legend of how St. Mary's Abbey had come to be built there, up on the rocky peak, in the middle of the thick, strange forest. Mother called it the cursed forest."

"I know. Even I call it the same. Tell me what you know about it. We have enough time." Bertha sipped from a cup filled with a black, strong-smelling brew.

"Mother said, at first the forest was an ordinary one. Like any other in the country. Then, some two hundred years ago, a great battle took place in it. A powerful lord opposed King Henry III, and his soldiers ambushed King Henry's son, Edward, when he passed through. The fight was a fierce one, a real bloodbath.

"At long last, Edward's fighters killed the lord. They chopped up his lifeless body and sent his head to his castle for proof of what would always happen to traitors. The King's son, also wounded but grateful he'd escaped alive, and eager to secure his spiritual salvation, swore to build an abbey on the place where he won the battle."

"Well, it might explain many things. I understand," Bertha muttered without giving Genevieve any further explanation. "Go on, I interrupted you."

"The legend also says that a couple of years after the battle, the forest housing the abbey became an evil haunted place. People heard strange cries and groans where the fight had taken place. Some people say, each year, dark blood stains the ground and trickles down the trees' trunks on the exact date the battle happened.

"Little by little, many animals disappeared from the forest. The only creatures left are some black birds and even those are found at the forest's border. And also the big trout, in a stream with the clearest waters people ever imagined. The deeper people advance among the trees, the more frightened they become. They know what they hear are not natural sounds and only whispers of voices. And, from time to time, agonizing moans." Genevieve stopped and glanced furtively over her shoulder at the grinning skull.

Bertha stood up and walked to the window. The storm still raged outside. "Yes, I've heard those moans too," she said and returned to Genevieve.

"Now and then," Genevieve resumed her story, "the villagers spoke of ghastly things, like red-eyed dogs, that were bad omens of terrible misfortunes to come. People called them the hell dogs or the ghost dogs because they disappeared once a tragic death happened.

"Above all, people spoke in whispers about the frightening eerie silence all around the forest, crushing them to the ground like a heavy, lead blanket. Breezes don't sway the branches, or rustle the leaves. Broken twigs don't make a sound. Nothing. It is as though the world is frozen in an eternal stillness—the very words Mother used to describe it."

Bertha shook her head. "I go to the forest by myself, though I must admit, not so often. It's quite far, and I'm no longer young. There alone can I find some of the herbs I need, so I can't help it, I have to go." She nodded and asked, "Would you like another cup of tea?"

Genevieve bit her lip and moved her head in a small jerk. "Yes, please." She shifted in the chair, bringing her feet closer to the stove.

"Here, you need it my dear." Bertha handed Genevieve another cup of the steaming, fragrant tea.

Holding the cup with both hands, Genevieve continued,

"I liked what Mother said about the stream, though she'd never seen it herself. Men alone go into the forest, she says. Never women or children. They go to catch the trout. The fish are so big, the biggest ever seen in a river, and they can catch them using their bare hands. The moment the fish jump out of the water, colored sparks are seen above the stream."

"Colored sparks?" Bertha shook her head doubtfully.

"Well," continued Genevieve, "people say if you are lucky, if you stay motionless and strain your ears, you can discern a sweet, soothing music coming from the stream's waters. A mesmerizing song."

"That's true. I heard it myself. Once. The only time I ventured as far as the stream. I haven't gone near it since that day. It stirred an odd feeling in me. Anguish? Worry? I can't say. Probably fear. Even an old woman like me can be scared."

"Many say the music gets into your soul and makes you forget all your worries, all your troubles, and you never want to return home. A few people say it is a blessed river. Most agree the river's the devil's work, and at night, the waters turn into boiling tar. Villagers also claim you can hear the wicked souls' moans and the sinners' groans while they boil in it."

Bertha shook her head. "Well, I think it's a bit of exaggeration. People have vivid imaginations when it comes to describing something they don't really understand."

After taking a mouthful of the bittersweet tea, Genevieve continued, "One day, three years ago, I begged my father to take me with him into the forest. I promised I'd help him carry the fish. He didn't want to let me. He denied me firmly, saying there's no place for a girl in the forest.

"He said I should stay home and help Mother with the household and the younger children. He didn't want to hear one more word from me. I'll bring you a spark from the magic stream. I promise, Father told me, patting my head. He left and headed to the forest. His dark eyes glittered, and he smiled. It's the last memory I have about Father as a normal person."

"Why? What happened?"

"I don't know. All the other villagers returned home in the evening, except Father. Hearing heavy footsteps coming closer to our house, I ran to the door, eager to welcome him and the promised spark. But it wasn't Father. It was our neighbor's husband, Geoffrey. He told us that Father left the others headed for the forest, and though they warned him not to go ahead alone, he wouldn't listen. They didn't see him again.

"Mother looked pretty upset and worried. I woke several times in the night and saw her in the dim moonlight. She knelt by the bed, her hands joined and keeping her voice low, to not wake the little ones, she prayed to God to protect Father from the forest's evil."

Bertha shook her head. "Prayers can't do a thing against the evil reigning there."

"Well." Genevieve sighed heavily. "Mother's prayers helped, I'm sure. When the first sunrays appeared, Mother told me Father was coming at last. I ran with her to open the door, but something in the way father walked told me things were not right about him. He kept his head bent, and his arms hung loosely at his side. He pushed Mother and me aside and refused to answer Mother's questions. The usual glint of life in his eyes was gone, replaced by a beast-like hate at times and empty, lifeless gazes at other times.

"The only thing my father told Mother, or any of the curious villagers the following day was, 'Leave me be. Leave me be. I've nothing to tell you.'"

Bertha nodded and patted Genevieve's arm, encouraging her to continue.

"For three years, things have become worse and worse. Each passing day we have witnessed him become more violent and brutal. Father has grown fond of drinking and turned into a filthy creature reeking of ale and dirt, often venting his fury on my poor mum. Today, out of his mind, he beat her and David cruelly. I reckon the beating and the fright was the reason why my brother got sick," Genevieve said in conclusion.

Bertha, a sad expression shadowing her face, nodded sagely, as if she listened to such a confession every single day. "Well, my child. Life's never perfect, and although I know what all the people say about the evil haunting the forest, I don't think it alone is to be blamed for the change in your father. As far as I can imagine, your father was a bully and a worthless man all the time. He wore a mask, a disguise."

The woman stopped for a second to cover Genevieve, who tucked her legs under her, with a soft blanket that smelled of lavender and lilac. It touched her exhausted body like a caressing hand.

Outside, the storm's savage demons played havoc among the trees and houses. Each time a wild howl, like from the darkest depth of hell, pierced the night, a strange apprehension clawed at Genevieve's heart.

Bertha continued in the same soothing voice, "The moment David feels better, escape to your grandparents, if they're still living. I'm sure they'll understand."

Genevieve, felled by exhaustion, nodded with difficulty.

Night gave way to day, but the untamed storm continued to rage outside.

Genevieve chewed at her bottom lip and went to the window. Her thoughts flew to her poor mother, alone by sick little David's bed. And all the rest of the children asking her for food and not understanding what had happened.

About midday, the rain and wind calmed down.

Genevieve and old Bertha struggled through the heavy mire of mud clogging the road on the way to Genevieve's house.

As they got closer, they saw a dark, thick cloud of smoke hovering above the tops of the trees like a death pall. People hurried to a place where something had been burnt overnight.

The iron claw of dread tore at Genevieve's heart. From the road she couldn't tell what was burning; she could only see that the smoke billowed from the direction of her house.

Once she and old Bertha reached the place, they stopped, rooted to the ground by the appalling sight before them. Stunned villagers swarmed in the yard of her house.

Her neighbor Martha, tears brimming in her eyes, shook her head and took hold of Genevieve's hands.

"I'm sorry, Gen. They're all dead. Your mum and the little ones. All gone." She gathered Genevieve to her ample bosom.

The pain of the hard truth--nothing left of her home, except some stones near the place the stove had stood and none of her family alive took over. Genevieve fell to her knees in the mud and howled like a wounded animal. She cried the names of her mother and sisters and brothers through the violent sobs that shook her body.

Bertha and Martha helped her up and tried as best as they could to calm her.

Fat specks of black soot caught in Genevieve's hair and touched her face. Specks of black soot was all that was left of her mother and sisters and brothers.

The soot's soft touch on her skin triggered a violent recoil in her, as if a snake had bitten her. Letting out another desperate cry, she dashed to the burning ruins, but the villagers wouldn't let her pass. Strong hands prevented her from jumping into the smoldering fire.

Her legs turned weak under her, and she fainted.

*** ·

Genevieve found it difficult to open her eyes. A terrible ache pressed her temples the moment she turned her head. She found herself in a strange bed, covered to her chin by a soft, lavender smelling blanket. The room felt warm, filled with the same pleasant, calming smell.

"Oh, praised be Lord's name. You are with us again." A hoarse voice made her focus. She turned her head with a huge effort and discovered old Bertha sitting on a chair by the fire. "You gave me such a fright. I thought you would go to join your family," she said and came closer to Genevieve.

Genevieve recalled why she'd come to the old woman the previous evening, and the carnage they were met with when they arrived at her parents' house. She sobbed and wailed, crying again her mother's name and the names of her sisters and brothers. Not once, though, did she utter her father's name. She didn't have any idea if he was dead or not.

"Now, now," old Bertha soothed her. She gathered Genevieve in her arms and let her cry out her sorrow.

Little by little her heartbroken sobs subsided into jerking spasms that shook her body. Genevieve lifted her tearstained face to Bertha. The only words coming from her parched throat were, "Why? Why? Why?"

"I can't answer that," Bertha replied. "You must also know something about what happened to your mum and the other children. I hate myself for having to tell you the horrible truth, but I prefer you to hear the cruel facts from me. Not from some idle tongue."

Grief and fear mounting in her breast, Genevieve didn't make a sound. She stared wide-eyed at old Bertha.

"The villagers told me about the terrible night's tragedy," Bertha started the sad story. "They say that late, during the night, your father returned home to find your distressed mother howling louder than the storm outside, with little David already dead. He bashed your mother's head with a wooden club and killed all the children in the same way. After that, he started the house on fire. The strong rain prevented it from burning completely down. Enraged, your father tried several times to start the flames again, but couldn't manage," the woman continued the horrible story.

"He told the villagers the voices in the forest and the big, black, red-eyed dogs urged him to do it. The reason? Your mum and the children represented the seeds of evil. 'Kill 'em. Kill 'em. Kill them all,' the voices chanted to him, he said. 'Set yourself free from the seeds of evil. Kill them. Kill them. Kill them. All!'"

Bertha paused to wipe a tear from the corners of her eyes, and then went on. "The lord of the manor judged your father, and the hangman executed him." She held Genevieve's hand tight, as if trying to instill some strength and courage into her. "I'm very sorry, my child. There's nobody left alive in your family and nothing standing of your house, as you yourself already saw," Bertha shook her head in sadness. "You are an orphan now, poor soul."

A terrible shudder shook Genevieve's thin body. She opened her mouth. Blinked several times. Closed her mouth. She could neither speak, nor cry. She trembled violently. She felt the blood drain from her face, and everything became a blur.

***

When Genevieve regained consciousness, the smell of herbs hit her nostrils. She opened her eyes. She didn't know how much time had passed or where she was. Except for a yellowish pool of light, cast by an oil lamp standing on the table, the room was dark. Her glance fell on old Bertha sitting by her bed. A grateful smile lit the woman's wrinkled face.

"Thank you, thank you, God, for sparing the child's life."

Genevieve didn't fail to see the film of tears covering Bertha's eyes, despite the old woman's attempt to hide her emotions. Bertha wiped Genevieve's face with a wet cloth smelling of fresh grass and lime.

"Why are you crying?" Genevieve asked.

"I'm crying because I'm happy. I was afraid, several times, you wouldn't make it. I thought you'd hurry to meet your mama and little David and all the others.

"You too suffered from the sweating sickness that killed your brother. Luckily, we managed to deceive the hideous lady waiting to harvest your soul, didn't we? Here, drink a little of this broth, child. It will strengthen you and bring some color to your pale cheeks."

Bertha caressed Genevieve's head with tender care. "You've struggled between life and death for more than a month. Fortunately for you, the precious herbs in the tea I made you sip, and obviously God's care, proved victorious over the merciless death waiting to harvest your life, too. Not this time, I told her. Go away. You'll have to wait for many, many years, still." Bertha patted again Genevieve's weakened hand.

***

Genevieve stood on her feet again. Fitful sleep and several days worth of good food proved more than helpful at restoring her health.

"There's something else I have to tell you," Bertha said. The old woman held Genevieve's gaze as she spoke. Her odd accent added a note of sadness to her words. "I talked to your neighbors. They sent word to your grandparents in Berkhamsted, letting them know what happened. We hoped they might take you in.

"The town priest let us know your grandfather died about two years ago. Your grandmother...well, the priest

said she suffered apoplexy and died on the same day as
your mum and the rest of your family. Not long before her
death, she'd made a will in which she left all her wealth to
a distant niece. Well, my dear child, this makes you an
orphan, indeed." Bertha's voice was tinged with
compassion.

Genevieve hung her head and suppressed the rush
of fresh tears. Her heart contracted. "What should I do
alone in this cruel world," she whispered to herself,
trembling with apprehension.

Old Bertha, who must have guessed Genevieve's
troubled thoughts, told her she'd be more than happy to
share her small house and food with her.

"I have no next of kin in this world. I came here
from far away, from a country over the seas, called
Flanders. My husband brought me to England.It was
unusual for them to see an ordinary woman who could read
andwrite better than many of them, and everyone treated
me suspiciously. Life blessed us with a daughter; but the
maid that went with her to the river one day said the poor
little girl crawled to the river while the maid was gathering
some mushrooms. She assumed the child drowned, though
we never found her body." Bertha's eyes welled with tears.
She swallowed hard and then went on.

"Some villagers said they saw a couple of gypsies
sneaking out of the wood with a little child who didn't look
like their child. Poor baby was just ten months old." Heavy
silence followed the elderly woman's words. Her chin
trembled and she wiped her eyes with the back of her
hand. She sighed and nodded looking at Genevieve.

"My gift of healing also brought me a lot of envy
and enemies. To escape the accusation of witchcraft, we
fled from our home. The only things we took were these
books." Bertha pointed to the large books on the shelf.
"And good old Hans." She patted the skull next to the

books as if it were an old friend. "Before reaching this village, my husband died of the plague."

"I'm sorry," whispered Genevieve. She placed her hand over Bertha's age withered one. The loss of someone dear became a shared tragedy between them.

"And," the old woman continued, dabbing her eyes, "I ran again for fear I'd be thrown into the grave near his dead body. People were afraid I'd caught the disease, too. I wandered along the vales and forests and, at last, I arrived here. The money I had proved more than enough, and I bought this cottage. And here I am. If you think you can put up with the foolishness of an old woman, you can stay here and be the daughter I've not had the chance to bring up."

Genevieve accepted the generous offer without any second thoughts. "Thank you. You won't regret having me stay. I'll work to repay your kindness."

Bertha shook her head. She flapped her hand and waved the suggestion aside with vehemence.

"I don't need any payment, my child. No repayment at all. You are the one doing me a favor."

***

Old Bertha taught Genevieve to read and write. She also taught her the proper hours of the day to gather certain herbs, and the way to turn them into the life saving potions she always kept handy.

The only time Genevieve found the strength to pass by the place where her house once stood was when Bertha asked her to take some ointment to a villager living close to Genevieve's place.

Appalled at the sight of the black charred ruin, Genevieve's heart contracted. She choked as she imagined she smelt the nasty stench of incinerated human flesh, a reminder of what was once her family. The persistent smell of death remained in her nostrils for the rest of her life; it had clung to her body and snuck into her soul.

Her stomach turned queasy. A flow of sorrow and regret engulfed her. The sharp anguish of having lost them all, and the anger against her father tore at her heart. If she hadn't left the house on that tragic evening to summon old Bertha, she'd have been dead like all the others.

Her mother's voice still rang in her ears. "Genevieve, it's bedtime. Let's take the little 'uns to sleep. I'll tell you a story. A new story I haven't told you before. Listen. Once upon a time, there lived an old king, proud father of three sons...."

Genevieve bowed her head, tears brimming in her eyes. Tears she couldn't restrain any more. "Why is life unmerciful and cruel," she whispered to herself. The only things left from her childhood were the stink of burnt flesh and bones.

And the memory of her family. The sole treasure she held onto.

Chapter Three

England 1990

Anne

Outside the tent, Anne shivered for a moment in the cold air, heavy with the fragrance of pine trees.

The strange woman didn't look back as she walked. It appeared that she didn't doubt Anne would follow her.

Anne glanced towards Neil's tent. The soft snoring coming from it meant Neil had heard nothing. He slept undisturbed.

She followed the stranger into the dark forest. The darkness didn't frighten her. Ghost stories never frightened her, either. On the contrary, such things fascinated her, and whenever she found the time, she enjoyed reading articles on magic and the paranormal. Her thoughts drifted, for a second full of tenderness, to the women in her family who, like her, had been gifted with special powers. Her grandmother could foretell the future by reading it in the cards, and her Aunt Megan had gained popularity among her friends for her clairvoyant abilities.

An odd feeling of infinite sadness and anguish Anne had ever experienced came over her. The sensation, no doubt, was connected to the young woman ahead of her.

The stranger stopped briefly among the trees, as if wondering what path to follow, and then turned and stared at Anne with a pleading gaze. Large, mute tears of despair, the color of blood, rained down her pale face. Without speaking a word, she continued on her way.

The farther they advanced into the forest, the dimmer the light of the woman's aura became.Anne cast a glance around. She had no idea how far she'd ventured from the tent. The red-haired girl walked in silence over the small branches fallen on the path. Genevieve's own footsteps didn't make a sound. She startled when a sudden noise reached her ears. At first she couldn't identify the sound. A river, a stream, something of the kind.

The mysterious woman stopped again. She'd reached the trunk of a tall, old oak and cast nervous, fearful glances around, her aura no longer glowing. She swayed as if on the verge of fainting,then moaned.

Anne's heart skipped a beat when the stranger, her hands joined at her chest, let out a terrible wail. Without turning back to Anne, the woman vanished.

Intrigued by the unexpected disappearance, Anne dashed forward to look for the woman behind the tree trunk. In her hurry, she stumbled over the tree's thick roots, lost her balance, and fell into a void. Anne reached out in a desperate effort to catch hold of the gnarled root, but the frail tuft of moss she grabbed couldn't prevent her fall.

The last thought, flashing through her mind, before she landed in cold water came as a revelation. The strange woman she had followed through the forest was not a real human being but some kind of an apparition.

A ghost.

***

A gentle, but stubborn nudge, shook Anne, accompanied by an insistent voice. "Anne, Anne. Wake up, my dear."

"Oh, not again," Anne groaned and slipped back to sleep. The nagging shaking didn't cease, and it became clear the voice belonged to a man.

Anne opened her eyes, blinking several times to focus her gaze. It took her some seconds to manage to get them open, and to recognize that the concerned man watching her was Neil.

"I think you had a bad dream. Your screams woke me up. I thought something had attacked you. You were twisting and tossing in your sleeping bag when I came in. Look at you. Your face is covered in sweat."

"I had an odd dream," Anne said and sat up. She rubbed her eyes vigorously and turned to look around her, bewildered. "I followed a woman, dressed like a nun, through the forest to an old oak tree. When she disappeared, I stumbled and fell into water. A stream, I think."

Anne raised a trembling hand to her forehead. "It all felt so real, even when I tripped and fell. I grabbed some grass to keep from falling."

"You're safe now, and I'm by your side."

She opened her palms and stared at them. Green and brown smudges of grass and earth stained them. "Here." She showed Neil. "How can you explain the stains? I've never been a sleepwalker." She paused. "Wait! I remember something else. The woman in my strange dream knew my name. And she looked like me. A different me, yet the same copper-colored hair and green eyes. An old-time version of me."

"All's possible in dreams." Neil's voice sounded to Anne like he didn't take the nightmare seriously, and he changed the topic.

"There's mist in the valley. After it vanishes and there's enough light, we'd better continue our way back to the main path. Let's have a bite of chocolate now. If we'd brought our mobile phones, things would have been solved in a jiffy. But you insisted on leaving them home," Neil said, and shook his head.

"I know I did. It's better this way," Anne said. She looked closely at her grass stained hands. "Let's see if we can find the oak tree from my dream and the stream nearby."

He attempted to protest.

Anne gave him a long, level look. Neil dropped his glance, and kept his mouth shut over whatever comment he had intended to make.

Hopefully, he was aware she was making a huge effort in trying to offer him a second chance after he'd betrayed her trust. Her pride didn't want to cede and forgive him so easily, though every time Neil glanced her way, a frightening urge to let him absorb her until she no longer existed as a separate, individual entity, swept through Anne.

Neil's betrayal had hurt her deeply. Imagining Neil holding Gillian curled in his arms, his strong arms subduing her, had still brought tears to Anne's eyes even a long time after she and Neil had parted.

His surprised, guilty look on that cursed day, two years ago, would never leave her mind. Her eyebrows knitted with the sudden, vivid memory of the unfortunate event.

Chapter Four

1468 - 1473

Genevieve

Life at old Bertha's cottage was a quiet one, and the housework was easier than it had been at Genevieve's own.

Little by little, Genevieve came to discover a kind and generous Bertha hidden under the appearance of a bearish old person.

Bertha told Genevieve again and again that she considered her the daughter she'd wished for all her life.

Genevieve's eyes misted over whenever the image of her dead family took life in her mind. She missed the pranks and laughter of the little ones. And above all, her mother's soft voice and her kind, brown eyes. The only one she didn't miss at all was her father. Even the recollection of her father's face aroused in her a deep resentment.

The old woman's affection overwhelmed Genevieve. Bertha doted on her.

Many women in their village considered Bertha their small community's 'wise woman' - a kind of good sorcerer.

Bertha didn't accept any money as payment from the people who needed her services: potions, ointments, or prayers. Women whose husbands gave up drinking due to her potions or couples able to conceive would have paid her anything, but she refused; still, she never refused other gifts. Any piece of meat - chickens, rabbits, fish - she received from those satisfied by the results of her knowledge would become, at once, a delicious dish for Genevieve. Something good, something new to surprise her.

Genevieve most enjoyed the herbal tea Bertha made for her every day. Watching Genevieve drink it with so much pleasure, Bertha said, "This will bring strength to your frail body and lift your mood." She shook her head thoughtfully and added, "You know, our past and our future are tea leaves in the cup of our present. I heard these words a long time ago, and never tire of thinking how true they are."

During the four years spent at old Bertha's, Genevieve learned everything she could from the kind woman. Genevieve leafed, with delight, through the pages of the leather-bound books on the highest shelf. Her favorite was a book written in English: a Bestiary, with fables about animals and birds. The beautiful illustrations of both real and imaginary beasts fascinated her. These allegorical stories, imbued by deep moral meaning and mirroring theological truth, were the ones that Bertha used to pass her knowledge of the written English word to Genevieve.

Not only had Bertha taught her to read and write in English, but she also passed on her knowledge of Latin. Both an avid curiosity and shyness urged Genevieve to turn the pages of the book representing the Latin text of St. Mark's Gospel, with stunning illuminations in vivid, bright colors ranging from red and pink, to purple. The book's beautiful pictures represented the Evangelists, and textured decorations, fusing animal motifs with spirals and trumpets embellished the cover.

Bertha once told her this book was a treasure in itself. It belonged to her family for generations. It had been stolen from an English monastery by Norsemen and later sold to some merchants before being stolen from them, too, by pirates at sea. After changing many hands, it came, in the end, to her kin in Flanders.

Another book on Bertha's shelf, written in Latin, that she learned from, was a Leech Book, a kind of ancient medical work containing much useful advice and countless remedies. Ordinary everyday complaints such as headaches, toothaches, burns and wounds could be cured with a simple herbal tea. A separate chapter in the book included ancient charms and short poems for good health.

Bertha passed on everything she knew about herbs and plants and their curing and healing powers. Most of the herbs Bertha gathered were those used by peasants from times immemorial: red nettle, garlic, radish, hollow leek – traditional folk remedies, while the prayers were Paternoster, Aves, or Creeds. People needed only a little faith to get well and healthy again, old Bertha said. If required she would often visit, the sick person's house and pray in Latin in the midst of their family.

Genevieve accompanied her on several such occasions and joined her in the prayers the old woman had taught her as well.

"Soon you'll be a better healer than I am. I'm glad to see you are already so skillful with the healing plants and herbs." Bertha smiled, content.

***

After a whole morning in the field, gathering herbs, Genevieve returned home.

The late April sun shone on the red nettle and hollow leek she'd gathered. Bertha needed them to prepare an ointment for a neighbor boy who cut his leg on a piece of wood. The red and swollen leg, had puss oozing from the festering wound. His mother, tears streaking down her cheeks, had come to ask for Bertha's help.

Genevieve entered the house, her arms loaded with the herbs. The sweet smell of cinnamon wafting in the room welcomed her. "Mother Bertha, you spoil me indeed," she exclaimed, hugging the old woman in an outburst of gratitude and love. Bertha had cooked her favorite cherry pie.

Large tears ran down the elderly woman's wrinkled cheeks, tiny rivulets gathering in a knot under her chin.

"What's the matter? Is anything wrong? Have I done or said something out of my way?" Genevieve inquired, her breath caught and held.

"Not at all, my child. Nothing's wrong. On the contrary. Take no notice of me. Bless not my ears if I ever heard a sweeter word than what you just said, 'Mother Bertha.' Nobody called me 'Mother' before. I feel as if my house is blessed. Now, I can die in peace," she replied in a husky voice, and dabbed her eyes with her apron.

"I'm also of the mind that you should never hold back the words you want to say, because you never know the hour when it is impossible to come out with anything. So, I'll say it now, lass. Since you came to live with me, I've known more comfort and peace than at any time since I lost my husband. And you've really become the daughter I lost. And you'll never know how much it means to me, the fact that you'll be with me, whether my life is going to be cut short or allowed to be long."

Genevieve embraced, with infinite warmth, the woman who was as loving and caring as her own mother had been, and she pressed her lips against Bertha's thin sallow cheek.

"Oh, don't say such a thing, not even joking. I don't want to lose you, too," Genevieve replied before hungrily turning her attention to the pie.

***

Summer came upon them bringing hot days. Healing herbs could be gathered only in the early hours while still covered by dew.

One Friday morning, Genevieve kept silent, while Bertha banged the plates and pots and rummaged in the drawers, throwing things out of them and mumbling something under her breath.

"What's wrong? Have you lost something?" Genevieve tugged at Bertha's sleeve.

Bertha shrugged, a groan accompanied the roll of her eyes to the ceiling. "I'll forget one day where my head is placed. Ugh! Old age...." was all Genevieve received as an answer. Bertha moved her activity to an oaken chest by the wall.

At last, the elderly woman cried out with satisfaction.

"Ah, here you are." She took a small white package out of the chest. She unwrapped the cloth and presented Genevieve with a strange looking knife, its blade curved, with shiny white hilt.She turned a relieved look to Genevieve. "I thought I'd lost my treasure."

"What is it? What do you need it for?" Genevieve inquired, scrutinizing the object with open curiosity. "What are these signs on the handle?"

"My grandmother gave it to me the day I left my country. She called it the boline and told me to use it for cutting herbs, especially the ones possessing magical powers. The signs engraved on the handle are magical sigils. I'll explain their significance to you one day, when I have more time."

"You cut herbs all the time using an ordinary knife. Why replace it with this one?"

"Well, dear child. Tonight's the night. I'll have to head to the forest by myself. I must be there before midnight. There's a particular plant I gather on this Friday of the year. Once in four years. I'll use the boline to cut what I need."

"The forest? The cursed forest?" Genevieve asked wide eyed, her breath catching in her throat.

"Yes, the very 'cursed forest,' I know. I find this plant, as I said, only once every four years. Four years ago, I couldn't fetch it. You were sick in my bed after the tragedy that hit your family. I didn't want to let you out of my sight for a second. Now it's that time of the year again."

"Can't you find this plant closer to the village?"

"No. It's a special kind of holly, one with smooth leaves. I gather nine such holly leaves and then wrap them in white cloth that's never been used. I make nine knots to tie the ends of this piece of cloth together."

"What is it for? What kind of illness does it cure, or has it some magical properties?" Genevieve inquired, her curiosity and worry roused at the same time. "It's not mentioned in the Leech Book."

"You're right. This is something I learned from my grandmother, back in my home country of Flanders. If I place these nine leaves under my pillow, the following night I'll have prophetic dreams. The next morning, I'll hang the leaves over the doorway to keep evil spirits out of the house."

"Mother Bertha, I won't let you venture in there alone. I'll never forget what happened to my mum and the little ones because he—you know who—spent the night in the forest alone. I'll come with you, no matter how scared I am of the forest."

Bertha nodded in agreement with Genevieve's words. "Dear child, I'm moved by your concern for me. I must be alone while gathering the nine leaves in the forest, but I'll allow you to follow me up to the forest edge if that brings you peace of mind. You'll wait for me there. Agreed?"

"Yes," Genevieve replied in a tremulous voice.

***

Genevieve, her arms folded under her breast, sat on the edge of a rock under an ash tree. She took a deep breath, frightened more than ever. What if something bad happened to Mother Bertha? She exhaled. Bertha was a wise woman. Nothing bad would happen to her.

At first, Genevieve counted the twinkling stars above to pass the time and not think about the evil forest. Soon she lost track of their number. Apprehension whispered over her skin. She bit her nails and kept casting worried glances to the place where Bertha had entered the forest. So much time had passed since the old woman had disappeared among the thick trees.

Genevieve stood up, undecided. She didn't want to upset Bertha, but what if something had happened to her? She hated the slight trembling of her legs when she advanced along the path old Bertha had followed. In the silver moonlight, a large shadow creeping away among the trees startled her. Her hand flew to her mouth to stifle a scream.

"In the name of the Father, the Son and the Holy Ghost," she said softly and crossed herself, cold with fear, but she didn't stop. She walked slowly on as she had to find Bertha.

After no more than two yards, her legs turned heavy. She couldn't step any farther. She swayed with an overwhelming sadness crushing her soul and heart. On the verge of fainting, she caught sight of a shadow coming hurriedly out of a cluster of tall trees. Bertha.

The woman grabbed Genevieve's arm and dragged her out of the forest. Once in the open, old Bertha stopped, breathing hard. Her eyes were wide.

"Oh, God, something's wrong. Really wrong. Can't... can't you feel it?" Bertha stammered.

Without waiting for an answer, or releasing the grip on Genevieve's hand, she said in a commanding yet worried voice, "Come. Let's leave this place and head home as fast as we can."

Genevieve followed her in trance-like silence.

Once home, Genevieve sat, still shaken, on the bed. Bertha, empty handed, sagged heavily in a chair, her head bowed and shoulders slumped as if burdened by all the worries of the world.

"Mother Bertha, what's wrong? Where are the leaves, and your special knife? What's happened?" Genevieve inquired, amazement growing in her voice.

"Shush, my child. Let's not disturb the night spirits. I don't want to frighten you more than you already are, but I think you should know the truth. I had just started gathering the first holly leaves and had tied them in the cloth when, I heard a moan. Startled, I stared among the trees where I thought I saw red points... shining red eyes moving towards me."

Genevieve gave a short cry. "The ghost dogs."

Bertha nodded. "Yes. At the same time, the branches of the tree above me turned into hideous hands and tried to grab me. I dropped everything and ran out of the forest."

"Could it have been your imagination or a shadow?"

"I don't think so. A red-eyed shadow? Trees with human looking hands? Never heard of something like that."

"Are sure you're well?"

"I don't know my child... I don't know... I hope so."

Alarmed, Genevieve studied the old woman. Bertha's gaze turned hazy and distant.

Swallowing hard, Genevieve managed to hide her own anxiety. Images with her father's similar gaze, after the night spent in the devilish forest, flashed in her mind's eyes. She frowned and bit her lower lip. Luckily, except for being a bit shaken, nothing bad had happened to Bertha. What a foolish thing for the old woman to do anyway, venturing into the cursed forest at night while aware of the evil lurking among the trees.

"You'd better go to bed, Mother Bertha. Forget the holly leaves. You'll gather others next time. Lie down, please. You need to regain your powers. Tomorrow morning I'll be the one to gather the dew-covered flowers we need for wounds. You stay here and rest." She unfolded the lavender and lilac smelling blanket.

Bertha caught Genevieve's hand in hers, and in a soft voice tinged by sadness whispered, "Thank you, my child. Forgive, please, an old woman for leaving you alone. Thank you for all the sun you've brought into my life."

Genevieve's eyebrows twitched in confusion at the old woman's words. Bertha closed her eyes with a heavy sigh and fell asleep at once, while Genevieve tucked the blanket over her.

Genevieve left early in the morning the next day. Before leaving, she checked, with misted eyes, on the sleeping old woman and tiptoed out of the house.

Several hours later, she returned to find the old woman still in bed. Vicious claws of fear gripped Genevieve's heart.

"Something's wrong," she said aloud, trying to brace herself. "No, no, dear Lord, let it not be true," she prayed, though, deep in her soul, she had known that would be the outcome of the old woman's visit in the forest. She gripped the rails of the bed in which Bertha seemed to be still sleeping.

Trembling and breathless, she turned down the blanket and touched Bertha's face. The stillness of death was almost tangible in the air.

The woman's ice-cold cheeks proved her fears right. Giving no sign of an ailment, Bertha had passed away in her sleep, as she'd wished.

In peace. Quietly. Without much fuss.

Genevieve took Bertha' s' cold, lifeless hand in hers, brought it to her cheek and whispered, "Mother Bertha, rest easy and wherever you are now, you know you take with you my love and deep thanks for all you've done for me." She, then, pressed her lips together to suppress the bitter sobs threatening to erupt from her chest.

***

A few of the village women helped Genevieve prepare Mother Bertha for her eternal rest.

Genevieve walked to the neighboring village's church, where the villagers traveled each Sunday across the hill for their services. She summoned the priest to come and perform the burial prayers for Bertha.

The priest refused. "Let her soul rot in Hell. She was a heretic. A witch. She doesn't deserve any prayers. I regret she escaped the stake here on Earth," he replied, his mouth twisting in a cynical grin.

The burial was a simple one. Only a few people stood around the grave. Genevieve, the gravediggers and two of the families Bertha's potions helped.

Over the grave of the kind woman,Genevieve, in a trembling voice uttered a few of the prayers Mother Bertha had taught her.

***

Genevieve hardly had the time to recover from the shock of losing someone so dear to her.The day after Bertha's almost pagan burial the resolute strides of two men drawing near her door forced Genevieve to put her broom down. Very likely they were passers-by, traveling through the village and wanted a mug of water or some information.

She inquired, raising her eyebrows, "Yes, how might I be of any help to you?"

They appraised her from head to toe, and the older of the two replied in a flat voice, "We are bailiffs. Someone told the lord that the woman who dwelt here died. He sent us to claim the house and see it freed at once for the new tenants."

"It can't be possible," Genevieve replied, staring at them in shock, her cheeks hot and her heart hammering against her ribcage. "This belonged to old Bertha, the woman who lived here. It was hers."

"Not anymore. She has no use of it where she is now, has she?" the older man retorted. He forced his way inside, shoving Genevieve away and ignoring her protest, followed by his younger companion.

Genevieve rushed inside, too, pain and grief choking her. "This was her house. She told me she bought this place many years ago." She tried a feeble argument. "The lord can't have it."

"Of course he can. Who are you, anyway? Any kin of hers? Show us some papers to prove your words." The older man, who did most of the talking, gripped Genevieve's arm. "Have you any proof?"

"No, I don't," Genevieve spluttered in frustration and nearly shrieked at them. "It belonged to her, no matter what you or your master says." She pulled away from him.

"Don't push your luck. Take your rags and hit the road," said the younger of the two bailiffs. "Furniture and carpets stay. The new tenants arrive this evening, and they'll need them. There's no use fighting, otherwise we'll have you arrested," he threatened.

With no alternative, Genevieve lowered her head and sighed. She tightened in a bundle the large books on the shelf.

She took the dried bunches of the herbs that were now ready to be turned into healing potions. She packed Hans, the skull, alongside Bertha's pestle and mortar. Genevieve possessed no other personal belongings, except the clothes she had on her back.

With her soul weeping and her heart shattered, Genevieve gathered the small bundle in her arms. Under the bailiffs' stern, unwavering look, she left the cottage, closing the door on another stage in her life.

Chapter Five

England 1990

Anne

Neil and she had been living together for three years when they separated. Nothing had predicted the disaster to come. She'd returned from a business trip one day earlier than planned and found him with her best friend and business partner, Gillian. In their bedroom—hers and Neil's.

"Gillian, good morning, to you," Anne said in a voice that didn't her reveal her real thoughts. "Well, since you're already present, and as far as I can see, there's no need for me to tell you to make yourself comfortable."

Gillian had looked paler than death when she came naked out of Anne's bathroom.

If looks could stab, Anne would have killed Gillian. "Should we discuss the results of the trip? A trip I only now understand why you refused to go on, Neil? Be a sport." Anne, eyes cold, stared hard at him.

His face, confused and crestfallen, drained of blood. He climbed out of the bed as though he'd been woken from a bad dream, as if the two women in front of him were ghosts from the nightmare. He stared hard at Gillian, with a sheet held in front of him, his gaze as black as a moonless night.

"Find a better use for that sheet. Too late for such outbursts of modesty, don't you think?" Anne addressed him contemptuously.

She .continued as if nothing out of the ordinary had happened "After all, what are you trying to cover? The fact you're turned on by the presence of both your mistresses? Do you, somehow, have in mind a ménage a trois? No, I assumed not.

"You'd better prove yourself useful in some other way. Please, hurry to the kitchen and fetch some coffee. I think we all need some."

The moment Neil left the room, Anne turned to her friend who was buttoning her blouse with unsteady hands, and in a cool, calm voice said, ."Even though I knew you were capable of being a selfish and heartless person, I'd hoped you'd be different toward me. I know you have your own shortcomings - we all do - but despite them, I considered you a friend."

In a stiff voice, Anne continued. "What a huge mistake. The irony of it still is that I don't blame you, and I don't blame him. Maybe I should have seen it sooner with all of Neil's visits to our office lately." She poured as much ice into her voice as she could.

Gillian pinned Anne with a blank stare. She didn't say a word. Only bit her lower lip.

"And now," Anne went on, " when I was gone, you wantonly offered your body, all the while telling me how much he missed me."

"He more than willingly accepted the offer.... Or was it the other way around? Anyway, I hope it's been a satisfactory experience for you both. By the way, in case you want him, you can have him and keep him. For good."

Gillian listened to Anne's words, a deep frown on her expressive face. Wisely, she refrained from any attempt to explain.

"I don't even want you to admit your guilt. It would be pointless. Finding excuses won't change my opinion," Anne added.

Only the whiteness of Gillian's strained face betrayed the fact that she didn't feel at ease under Anne's unwavering gaze.

A sign of poisonous jealousy flashed over Gillian's features. Very likely, she was thinking fate always favored Anne - loving family, prosperous business, a sharp mind, good business sense and a faithful lover... until now.

"Here's what we'll do," Anne continued in the same voice, stiff and loud.

Neil, no doubt, heard her words too, through the door he'd left ajar.

She stood perfectly still, her eyes steady, her hands clasped on the handles of her briefcase. "Let me give it to you straight. I'll buy you off. I've enough money to buy your shares of the company. You can't refuse me under the circumstances."

Gillian caught her lip between her teeth, opened her mouth on the verge of replying, but kept silent.

Anne spoke on, "From now on, I'll only speak with your lawyer about signing the necessary documents. And since it's obvious you're more than familiar with the house and my bedroom, see yourself to the door."

After Gillian's hasty departure, Anne didn't cry, shout, throw things against the walls, or slap Neil's face. She stood for a long time staring out the windows of her beautiful house and swallowed the tears threatening to burst free. She turned to Neil, who stood sheepishly holding a cup of hot coffee in his hand. He'd dressed in a pair of jeans and a T-shirt.

He at least had the decency to blush, and Anne's unwavering stare deepened his color. An anger Anne found difficult to imagine built within her. She regained control of herself and in the same calm, undisturbed voice she addressed him. "It's clear that you have used me, my house, and my connections. Apparently it wasn't enough. You also wanted to use my best friend. Are you satisfied? Please, I want you to leave, too."

Anne raised her hand against Neil's feeble attempt at an explanation."No. Spare me the sordid details.I would hope you would know me better. I'm not interested in any explanations. Keep them for others.

"And I'm not the type to swallow the story of male hormones being more frolicsome than women's. Imagine things the other way around. You coming home and finding your lover and your best friend. Naked. In your own house. What would you have done or said? What would you have felt? We've nothing left to tell each other."

She hurried out of the room to her garden, leaving him to gather his belongings, afraid the last shreds of her pride would vanish. She wouldn't humiliate herself by begging for his love if he wasn't willing to offer it any longer.

Anne also didn't want to offer him the satisfaction of seeing her suffer. Under her steady voice and expression, her heart was wounded, and she wept silent, bitter tears. She pressed her hands over her ribcage as though her heart had broken and she wanted to stop the shards from falling to the ground. Fate, very likely, had offered them the chance, the once in a lifetime chance, to live true love, a chance Neil stupidly wasted by sleeping with her once best friend.

Anne didn't understand how he'd ended in their bed with Gillian. He'd told her more than once that he didn't even like Gillian. That she represented the opposite of everything he loved in a woman... in Anne.

He'd said he distrusted Gillian. He even tried, once, to open Anne's eyes and tell his suspicions that under Gillian's thin, urbane veneer she was not the honest, trustworthy, dedicated friend she claimed to be.

Anne had laughed at him. She'd told him she was aware of Gillian's selfish and spiteful character. She added she could handle Gillian and her moody character.

***

Following their confrontation, Gillian sold her shares in the company to Anne and left town. She made no attempt to talk to Anne in person or to mend things. It would have been useless to tell more lies. Gillian left a short letter apologizing for having hurt her feelings and told Anne she still considered her a friend.

"In the long run, all bitterness lessens, and you'll no longer think about me with venom or hatred," were the words with which Gillian ended her short note.

Mutual friends told Anne, several months later, that Gillian opened an advertising company in New Zealand, and married an obscenely rich cattle owner, twenty years her senior. Furthermore, she'd given birth to a girl she named Nellie.

Chapter Six

1473

Genevieve

With the small bundle under her arm and the tears brimming in her eyes, Genevieve swallowed the hard lump choking her. She stood for a while in the middle of the road. Her legs betrayed her, and an uncontrollable tremble shook her whole body.

"I'm alone. Again," she murmured, dismayed. "Where to now? Where?" She brushed at the hot well of tears running down her face. Her prospects looked dreary.

She sighed and headed to the alehouse at the end of the village. They might need a servant in the kitchen, or upstairs where the owner kept four rooms ready for passing travelers. She'd never entered the drinking establishment before, although she had passed by the place several times while going to the fields to find herbs for Bertha's potions.

On those occasions, loud laughter and swearing had reached her ears through the open windows and door. She clearly remembered the riotous, drinking men's lewd, offensive words.

The old owner, the one who used to provide her father drink on credit, died not long after the horrible event that took her family from her. His eldest son ran the inn now.

It was after midday, and she'd not eaten anything since the morning, before the bailiffs came. Her meal had consisted only of a slice of cold mutton left from the food some charitable wives had prepared for old Bertha's funeral.

At the alehouse, known by all the villagers as The Sly Fox, Genevieve stopped in front of the entrance. Her heart thumped in fear. There were less noise, less laughter, and louder speaking than at other times. The usual guests might not have awoken from the previous night's carousal.

Reaching for the door handle, ready to enter, she gathered all her courage and stepped inside. The stench of beer, human sweat and smoke from the quenched candles invaded her nose. Genevieve blinked several times to adjust her sight to the dim light and smoke in the room.

There were only two customers who sat at one table and judging by their half-opened eyes and the way they swayed on the wooden chairs, they'd reached the stage in drinking when everyone spoke and nobody listened.

She found the owner in the middle of a heated argument with one of the inn boys, who'd broken an earthen jug full of cider.

She cleared her throat, but her voice came in a tremulous whisper. "Good morning," she addressed the man. She couldn't have come at a worse moment. He would refuse to hire her most likely.

The man stopped his bellows and, turning his glance to her, he answered between his teeth, "Mornin'. What's it you want? I think I recognize you. The daughter of the witch. We've nothing for beggars. Nothing to give away," he grumbled. "Take yourself off," he spat at her.

People had already forgotten Betty and John and their children. She'd become the 'daughter of the witch.' A beggar. Yes, nothing else than a vagrant begging for a roof over her head and a piece of bread to appease her hunger. Genevieve reflected on the bitter truth. She forced her lips to keep a smile, her mood far from feeling it.

"No, no, sir. I don't want to beg. I'd like to ask you if you have some work to be done here. I can clean and cook. I'm strong and not afraid of work. I want nothing in exchange, just a place to sleep and food to eat."

"Work you say. No," replied the man, clicking his tongue. He waved his hand and continued, "Nothing, for the time being. Well...still I think there may be something. Yeah. But not here. I've a good cousin who owns a large inn, over the hills. In South Dalestride. The Golden Stag, they call it.

"My cousin, Master Morgan, sent me word some days ago. Two of his servants left and found work at the lord's castle, and he needs some new hands. Tell him I sent you, by all means. They might find something for a clean skivvy like you to do. He has an eye for the fresh ones. Ha, ha." The man roared with laughter, slapping his thighs.

His roars sent icy shivers down Genevieve's spine. She recoiled, as if touched by a toad, catching his meaningful wink.

"Go right ahead," he instructed her. "Follow the tracks left by carts on the road, and you'll reach him, no doubt." The innkeeper ended his explanation and turned his attention and shouts back to the inn boy, who hadn't dared move all that time.

"I bid you good day, sir. Thank you. I'll tell your cousin you were so good to send me to him," Genevieve said, leaving the inn, grateful in a way that no work was available for her there.

She followed the directions The Sly Fox's owner gave her and continued her journey to the hills, in the distance. She glanced ahead at the long way left to walk, that to her, a country girl who never left her home village, seemed to stretch endlessly. She followed the deep tracks left in the dry, crumbling ground. She couldn't afford to lose her way.

All along the road, red poppies and bluebells swayed their delicate heads in the slight breeze. She'd have liked to rest in the tall grass and listen to the grasshoppers' song; however, she needed to reach The Golden Stag first and find shelter for the night. Genevieve hurried her step. She still had a long way left to walk.

The sun had nearly set when she arrived, on weak, tired legs, drenched in sweat, at the inn.

The Golden Stag was situated at the very entrance of the village, and she arrived just as the purple light on the horizon gave way to the coming night's dark colors.

Judging by the loud noise coming from the inn's main room, and from the many horses in the stables, it was obvious that several travelers had arrived and very likely they would spend the night at the inn.

Genevieve asked a boy, who passed by her in a hurry, where she could find the innkeeper. The boy held a pair of fowls in his hands, blood oozing from their slashed necks. He mumbled something under his breath and, in too much of a hurry to stop for a detailed answer, pointed to the inn with his head and disappeared through a door she guessed to be the kitchen.

Genevieve paused before her hand touched the door handle. What if this proved to be another dead end? She inhaled deeply and entered the inn.

The boisterous laughter coming from a group of noisy soldiers, roaring and slapping each other's backs as if celebrating some victory, attracted the disapproving looks of three nuns sitting at a table in a corner.

Judging by the empty plates in front of them, the nuns had already finished eating. They stood up and left the room, climbing stiff-backed up the stairs to their chambers.

The soldiers ceased their amusement for a moment, only to listen to a loud, irreverent remark thrown by one of their companions regarding the three black clad women.

Roars of laughter rang out again, the men oblivious to the nuns' indignant faces.

Genevieve approached the innkeeper, who was busy with the drinks for his customers. "Good evening, sir," she addressed the man. "I'm sorry to barge in at such a busy time. I'm a stranger here, and I'm looking for work. Your cousin, the owner of The Sly Fox, told me you were short of hands. I'm strong and I need little, just food and a roof over my head."

The innkeeper, a stout man, broad-shouldered and with enormous spade-like hands, ceased his activity to scrutinize her with a shrewd gaze. He rubbed his hands together, inspected Genevieve again, from head to toe in hard-eyed speculation.

He measured Genevieve in an appraising glance as if she were a calf or horse to buy. Genevieve's whole body turned to a slab of ice under his insistent, pert gaze.

He must have found her appearance satisfactory, because he nodded."Yeah, yeah. Right. We're in need of working hands. Things are very busy. Hurry to the upper floor where my wife's preparing the rooms for the guests."

Relieved she hadn't been turned down, Genevieve climbed the wooden stairs, in search of the innkeeper's wife. Yet, something nagged her mind. While the innkeeper spoke, cold waves emanated from him and caught her in their icy claws.... Just like the ones that came from her father after his stay in the cursed forest.

Chapter Seven

England 1990

Anne

Backpacks fastened tight on their backs, Anne and Neil left the place where they'd spent the night and entered the forest, Anne following the path of her own thoughts, Neil frowning and silent.

Anne didn't harbor any doubts that he hoped they'd find a path leading to the modern facilities of the chalet. Or, at least, meet some people who could show them the way to the mountain hotel where they had their reservations.

Anne chewed her bottom lip. What would happen if the dream proved real and not a dream? What might such revelation lead to?

A faint scent of lavender, Neil's favorite aftershave, reached her nostrils. The fragrance invaded her senses and her soul, stirring to life the memory of how they first met and what dreams they shared together.

It must have been fate, no doubt, that brought them both to the same place on the same day.

She had been in a bookshop, looking for her credit card in her handbag. While she was hurrying to the cashier's desk, she bumped into a man. It was Neil.. He dropped the pile of books he had in his hands. Embarrassed for having been absent-minded, she apologized while trying to help him pick them up from the floor.

"Never mind," Neil had answered in a bright voice, striking a chord in her soul.

She glanced up and the moment their eyes met, his gaze rocked her world. The warmth in his eyes contained a sensuous flame, his eyes bringing an immediate softening to his handsome features. Muscles rippled under his white shirt, his firm and sensual mouth stretching in a wide smile that quickened her pulse.

Right then, she'd decided he was the man she wanted to spend the rest of her life with. A man she'd seen in her mind's eye, long before ever meeting him. That very second, she fell in love with Neil, the man she believed she'd known forever.

"Oh," she managed to utter at last, moistening her dry lips. "I'm sorry. Please, accept my apology."

Neil appeared a little baffled too. He held up a hand. His gaze stayed glued on her.
"No harm done. It's my fault too. I know you might say it's a cheap line, but have we met before? Your face looks familiar to me."

Taking a deep, unsteady breath she replied, "I was wondering the same thing. You remind me of someone, though I can't say of whom."

"Someone nice, I hope," he replied playfully, and flashed his irresistible smile. "By the way, my name's Neil," he said, reaching out his hand. "Neil Blackwell." The faint scent of good tobacco and lavender aftershave enveloped Anne.

"Anne," she answered shaking his hand. "Anne Ellett." She would often afterwards, for the swiftest second, have odd flashes of memory, of the face of a man. Thick lashes over kind brown eyes, a square, dimpled chin, very similar to Neil's, yet slightly different. Maybe sometime, in another life, she had met and loved him.

Unfortunately, the flashbacks didn't last long enough to offer her more clues and after a while, she gave up trying to force her mind. She and Neil were different, yet at times so alike—the very key to her attraction for him. The chemistry between them sparked into love.

The surrounding old trees claimed Anne's attention while she advanced through the forest and kept close to Neil's heels, worried she might stray away from him. She glanced at the strong, thick roots grabbing the earth with their powerful wooden, claws, like vultures grabbing their prey, unwilling to let it go.

A smile stretched the corners of her mouth, as something Neil did once came back to her mind. A tender man, he often touched her heart with unexpected gestures.

Neil earned his living as a freelance writer tackling various subjects, mostly documentaries. He traveled frequently around the country. Once, on his return, he brought her a wood anemone. A delicate, white-ivory flower, she pressed in an album – ivory being her favorite color.

"You know," Neil had told her, "when I found the flower I thought about you. Frail and delicate in appearance, yet so strong and determined at heart. Our guide told us the flower could resist very harsh weather."

Despite his attention and care towards her, all through their years together, he'd never proposed to her.

"They say marriage is the perfect murder for love," he stated, half joking while they were in the company of friends. "Why should we destroy our beautiful relationship and chain it into marriage?"

Anne never commented on his 'joke,' yet she didn't hide the feeling she disliked it.

Mutual hobbies, like mountaineering and reading, tightened the bond between them. He was fond of antiques: furniture, jewelry and books. He also liked fishing.

She enjoyed sitting by his side and watching him fish while her mind buzzed with the many problems at the office. She ran a building company. Fresh out of college, she inherited the business after the tragic death of both her parents in a plane crash.

With her sharp mind and being a dedicated person, Anne proved all the skeptics, who predicted the company would suddenly collapse when she took the lead, wrong. On the contrary, Anne managed to expand the business into new areas, and drew the bottom line well above a comfortable profit at the end of the financial year.

Later, she became interested in other profitable things, one of them was advertising. She bought half of the shares of an advertising company, the other half belonging to an older acquaintance and friend of her father's, Mr. Emerson. In fact, she bought the half to help the owner solve his financial problems, believing her father would have done the same. Soon after she became involved in it, things bloomed. Her new partner, Mr. Emerson, praised her and said she possessed 'a gold touch.'

Fate wasted his life two years later in a car crash, his half of the company going to his sole heir, a daughter, Gillian, a tall, gorgeous, passionate brunette. A sparkling, sophisticated, sensuous woman who broke the hearts of many men.

Opinions differed, according to who commented on Gillian. Men said she possessed it all: looks, brains and an inborn capacity to adapt to any kind of circumstance. Women admitted she looked gorgeous but added she acted spoiled and possessive. And she used phony charm to ensnare other women's men; they also spoke of her beauty as secret and dark. Her dark blue eyes spoke more of a devil than of an angel.

Anne and Gillian became close friends. They'd known each other for a long time, and the bond became tighter when they started running the company together.

They shared the same hobbies. "Even the same man, in the end," Anne told a friend later, after the incident.

Theirs, she'd believed to be, up to the ill-fated day, a relationship based on mutual understanding, respect, compassion, and above all, love. She defined their relationship as a comfortable, quiet love. Love coming from the small, kind, tender gestures bringing a warm, bright smile on the other's face.

Anne dated other young men after her abrupt, painful separation from Neil. She always watched them with a critical, analytical eye and wondered what their Achilles' heel was. None of the dates ended in a serious commitment. She wasn't ready for it.

At times, Anne asked herself what she wanted from her life. If she had had to choose anything right then, what would her choice have been? The answer left her no doubt. Neil. All she wanted was Neil. She came to the conclusion it would be easier to forgive Neil's one mistake and accept him back, than try to adjust herself, her life, and her time to another man. God knew what other failings would be possessed under his polished, urbane appearance.

Mutual friends' insisted they were the perfect couple. Her own belief that something wasn't as it appeared on that unfortunate morning, caused her to grant Neil one more chance.

She found no explanation for her present reluctance to be very open towards him, at first. They booked a room at a luxurious hotel, and here they were, in a kind of renewed romance, lost in an odd forest, far from any human settlement; now, trying to find their way back to the noisy modern world, as well as in their old relationship.

Lost in her thoughts, she bumped into Neil, who'd come to a sudden halt. He turned a concerned and uncertain look on Anne. "We've been groping along for more than two hours and there's no proper path in sight. Does anything look like the road you followed in your dream last night? I for one can't call the small run between this thicket of trees a 'road.'"

Anne shrugged skeptically and turned to face what she hoped would be the right direction. "I don't know, Neil. I can't tell one tree from another. The huge oak in my dream looked different from these. I remember I passed a kind of crossroads before I saw the woman disappear into the tree. Maybe we'll get lucky and find that tree."

Neil checked his wristwatch again. "There's no sign of the crossroads you're talking about. I just noticed something. I was concentrating on finding the main path and didn't notice it until now. I don't hear a thing; no birds, no animals, not even the sound of branches in the wind."

"Now that you mention it, I think you're right. Hope it's not a bad omen. I don't know what to say. I feel guilty I insisted on checking out the things I saw, or dreamed, and it's too late to turn back now. Let's follow the path to our right first. That way, we can't get lost again." Anne stepped with renewed resolution among the old trees.

"Here. It looks like the one I told you about. If we turn to the right and keep on walking for five or six meters, we should run into the oak tree."

"At last. This place finally resembles a normal route," Neil exclaimed, relieved. "If we follow it in one direction or the other, we may get out of this spooky place."

Anne pointed to a tree. "Look over there. The huge tree in my dream; the thick root stretching over the ground." Anne's voice came in a controlled but excited tone. "And over there, behind the tree, a few steps down it the stream from my dream. What kind of fish are those? They're huge."

After an attentive glance, Neil nodded. "It's trout, tasty grilled. I'll try to catch some, later."

Neil looked up into the tree. "Is this the branch you told me about?"

"In my dream it was closer to the ground. The tree looked shorter. Well, what do you say about my dream now?"

"It appears more like sleepwalking to me."

"What about the woman? She called me by my name. She wanted me to come here. Why? And for what?"

"We'll find the answers to your questions, sooner or later. The only certain thing is that we lost our way. Let's, at least rest by the water and enjoy the stream for a while. After that, by following its banks, we should find some signs of human life. I hope."

Anne heaved a concerned sigh. "Yes, I think you're right. Let's rest here for a couple of minutes. I hope the people at the hotel have realized we haven't shown up," she said and put down her backpack.

"I doubt it. We pre-paid for the room. Our absence won't bother them. You know these things. Money is all people care about."

"Quite encouraging," Anne muttered.

They sat on the soft grass and lunched on the packet of crackers and some chocolate. Anne was glad to rest her worn-out feet. Neil sat next to her. He leaned back against the broad trunk of the oak tree and heaved a tired sigh, stretching his long legs out in front of him.

"I missed you so much, my wood anemone." His voice faded to a whisper.

Anne remained silent for several seconds, her gaze steadily fixed on his. She touched his cheek. "I missed you too." She turned her thoughtful glance to the stream.

Sunrays sneaked through the trees' dense crown and gave the place a peaceful look - sunny, warm. No ghosts, no fears, no secrets, no worries.

"An ordinary stream, in a normal, ordinary forest," Anne said and bent over the water to watch a busy looking trout. The fish slid with determined movements among the stones on the riverbed to a destination known only to it.

Anne closed her eyes and lay in the grass. The only sound was the sloshing ripple of the running water over the stones. An uneasy shiver ran down her spine, as if someone was watching her.

On the verge of turning from the water, her gaze met the woman's face reflected in the stream's clear mirror. The very woman who had haunted her dream the previous night. Her eyes were the same green as Anne's. She had auburn hair as well.

Even her face was not much different from Anne's. Long, prominent cheekbones and a full mouth gave her an attractive air. But, the face wasn't a reflection. The woman watched her from beneath the water mirror. Silky lashes shadowed the large, sad eyes. Their look filled Anne's soul with a torrent of mixed emotions: wonder, sadness and apprehension. A pleading glance from the stranger, full of despair and anguish. And, no doubt, she wanted Anne's help.

"Neil, Neil, come and see. The apparition, the woman's face is in the water." Anne's agitated tone startled Neil from his light sleep.

Too late. The image had already vanished. Neil glanced at Anne, mounting concern glittering in his eyes, and shook his head.

"Nothing's wrong with my mind, or me, if that's what you think. I saw her there, under the water surface. I have no clue what she wants from me," she added breathlessly. "Or why she chose me. We found the tree and the water I saw in my dream, or whatever that was last night, haven't we? You can't say what happened to me is nothing but a figment of my imagination."

"Well, something strange is happening here," Neil said agreeing with her.

"I think we'd better examine the hollow. Maybe there's something in there connected to the woman. I told you, in my so-called dream she vanished *into* the tree, not behind it or into the air. Let's find a long branch to stir inside and chase away any critters." Anne looked at the tree hollow.

"Do you have your flashlight? My curiosity's aroused," Neil said. "Let's try it. Even if only to put your mind at ease." He searched around for a loose branch. It wasn't difficult to find one. They threw some pebbles Anne brought from the stream into the hollow and waited. Nothing crawled, flew, or jumped out of the tree trunk.

Neil climbed up closer to the hollow and poked the branch in, moving it around several times. Anne gave Neil the flashlight, and he leaned half inside. She kept her gaze on what Neil did with an indefinable fear of what he might discover.

Neil's alarmed voice almost frightened Anne. "Sweet God. Oh, Anne."

"What, Neil? What's wrong? What have you found?" "Promise you won't scream. Or run away."

"You're already scaring me. What's up there? Hope you aren't joking."

"Not at all. I've found something. Some bones. They are no doubt human bones, judging by the skull. I can't say if they belong to a man or to a woman."

"My goodness. What a strange place for a grave. Let the bones rest there. I don't know what we should do in these circumstances. For all we know, someone was killed and the body hidden inside so it wouldn't be found."

"Hey, what's this?" Neil asked. "I can see something sparkling under the bones. I think it's a piece of jewelry."

Neil pulled his hand out of the hole.

Anne gasped in horror at the sight of the object hanging from the tip of the branch. She experienced one of her quick mind flashes. This time, the flash brought the image of a mean stare and vicious smile thrown at her by a tall, dark-haired woman, dressed similarly to the first apparition. A gem encrusted cross glimmered around her neck. The image vanished as suddenly as it appeared.

Anne controlled her apprehension as best she could.

Neil wiped dirt and bits of tangled leaves off what proved to be a beautiful crucifix, hanging on a thick golden chain with a large ruby in the middle.

"Wow, what a treasure," Neil exclaimed, examining the cross and its chain with the keenest interest. "The owner must have been a rich person, or an important cleric to possess it, and it looks old," he added, inspecting the exquisite object.

"Why not a prince, or a wealthy lady, or an outlaw?" Anne asked, unable to master the distressing sensation the sight of the embellished cross caused. It resembled the one she'd seen in her vision just seconds ago. She made no attempt to hold the object.

"It could have belonged to anyone."

"Is the skull broken or in pieces? How does it look?" Anne wanted to know.

"I'll examine the bones again." Neil agreed and returned to the tree trunk. After a short examination, he climbed down to Anne.

"The skull has a large crack in it. I suppose someone may have hit this person with an axe, or something similar. The teeth of wild animals can't open such a wide gap. I think we can call it murder. I'm sure of it. It occurred a long while ago, no flesh left on the bones at all."

"We'll have to inform the authorities."

"Right. The experts can tell if it was murder or just an accident."

"They'll even be able to tell the gender and the year it happened." Anne nodded.

"We'll keep the cross, if we're allowed, and offer it to a museum or something. But first, we need to find our way back to civilization. I don't feel comfortable at the thought that someone or something's waiting for us behind a tree to crack open our heads. It gives me the creeps.

The sooner we get out here, the better. I have the feeling the trees have closed in on us, like they want to catch us in a trap. I can't even see the path that lead us here," he said in a worry tinged voice, rubbing the back of his neck with one hand.

Anne nodded. "It seems we're the forest's captives."

"Weird. Don't like it at all," Neil added, his forehead puckered.

"Let's walk north, along the banks of the river."
"Upstream? Why not down?"

"There's still something nagging at the back of my mind. Something is urging me to go that way. I have a feeling we're not finished with our discoveries."

"It's already two o'clock; the weather's changing. I'm not happy with the idea of a storm catching us here."

"You're right. We'd better hurry," Anne said, watching a patch of cloudy sky visible through the branches.

"Here," Neil said and held the cross out to her. "Put it somewhere safe."

The feel of the cold object brought Anne a new brief flash of memory. The same cross in the outstretched hand of a young man. She raised her gaze to Neil, trying to separate reality and the unsettling sensation the golden chain left in her hand. She wrapped the necklace in a handkerchief and placed the small bundle in one of the rucksack pockets. All the time she handled the exquisite piece of jewelry, its touch raised gooseflesh, and left her the feeling similar to what she'd experienced the previous night while following the mysterious red-haired woman. Malevolence crawled over her skin, and she fought the desire to throw the object away.

Casting a last look towards the old oak tree, Neil walked ahead along the river's bank.

Anne shook her head, concerned, and glanced up at the sky again. Hopefully, by the time night fell, they'd find a populated place. Village, or camp, or chalet. Anne regretted they'd not brought their mobile phones. A rescue party would have started a search, and they'd have been out of this strange forest in a couple of hours. She chanced a furtive glance at the stream, and stepped back, appalled, at the image she saw.

Chapter Eight

1473

Genevieve

Genevieve found the innkeeper's wife making the beds in one of the chambers.

The room wasn't very large. There was enough space for a four-poster bed, a wooden stool, and a large water carafe on a washstand.

The woman grumbled under her breath about ungrateful people, and how one shouldn't be generous towards the servants. Ready with the sheets, she turned, and gave a startled cry.

"Oh, sweet God, girl, why don't you speak? You frightened me. What is it you want?" she inquired, raising her eyebrows, intrigued. Genevieve obviously didn't resemble a guest.

Genevieve curtsied and addressed the short, fat lady in front of her. "Good day to you, madam. Your husband said you were here and told me you needed a helping hand. I'm an orphan, and I've come from over the hill looking for work. Your cousin at The Sly Fox sent me to you, knowing you are short of servants. I can do anything. Sweep the floors, do the laundry, help in the kitchen, sew and iron, carry the pails of water. Anything," she added, eager to please the owner's wife.

"Yes, indeed. We need some help. Badly," the fat woman replied. A wart on her left cheek, displaying a tuft of hairs, moved at every word.

"We had two ungrateful servants. Two urchins…. I fed and dressed them since they were six, and after they grew up and were good for work, they left us. Went to the castle to be maids, they said. Humph. Whores. Yes, nothing but whores they'll be there, in the big house. The master's whores."

The woman punched the feather pillows as if they were the ungrateful servants.

"So what if we asked them to keep company, from time to time, to some of our guests, soldiers, or traders? What's the big fuss about? No, they preferred a tumble in the hay with the filthy lads from the village.

"They even jumped into my husband's bed, the moment I was gone to attend my mother's funeral. Bad, very bad girls," the woman continued without a break. At last, she seemed to remember the reason for Genevieve's presence.

"Hear me well. If you want a bed and a piece of bread from me, you must obey my orders. Every morning, you help the kitchen woman. Afterwards, you tidy the yard and the inn hall. After the guests wake up and leave the rooms, you have to empty the bed pots. Clean and air the rooms, make the beds, take fresh water to every room and the sheets to the laundry woman. You shall also help with the washing.

"After you are finished with your morning work you return to the kitchen and wash, chop or peel what is needed for lunch. If there are too many guests for the servers, you help my husband and wait on the tables. Any money the guests might leave to you, you must hand over to me. Do not forget!

"And another thing," she added, pointing a threatening finger at Genevieve. "If I catch you once, only once, becoming too sticky to my husband's fingers, I throw you out to the dogs. Don't say I haven't warned you. You shall always address me as Mistress Morgan, you hear me?"

The woman was all red in her large face from her long speech, her double chin shaking in an agitated way. The headdress on her head sat akimbo, giving her a pathetic appearance. Her huge bulk swathed by a plain, black dress made her look like a draped barrel.

No wonder her husband is looking for a bit of fun with the slim, young servants they hired, Genevieve thought, and then she jerked her look away, embarrassed at the nasty turn of her own thoughts.

With a hefty push, the woman unfolded a dark green quilt over the bed. Her small eyes pinned Genevieve in a cold, penetrating stare.

"Come with me," Mistress Morgan barked an order. "There are three more rooms to be made ready. Follow me. I hope you're not one of those good for nothing, lazy creatures who want only to be fed for free, and pretend they're sick when there's work to be done."

"No, Mistress Morgan, I'm not lazy. You'll see."

"Leave your things here. After we've finished this room, go and meet the other servant, Mary. You'll share the same bed in a fine room close to the stables. The other servants will envy your luck."

***

Mary, a fair-haired girl about the same age as Genevieve, greeted her warmly. "I'll show you our palace." She laughed.

Genevieve followed obediently. The 'fine room' was a small shed with worn, peeling yellow paint and smelling of mice and sweat. The dark and stinking dreariness of the place alone would have made her leave at once, but the fact she'd not be alone instilled a bit of courage into her .

"My, how glad I am I'll have company." The blond girl nodded. "We'll keep one another warm during the cold winter nights. Leave your things on the bed. You'll see to them later. First, let's return to the kitchen. We must be ready with the food for the guests. Otherwise, our masters will raise all hell's demons. Come. You'll wash the potatoes. The cook is happy for new help. We'll talk while finishing work."

"Yes, please. It's so nice of you," Genevieve replied in a small voice, keeping close to Mary's heels while they entered the kitchen.

Great billows of steam and the tempting aroma of food enveloped her. Her empty stomach protested angrily.

The elderly cook raised her gaze, irritated at the intrusion, and seeing Mary, she grumbled, "At last you returned. You know we're short of hands around here. Everyone wants to eat right now, and I have only one pair of hands. Who's this?" She jerked her head to Genevieve.

"It's the new maid. Genevieve. She'll help us for the moment, and then go to the tables."

"Well then, there are ducks to be made ready," the cook added. She turned to the hearth and took a batch of wheat bread out of the oven and placed it on the table to cool.

Cabbage, onions, lentils and potatoes stood waiting to be cooked on a corner of the table in the centre of the room, next to slabs of salted game, pork, and the fowls brought by the boy who stood in front of the turnspit waiting for the meat to roast.

Mary gave Genevieve an apron and pointed at a stool for her to sit on."Here. Take this and grab a duck. We mus' hurry, or the cook won't give us a piece of fresh, warm bread. Well, there's one thing you mus' know. Around here, never be shy or show you're afraid. You need blood in you, or they'll trample all over you. I learned things the hard way, though I'm related to Mistress Morgan."

"Are you? Why are you only a maid, then?" Genevieve's asked, her eyebrows going up.

"Oh, nothing comes for free in this world. We're close relatives, but I mus' work hard for me bread and a few coins. Me father and Mistress Morgan is cousins. Was, I mean. He died some years ago and me mum's a widow having to feed six bairns, except me," Mary offered the information while plucking vigorously at one of the ducks.

"I've me luck. I'm not one to complain," the girl went on, removing a strand of hair that escaped her cap. "The only favor for me is that I'm to help only in the kitchen. Not like you." The girl's eyes filled with pity as they fixed on Genevieve. "Well," she continued, "during winter it's real heaven to sit by the large stove, drowned in the smell of food, and peel potatoes or pluck some chickens. Things are not so nice in the summer… you feel your brain boil in your head." "Lucky of you to work only here, anyway."

"I guess. Only if the inn's short of hands, I have to wait on the customers. There's something else you should know," Mary lowered her voice not to be overheard by the cook. "I mus' also tell you a word of warning about me uncle, Master Morgan the innkeeper. He's a lecher. None of the girls who'd been hired hands at the inn escaped his 'attentions.' He even forced his luck with meself," Mary confessed to a bewildered Genevieve. "To me luck, me aunt appeared in time to prevent a disaster."

Genevieve listened, appalled to Mary's words.

"You can't even imagine what hell me aunt started. There followed a violent row. Yells and screams shook the windows, though the masters fought behind the closed door of their bedroom. Me aunt reproached him he could never keep his 'stick' in his trousers and enough's enough; he'd crossed the line.

"From that day on, Master Morgan chose to ignore me. He never dares to come to me room when she's not present at the inn, as he'd done before the scandal. And, Mary continued, nodding, "I pretend I don't see his hateful looks and just carry on with me work. As for the other girls who worked at the inn, me uncle continued to enter their beds. That's why they never stay, and look for work somewhere else. There's rumors he has two children in the village. And even me aunt knows about it."

Mary again shook her head. "Take great care around me uncle. Your hair, like the glowing fire in the stove, and those green eyes will attract him like the flames lure the moths."

Genevieve shuddered.

"Thank you for warning me. I'm so glad we share the same room. I feel safer already. The moment I asked him for work here, I pretended not to see his lustful gaze crawl over my body. Knowing you are by my side, he won't try to visit me at night. He can't risk it. Mistress Morgan might learn of his attempt from you."

***

Genevieve did not complain about hard work. The chores became her daily routine. She did everything without any word of lament, dead tired by the end of the day, her back and hands aching like hell.

Things followed the same daily routine for five months. Although the Morgans didn't pay Genevieve anything, she was content to have a place to live in and something to eat.

There'd been times, at first, when she missed kind, old Bertha very much; above all, she missed her mum and the little ones. She closed her eyes and brought their image to her mind. Only by suddenly remembering them and how much they meant to her, did Genevieve come to grasp the meaning of death.

Sad, eternal nothingness. She feared her heart would break into pieces.

Following Mary's advice, Genevieve hid her brilliant auburn hair under a kerchief, not a strand out of the neat plaits. She avoided any close encounter with the inn's male customers as much as possible. She had no doubt her frail body presented no obstacle to the strength of a drunkard looking for fun. The maids of the inn were always easy prey, advised by the owners not to refuse the customers.

The scandal started one cold November afternoon. Genevieve blamed the damp cold for the men's continuous orders of more ale and wine. To keep them warm, they said.

Two groups of travelers arrived. Some tradesmen who had returned from the yearly cloth-and-meat market. They had sold all their goods and had gained a nice profit. They were willing to buy the best wine the innkeeper offered, and ordered some kidneypie and game. Waiting for the food to come, they swilled the wine that the shrewd innkeeper proffered as the finest. Soon, they were drunk, their loose tongues turning more and more offensive with every cup.

Two other strangers came too. Genevieve recognized one of them as the younger of the bailiffs who'd kicked her out of Mother Bertha's home.

He stared at her, but gave no sign of having ever seen her. Very likely, he didn't want to acknowledge the servant waiting at tables as the girl from the neighboring village they had thrown out into the street, Genevieve thought.

The two groups of guests were already having their meal when another group arrived.

Four nuns on the way to the St. Mary Abbey.

The nuns let the innkeeper know they didn't intend to continue the trip that night. It was already late, and they'd stay overnight at the inn as they did, most times, on their way to and from the town.

Only Genevieve attended the numerous guests. Mary left the inn, summoned to her village for her mother's funeral.

Mistress Morgan was upstairs, preparing the chambers for the nuns. Genevieve received the order to stay downstairs and help the innkeeper and Johnny, the stable boy, at the tables.

She brought the traders their meal and turned to leave when one of them, a lewd grin spread on his lecherous face, used filthy words. He invited her to his room and slid his hand in her blouse.

Shocked, Genevieve slapped his face hard. She stepped back, away from him and his groping hand, only to trip over the stretched legs of one of his companions. No doubt the man had stretched his legs on purpose. She fell in a graceless heap, to the derisive laughter of the three men who continued to speak obscene words.

Hot tears of humiliation and hurt welled up in her eyes. She attempted to gather herself up from the floor, but one of the traders pushed her back down.

A voice thundered by her side and, at the same time, a hand helped her rise to her feet.

"You should be ashamed of yourselves. Leave the lass be, the stranger addressed the boozers through clenched teeth. His voice possessed a commanding tone, and he towered over the three men.

Two of them turned to their food, voicing a meek protest that they hadn't meant any harm. The one who'd asked her to his room didn't want to abandon his prey and stood up in a swift movement, upturning his stool in his hasty gesture.

He raised his fist to hit Genevieve's savior. To the trader's bad luck, the man was sober and much stronger than him, and a slight push sent the drunk tumbling over the upturned chair.

"If you want more, I'm ready," the stranger said in a calm, cool voice, but the other two traders helped their companion to a sitting position and calmed him down.

Genevieve raised her glance, her cheeks burning like fire, to thank her unexpected benefactor and to her surprise she discovered he was none other than the bailiff.

He gave no sign of having recognized her.

Genevieve thanked him and retreated to the kitchen as fast as possible to check if the cook had prepared the nuns' meal. Once inside, she let loose the dam of her tears. She'd never been humiliated like this by anyone.

"There's no use crying," the cook told her, shaking her head. "Dry your tears and pretend nothing happened. Someday, either one of the guests at the inn or our master will enter your bed. You're too pretty for your own good, child."

Genevieve couldn't rid her mind of how the innkeeper who'd witnessed the entire scene, had done nothing to help her out of trouble, though she worked her fingers to the bone for him. His sly gaze had only riveted on her, giving her an uneasy feeling. She could swear Master Morgan regretted that the bailiff interfered.

Of course, it's in the innkeeper's interest not to antagonize the customers who spend their money at the inn. Why should he help her, after all? She shuddered and following the cook's advice, swallowed her bitterness and continued her work, avoiding the gazes of the innkeeper and the traders.

***

A freezing wind howled outside, bringing the smell of snow and ice with it, an unmistakable sign of the coming winter. Genevieve finished her chores long after midnight, after all the guests had retreated to their beds. Genevieve's small shed was filled with the banging of a loose shutter at the window, shaken by the furious gusts of wind. The room was cold, fire being allowed only for the guests' rooms. Servants had no need of warmth, Master Morgan said. Too much warmth turned servants lazy.

Dead tired, Genevieve wanted nothing but to stretch her exhausted bones for the few hours left until dawn. Soon enough, she'd have to be up again, to sweep the fallen leaves from the yard, tidy the common room, and then hurry later to the kitchen to help the cook prepare breakfast for the nuns and the other guests. With Mary away, things had been hectic in the kitchen, too.

Worn-out, Genevieve fell asleep before her head even touched the hard pillow.

With a sudden start, she woke up, confused and alarmed, unable to tell how long she managed to sleep. She couldn't see anything in the freezing darkness, though she sensed another person's presence in the room. She must have forgotten to block the door latch. Disoriented and frightened, she bolted upright and clutched the thin blanket to her chin.

An icy claw gripped her heart. She held her breath. Cold waves emanating from whoever sneaked into her room engulfed her, as if she slept outside. Danger. She was in danger. Genevieve's heart thumped so loud she imagined the intruder also heard it.

She opened her mouth to scream, but no sound came through her petrified throat. No doubt the drunken trader came to take revenge on her for refusing him and because the bailiff had proved him a coward in front of the other people in the room.

It was pitch dark in her cubicle, but fear made her hearing acute: a man was breathing hard in her room. A man, representing danger, was closing in on her.

Spurred by her terror, she jumped out of the bed and attempted to reach the door, only to bump into a body blocking her way out. The man grabbed her, pushed her back onto the bed, and jumped on her. She smelled his sweat and his foul breath while he, panting, managed to part her legs. Genevieve's fists hit him and she clawed at his face and hands, screaming, as loud as she could for help.

The man stopped for a second and slapped her face hard. Obviously, he couldn't see a thing either, and he missed the first blow, striking his hand on the iron bed frame. He moaned and hit her again. The second hit caught her mouth and nose. Her lip split and warm blood trickled from it. She twisted under the man's weight and screamed again.

The door flew open and someone holding a lantern entered the room, the swaying light threw long shadows on the mold covered walls.

"Well, well, here you are, dear husband," Mistress Morgan's stentorian voice came out of the darkness. "I knew you were up to something nasty, since Mary's not at the inn. You bastard. You despicable fornicator. You thought me too tired to feel you slip out of our bed in the middle of the night. I know all your tricks. You can't deceive me. You, you villain!Take yourself off. At once. Wait for me in our room."

Her voice rose with each word, ending in raging yells. In a last outburst of fury, Mistress Morgan hit her husband, using a pot she held in her other hand.

Genevieve managed to cover herself. Cold and frightened, she trembled like a leaf in the wind, her teeth chattering as she sagged on the bed. As soon as the innkeeper departed, his wife turned her hard stare on Genevieve. Mistress Morgan's unflinching, hateful glance bore holes in Genevieve's soul.

The woman shook her head disdainfully, her icy voice reproaching Genevieve."Now, girl, I'm sure nothing of this would have happened if your false smiles and lust-filled looks didn't lure the poor man. Wash your face.

"You're making a mess on my sheets. In the morning, you'll do your usual duty and help the cook prepare breakfast. And then, you shall leave our place. For good. I don't want to see you around my home and husband anymore." The enraged woman turned and left without any further comment or allowing Genevieve an explanation.

After her trembling subsided; Genevieve summoned what seemed a superhuman effort of will and got out of her bed. Using the half frozen water from the jug next to her bed, she washed her bruised face with difficulty. She touched her fingers to her swollen lip and sore nose. The bleeding would stop soon.

By pure luck, the innkeeper hadn't broken her teeth. Too shocked to be able to go back to sleep, she sat for a long time in a stupor on the bed's edge, unable to cry or to think of what to do next. An unmerciful headache made her temples throb. She passed her hand over her eyes to clear her mind.

A deep sigh escaped her as despair settled in. She had no one to care for her. It was useless to return to her native village. The house where she'd been born and spent her childhood years was gone. New tenants had already taken over old Bertha's house, and the village people were too poor to need a servant. Nobody would accept another mouth to feed. They didn't have enough to fill their own bellies. Hot, bitter tears ran down her cheeks.

For the first time in her short life defeat choked her.

"Oh, mum, I wish I'd been home the night father took your lives. I wouldn't suffer such indignities at the hands of strangers. What good's my life here, alone without you? Oh, mum, dear mum. I wish I were dead, too."

Her crying deepened into distress. Deep, racking, violent sobs, shook her shoulders. Her body jerked spasmodically as she gasped for air.

Then, she felt small, firm hands grasping her shoulders gently, holding her at arms' length. Sister Benedicta, one of the nuns staying overnight at The Golden Stag sat next to her.

"Hush, my child. Seal your lips. You're too young to die," the woman said, taking Genevieve in her arms, and held her close to her bosom. "Hush. Don't cry any more. We're all mortals. Only God decides the time for each of us to leave this world and go to face our judgment.

"I couldn't sleep, and I overheard the disturbance. The innkeeper's wife yelled and threatened she'd send him to sleep in the small room in the attic with the boy servants, separate from him, if he continued his shameless gallivanting. This shut his mouth at once. It's no secret the inn and all the money belong to her, no matter what the law says. Her husband mentioned your name and blamed you for what happened. Such a coward. Starting tomorrow or better said, today she said you would be gone, and she didn't care if you were an orphan. Since the ruckus ceased, I imagined they made peace," the nun continued, shaking her head. Her kind eyes appraised Genevieve.

"I thought to come and see how things were with you. I knocked, but you obviously didn't hear me. You don't need to despair. Almighty God won't let you perish. He always offers us choices. And you must know something else. He never knocks at your door, but the moment you're in need, and you call His name, He's already by your side." Sister Benedicta patted Genevieve's head in motherly fashion.

"In fact, I've come to tell you we're preparing to leave The Golden Stag and head to our abbey. We won't wait for our breakfast. We fear winter is taking hold of the land, at last. We must pass through the forest, and it's a very long, tiresome trip. If you want, you are welcome to accompany us. Our abbess, Sister Dominica, will be glad to offer you a roof over your head at the abbey. Our Mother

Superior is a wise woman, and she'll know what to do. I've already mentioned you to her," the nun's soothing voice continued as she embraced Genevieve.

Genevieve sighed.

Every two weeks, the group of nuns, always led by Sister Benedicta, came down from the abbey to buy provisions and special silk and gold threads for the famous embroideries they made. Each time, on the way to and back from the town, they stayed overnight at The Golden Stag.

One morning, after the nuns had spent the night at the inn, Genevieve entered their room. She wanted to ask if they were ready to leave. She brought them food from the kitchen for the trip: some apples, smoked meat and a loaf of bread.

Sister Benedicta held a book in her hands: the Old Testament.

Genevieve's glance had been interested and avid. The nun handed her the book. Benedicta's eyes widened when, opening it, Genevieve read from the page in fluent, articulate Latin.

"You can read Latin?" the nun interrupted her. Genevieve nodded, smiling. "Yes, I can read and write." "Good for you, though quite unusual for an ordinary, peasant girl. Where did you learn the language?"

Genevieve told the nun she owed her knowledge of Latin to an old lady who looked after her for about four years, before she came to work as a servant at The Golden Stag, having no other choice.

"Why do you waste yourself here? It's time for you to leave this disreputable place," Benedicta added.

Genevieve shrugged. "I've no place to go. No one left in the world. All my family perished some years ago."

"If you ever find yourself in a difficult situation, think about coming to us. Coming to St. Mary's Abbey."

It had been the only time Genevieve spoke to Sister Benedicta until today.

"Come to St. Mary's. It's the best thing for you to do, my child. If you later find our life not to your liking, you'll be free to leave anytime. I cannot force you to come, but I think it's the only way for you."

Genevieve nodded at the kind woman's suggestion. Tears threatened to choke her again. She swallowed hard and managed to tell Sister Benedicta in a whispered voice, "Thank you, Sister. I'll accompany you." Her voice trailed away into another spasm of sobbing.

Sister Benedicta waited until Genevieve regained control before speaking. "We'll leave early."

Genevieve nodded. "It might be God's will for me to follow you to the abbey." She repeated, as if to assure the nun she wouldn't change her mind. "Thank you, Sister. I'll join you."

"Good. I knew you'd make the right choice. A wise decision. Pack your belongings. We follow the longer route to avoid passing the whole way straight through the forest. We still have to walk about a mile across it. The abbey is deep in the wood. Have no fear. I know about the legends people used to whisper, regarding the evil lurking in the forest. I can't say I believe them, yet we don't want to find out if it's true or not."

Genevieve frowned. "Yes, I forgot the abbey's in the forest. The cursed forest. It's waiting for me. It still has some things to settle with me," Genevieve whispered, resigned, her heart thudding fast.

Chapter Nine

England 1990

Anne

Anne's gaze was riveted on the small river. The stream's waters suddenly became murky, writhing as if the whole stream boiled.

Furious. Threatening.

In a flash, as suddenly as it started, the writhing stopped and the water cleared. The face of the woman from Anne's dream appeared below the surface. Her eyes closed and large tears flowed down her face, mingling with the waters of the running stream.

"What in the name of God is this?" Anne whispered to herself. She opened her mouth to call Neil back, but the image disappeared.

The stream continued to run undisturbed through the grassy banks.

Anne glanced at the sky. Big black birds, stretching their large wings, flew from the crest of the old oak tree. Baffled, Anne followed Neil.

They walked quickly along the banks and advanced up the stream that had narrowed to a mere silvery tongue of water, jumping over the smooth stones. The trout could be seen more easily in the shallow water. Two hours passed and there was no sign the forest would ever end.

"It's already four o'clock," Neil said. "If we don't find another human being, I mean a live human being, in another hour, we should head back the other way. Who knows how large the forest is, and I don't want to be attacked."

"Well, I think we don't have to fear animals. As you said before, there's no sign of them. Except some big, black birds I saw circling for a while over the stream. I wanted to show them to you, but they'd flown away. Anyway, I totally agree. If nothing comes up in the following hour we'd better go back.

"Sunset's around eight o'clock during the summer. This leaves us time enough to at least reach the point where we began to look for the way out of the here. I still feel something urging me on, and I wonder if it's sheer curiosity or premonition. Both, very likely."

She marched on, forcing a more alert rhythm to her steps. She always enjoyed a weekend in the open, especially after the long straining hours spent in the office, at herdesk among files, figures and all the paraphernalia of a big company. She'd intended for the short vacation to be an idyllic one, with Neil wooing her again and renewing the broken bond between them, not treading along unknown,dangerous mountain paths, chasing a ghost.

On the other hand, maybe it's for the better we lost our way, Anne considered, stepping ahead. God knows who we could have bumped into at the chalet, considering that one of our mutual friends had recommended it to him. Can it have been fate's hand?

"Look over there, on your left, behind the tall pine trees. I think I caught sight of something resembling man-made walls. It might be a hunter's lodge. Let's find out."

They found an area strewn with the dilapidated remains of a building. Screened by a large cluster of trees, as though hidden from inquisitive, prying eyes.

Anne glanced around, amazed. Fragments of memories flooded her mind. Nothing clear, nothing that remained long enough to make sense.

There were some pieces of wall still standing, most of them covered by vegetation, while in other parts there were heaps of half burnt stones. From place to place, stone pillars, supported ribbed arches. Vestiges indicated that the ruins had not been a hunter's lodge or a peasant's house. Grass, wild flowers and weeds had conquered the whole place.

"Judging by its present derelict state, the building must have been quite impressive, with many rooms," she remarked.

"Could it be the ruin of a castle, or a church? Or a manor house? I'm certain you know more about this than I do," Neil said.

"I can't say for sure. Taking into consideration the surviving arch, there on your right, it seems to me the ruins belong to a church or a monastery of some kind, rather than to a castle. There's no sign of a moat or any fortifications, customary in castles built during the Middle Ages. Here, so far in the wilderness, it might have been a clerical establishment of some kind, although quite unusual to be so remote from any populated area." Anne offered her viewpoint. "Experts in the archaeology maybe could identify it and trace it back to the period it was built."

Walking among the ruined pillars and former walls, Anne and Neil discovered, to their great surprise, a room mostly intact at the north side. They stepped inside the small room, the stones carpeted by moss and daring tufts of grass. The confined space made Anne physically aware of Neil,in a strong and pleasant way. The aroma of his aftershave caught in her nose.

Close to what appeared to have been the window, a single wood anemone's ivory petals sparkled, like a tiny candle lit for penance by the room's former inhabitant. Anne shivered, the air suddenly cold on her bare arms.

"What a strange coincidence, a flower similar to the one you brought me some years ago." Anne touched the small flower's delicate petals.

Neil examined the entire area and found traces of the whole square-based building.

"I'd have never imagined people would build such a large construction on a mountain slope, in the forest," Anne said shaking her head.

Neil left to search beyond the ruins. He came back to Anne, who was sitting on a stone and lost in deep thought, to let her know what he'd found.

"I walked for about a hundred yards ahead and I discovered the mountain ends abruptly, in an abyss whose slope is like a straight wall. The person who built here was wise."

"Why?"

"Very likely they erected the establishment here realizing that, at least on one side, it couldn't be attacked by anybody."

"Clever, indeed." Anne gazed up at the sky.

Dark, ominous clouds, lowered over the forest. The air smelt of rain. A clap of thunder banged deafeningly close.

Anne gripped Neil's hand.

A second thunderclap fell closer, wrapping itself fast over the first.

"There's no chance for us to go back now. If the rain starts, we'll be soaked to the skin, not to speak of the danger of being hit by lightning if we seek refuge under the tall trees," Neil remarked in a concerned voice, entwining Anne's fingers with his.

"I'd rather we find shelter in that stone room, than stay here in the open," Anne added, already on alert because of the coming storm.

She wasn't a coward, although she didn't consider herself as a very daring or courageous person. She feared thunderstorms, though. No matter her whereabouts,whenever, menacing dark gray clouds gathered in the sky, her heart thumped at an alarming speed and her whole body froze.

Every time the wind snatched branches from the trees and whirled the dust high up in the air, she became jumpy and her pulse accelerated. She didn't deny it was an illogical fear, but nevertheless she couldn't control it.

She recalled Gillian telling her that once, surely in another life, Anne had suffered or died in a thunderstorm and this traumatic experience still lived in her present day spirit. Anne laughed at Gillian's explanation, though there were moments she tended to agree.

The wind, howling and roaring in the nearby trees, gained force and the first icy raindrops splashed down.

Anne and Neil took refuge in the tiny stone cubicle, grateful for the shelter and security it offered.

They managed to cover the small square hole that was once a window by putting Neil's rucksack in front of it.

When they entered the room, a powerful bolt struck the place where Anne had been sitting several seconds before. The terrible crack deafened them and the blast caught Anne unaware. She lost her balance and tripped over Neil. He caught her and took her in his arms.

The ground vibrated again with the heavy crashes of trees hitting the forest floor. A bright fork of lightning dashed from the belly of a dark cloud and hit the ground close to the entrance of the small room in another deafening explosion.

Anne cried and covered her ears, closing her eyes.

Neil embraced her in his strong arms and held her close to his chest, whispering encouraging words. It was the first time in two years he'd held her.

His touch triggered in Anne a sweet, dizzy sensation. The two years of separation disappeared in the dark remote depth of a bad dream.

The strong circle of Neil's embrace helped Anne forget the unleashed storm outside. A surge of emotion and a spark of courage and confidence overcame her. He'd held her in his arms so many times before their separation, but this time was different.

A scorching desire rose in response to his embrace.She regretted having lost so much time away from the man who meant so much to her.

The warmth of his body next to hers brought to the surface, from the deepest corner of her heart, a flood of pleasant memories. Tears came to Anne's eyes and they slid down her face, dropping on his shirt, as she melted in his arms.

"Don't cry honey," Neil whispered. He dusted her lips with his. "Don't cry. I'm here. I'll always be here for you. Forgive and forget my foolishness, please. You'll never regret it. The last two years were the most miserable years of my life. I behaved like a complete fool. Offer me a chance to prove I'm not such a villain. You can't deny we lived a good life until that unfortunate episode."

The knot of tears in her throat prevented her from answering at first. Neil must have thought the rain's loud drumming wouldn't allow Anne to hear him, and he repeated his plea.

"Have you considered you might possibly be able to forget the past and learn to love me again, as I love and have always loved you?"

She nodded and raising her face, stared straight into his eyes, relieved to find her own love and desire mirrored in them.

"Has my past behavior destroyed all chance of that happening?"

She stood breathless and the beating of his heart next to hers little by little wiped away the pain of his betrayal. She nodded again and whispered, the same as he'd done before,

"Yes, I forgive you. I've offered you a second chance and you'd better not spoil it again." Anne kissed him full on his mouth.

He returned her kiss with the same eagerness and passion as hers, a huge wave of relief washing over her. It was as if a secret spring within herself had been released and a great hunger let loose.

His grasp on her tightened. Neil's hands on her hips pulled her body to his. For a moment she imagined their clothes didn't exist. An inner liquid heat engulfed her loins.

Their entwined lips and tears sealed the reawakening of the world's most sacred gift and miracle, giving the universe its meaning – unconditional, everlasting love.

Outside, the heavy unrelenting rain scourged the ruins where they'd found shelter, as if trying to clean the stones of the former inhabitants' sinful touch.

A long wail broke through the howling wind. Weak at first, growing louder with every pail of the rain.

"Anne...Anne... Anne...."

Chapter Ten

1473 - 1477

Genevieve

The nuns, accompanied by Genevieve, left the inn behind as soon as dawn's first timid light replaced the night's cold perilous darkness. A long trip awaited them and the strong air of the gloomy November morning and the slush of last night's drizzle increased Genevieve's apprehension, like an omen....

A bad omen.

***

"Welcome among us, my child. I do hope you'll soon consider our abbey your home," Sister Dominica, Mother Superior at St. Mary's Abbey, addressed Genevieve.

A dark gray, long habit, tied around the waist with a leather belt, clad Sister Dominica's slender body. No wisp of hair came loose from the wimple on her head. A hint of a smile pulled at the corners of the woman's mouth and her kind brown eyes searched Genevieve's face.

"Sister Benedicta told me some weeks ago about a nice, bright girl who worked at the inn. And she has already told me how mean and cruel the inn owners treated you. Both I and all the nuns here are touched by what happened to you.

"It came as no surprise to me, you should know," the nun continued, shaking her head, a world of understanding in her voice, "I have heard many bad things about the Morgan couple. Anyway, it might be for the better. A decent girl like you has no place living and working at The Golden Stag. Sister Benedicta told me about your predicament in life. Never lose hope, my child. I like your neat and serious appearance, Genevieve. And I am glad you decided to join our community."

With a trembling hand, Genevieve tamed a coil of her rebellious hair that had escaped from the cap.The friendly, open smile of the elderly woman in front of her brought to Genevieve's mind the talk she and Sister Benedicta had on the way to the abbey.

***

"Your frown tells me you are worried, my child."

"Yes, Sister. A bit."

"Don't be afraid. Sister Dominica, our Abbess, is the kindest person I've ever known. She is a special lady. We all love and respect her. You know, in her lay life, she was indeed a lady, the daughter of a nobleman. Catherine de Westerville."

"Why did she become a nun? Was she an orphan like me?"

"Not at all. Even as a young girl, Catherine vowed to pursue a life of celibacy, never to marry or bear children. Her family's interests differed from hers and they didn't want to listen to her pleas, forcing her into an arranged marriage."

"How did she manage to join the abbey? Did she run away from home?"

"Not exactly. Dedicated to her faith, Catherine refused to consummate her marriage. The Archbishop of Canterbury, impressed by her willpower and strong determination, granted Catherine the annulment of the marriage to the great dissatisfaction of her whole family. She left her parents' manor house and joined the nuns at the

St. Mary's Abbey, becoming Sister Dominica. A few years later, the Archbishop appointed her as the Abbess here.

She's an ardent believer and a hardworking person. She's filled with a deep understanding for the pain of human life, with the deep conviction lying at the heart of our spirit: that God is omnipresent. God is among us. Her warm smile is a blessing for any troubled soul. You'll soon see it for yourself. Yet, don't let yourself be fooled by her grandmotherly appearance. Beneath it lies cleverness and force making her respected among the nuns. And she doesn't go easy on idleness or gossiping."

***

Sister Dominica's voice carried an evident trace of sympathy in both her serene face and words. "Come closer. Have no fear. You may call me Mother Superior." The Abbess patted Genevieve's head.

Genevieve raised her gaze to the frail wisp of a woman who was the one to decide her fate. Warm waves enveloped Genevieve. Warm and pleasant like Bertha's soft, lavender and lilac smelling blanket.She blinked back long repressed tears.

What will become of me if I can't adjust to their way of life? A homeless tramp? Oh, but I'm already homeless. How silly I can be, she scolded herself silently. She swallowed the lump of tears ready to choke her, focusing on what the Abbess was saying to her in a warm, soothing voice.

"You'll meet the rest of our small community at the evening meal. For the moment, if you don't feel too tired, you may take a tour of our home. Sister Francesca here will show you around. I'm sure you two will become friends in no time, won't you?" the Abbess addressed a young nun wearing a white novices' veil, who riveted Genevieve in a curious gaze.

"Come," the young novice said. "Follow me. I'll show you the whole place. You can ask me anything you'd like to know."

Genevieve bowed in front of the Abbess. She considered herself lucky to have met such a kind person who, in some ways, reminded her of Bertha.

Glancing around in awe, Genevieve followed Sister Francesca. The large building of her new home impressed her. The space was divided in a wise way for each activity: the church proper, the kitchen buildings, the wooden belfry and the nuns' chambers; there was even a small graveyard for the abbey inhabitants who had died within its walls.

"There's a lookout tower, though it's never been used," Francesca explained to Genevieve who expressed her bewilderment on seeing the tower.

"Nobody has ever ventured here, up the mountain, to attack us. The abbey's location, between the mountainous abyss and the unwelcoming forest, deters any attempts at ransacking it.

"You know the legend about the ghost dogs, and the song of the stream, and the evil hiding among the trees? It helps, somehow, in keeping malevolent people away from us. And there are some treasures under its roof many would like to lay their hands on," continued the young nun. "Sometimes, I think the cursed forest protects us, in a way, if you catch my meaning."

"Yes, I know about the cursed forest."

"I can tell you lots of interesting things about St. Mary's. Everyone here knows its history. There's an old book, a kind of chronicle, telling it all. It says the most skillful master masons, sculptors, architects and glaziers worked to erect our abbey.

The pointed arches, ribbed vaults, and foliage motifs had never before been used in English architecture. The stained glass fitted into the church windows, the fine stone, and the rich decorations made St. Mary's Abbey an exquisite masterpiece. When we have our meal later, you'll see the beautiful table silverware donated by Edward, earl of Gloucester, the abbey founder."

Sister Francesca paused in her chatter to allow Genevieve to admire what she'd pointed out to her.

"I've no doubt all these details will be familiar to you soon," the young nun spoke on. She took Genevieve's hand and led her outside into the yard. "Here's our garden, divided into two distinct areas, one for flowers and one for vegetables. There's a space for poultry and sheep too. An old man, who has his lodgings in a small cubicle near the abbey gate, helps us tend the garden and the animals. Ryan is his name and he came to work as a gardener here many years before. We call him 'Uncle Ryan'. I think you already met him, on your arrival."

"Yes," Genevieve managed, at last, to interrupt Francesca's flood of words. "He was at the entrance cleaning the yard of broken twigs and branches. When he noticed me, he stared at me in a strange way, frowning. He appeared a bit dismayed,. as if trying to remember a long forgotten face... as though he'd seen me before. He has a long ugly scar on his cheek. What happened to him? Did someone try to cut his throat?"

"It's an old story. A nun told me, in a moment of despair, he attempted to take his own life, but didn't manage. The scar remained as an eternal memory of the terrible event."

Genevieve's eyes widened in wonder."How awful! Why?"

Francesca didn't answer. She'd already advanced to the imposing main door, waiting for Genevieve to join her.

***

Sister Dominica smiled her warm smile at Genevieve. "Now that you've become familiar with the abbey, I hope you'll soon find your stay among us satisfactory. You should know St. Mary's Abbey was designed to promote piety and worship, not only among its tenants but also among the population of the nearby villages. It's also a refuge for widowed, abandoned or persecuted women and girls, the very reason for which we can offer you a shelter here. Of course you'll have to follow the same routine, or 'horarium' like all of us."

"Yes, I understand," Genevieve replied.

"Sister Benedicta told me about some books you inherited from the woman who taught you reading and writing. What books are they? May I see them?"

Genevieve handed her the only treasure left for her in the world. The Abbess studied them with care and even reverence. Nodding, she confirmed old Bertha's words. Both the Gospel's Latin version and the Leech Book were real treasures.

"Yes, your books are valuable. I'm glad you are such a capable young lass. Of course you may keep them in your room. They are yours. Even, what do you call it?" Sister Dominica pointed to the skull.

"Good old Hans," Genevieve replied in a small voice, afraid she would have to throw it away.

"Good old Hans... yes, you may keep it too. The words written on it are a permanent reminder of our transient status here on earth. I also understand you are skilled in preparing potions and healing ointments from plants?"

"Yes, Mother Superior," Genevieve replied, already at ease in the presence of the abbey's head. "After the tragic death of my mum and her little ones, I lived with a kind old widow, Bertha. She taught me a lot of useful things, and everything she knew about plants. Old Bertha, as everyone used to call her, said I had in me the gift to find the proper plants and to prepare them like she had."

"Got a head on your shoulders. I like that in young people. I'm glad to hear about your gift with plants. God has led you to us. I always say He has His unknown ways to lead us on the right path. The sole nun skilled in nursing the sick, a kind of doctor in our abbey, died about six months ago. None of the other sisters are able to remember how she made all the remedies along the years.

"Well, my dear. Enough with so much idle talk. You must be tired. We'll meet later this evening. Francesca, lead Genevieve to her room." The Abbess concluded their conversation and allowed Genevieve to leave.

***

"Here's your room," Francesca invited Genevieve inside with a large gesture of her hand after opening a solid oak door. "It's similar to all the rooms where the rest of us live."

Genevieve entered and inspected the small room, her new home; a plain room with a minimum of furniture and an atmosphere appropriate to praying and reflection

"Well, what do you say?"

"It's a palace compared to the hole I lived in at The Golden Stag."

"All the nuns here deal with the same activities here. We take turns in preparing the meals, doing the laundry, sewing our own clothes, stacking the wood brought from the forest, and milking the sheep that provide us plenty of milk and wool."

"It's fine with me. I'm used to all kind of work."

"Another thing, we specialize in embroidery here at St. Mary's. Not only high-official clerics, but also noblemen and wealthy merchants buy it. Tomorrow I'll keep a seat for you next to mine and I'll teach you how to do it. Regarding the rules at the Abbey and the prayers, Sister Benedicta is the one to instruct you. Nothing complicated, you'll see.

"I'll leave you, and if there's something else you'd like to know, don't hesitate. Come and ask me. My room is next to yours."

***

Here at the stately, two hundred year old abbey, with its thick, gray, stone walls and narrow slits for windows, keeping the air damp and cold even in the hottest summer days, Genevieve, like all the other nuns, had her own room, a wooden bed, a chair and a small table.

A rosary, a crucifix and a candle, burning day and night, were the only decoration within the room's cold walls. Each room was a mute, an indifferent witness to the pain, suffering, giving up, penitence and renewed faith of its transient, ephemeral tenant.

Genevieve divided her time between the regular daily prayers and the more mundane activities of cooking, laundry and, what was for her real, relaxation, embroidering. She soon became an expert in the delicate skill.

In a short while,the Abbess herself praised her for making some of the finest "Opus Anglicanum," a piece of embroidery enhancing the priests' vestments.

The beasts' liveliness, the Biblical figures depicted amid decorative frameworks, and motifs of silver and gold thread were the most poignant characteristics of the exquisite work.

On Sundays, after attending Mass, she would bring out the illustrated fables book and read some of the stories aloud, taking turns at reading with Francesca who, just as the Abbess predicted, soon became Genevieve's best friend.

***

Genevieve turned eighteen in the spring. She'd lived four long years at the St. Mary's Abbey, since Sister Benedicta brought her there.

She worked beside the other women and attended all the religious services. She joined the nuns' line, holding lit candles in their hands while they walked inside the abbey church, raising their fervent prayers to the creator and thanking Him for the priceless gift of a new day of life He laid in front of them.

Her soul would turn easier and her body light, as if a miracle happened. She'd always been a faithful person, but except the Sunday religious service she attended with her family, she'd never gone by herself to any church until arriving at the abbey.

Sister Dominica's deep piety, her exemplary life here, offered Genevieve food for thought and, at last, she made up her mind. She petitioned to take her permanent, solemn vows and to be confirmed in the creed, after a long period of living the life of novitiate and of the temporary vows. She spoke to Sister Dominica and let her know about her decision.

"Are you sure?" the elderly woman inquired, keeping quiet for a moment, appraising Genevieve in a serious, thoughtful glance from head to toe.

"Don't take my words the wrong way, please, my child. Your vivid emerald eyes, bright auburn hair, your slender figure and your clear, melodic voice are as many signs pointing to the dormant volcano of passion and sensuality beneath your untouched innocence. A volcano in danger to erupt, one day, in a sea of scorching flame if the right man stirs it, though a very unlikely event in our circumstances, for the moment."

Genevieve's cheeks turned hot.

"Do it, my child, only if you feel you're ready for this sacrifice, since it's indeed a sacrifice, at least for some people. You shall abandon all the dreams you would have in your lay life. You'll forget about all desires and, above all, your body's drives." The wise Abbess very likely sensed Genevieve's embarrassment.

"You are a bright girl and you understand, of course, your vows are sacred and you'll remain a nun until the last day of your life. Only God will be your bridegroom and you'll be God's bride. If you don't want to join the creed and one day you decide you want to leave us, to go down in the village, nobody will stop you. I force you into nothing,"

Sister Dominica added. "Nobody forces you to join the creed. You may live here for as long as you wish. You've been our companion quite a long time and I hope you don't regret having lived here. You know there's nothing for you to fear. It's a choice you make of your own free will. It's up to you."

Sister Dominica's words disconcerted Genevieve for a few moments. Did the elderly woman, who usually treated her with the utmost kindness and generosity, consider her unworthy to become one of them? Was it something in her, different from the rest of the nuns? She was always hard working, obedient, and ready to bring her small share of work to the benefit of all in their close community.

Genevieve hadn't asked the Abbess these things, yet her questioning look said it all. The old woman shook her head and left Genevieve alone, telling her to think, very seriously, for a few days about it.

Two months later, Genevieve officially became a nun. Sister Dominica allowed her to keep her lay name, a rare thing in an abbey.

The religious service was a special one, as usual on such occasions. The atmosphere, the prayers, the whole ceremony gave Genevieve a feeling of elation.

"I'll never disappoint you," she promised the Abbess at the end of the ritual.

Sister Dominica's gaze riveted Genevieve, again, and nodding her head, she answered, "I hope so, my child. I do hope so."

The Abbess turned and left the room.

Genevieve stood staring after the old woman, her eyebrows raised in dismayed inquiry, her hands clutching her Bible to her chest.

Genevieve's skill in preparing healing potions proved its usefulness whenever the nuns had to be treated against severe headaches, colds, or joint pains. The warm season was very short, with the abbey being in the mountains.

But none of the remedies she'd learned from Mother Bertha or from the Leech Book would be of any use, one winter day. Sister Camilla came in a hurry and summoned Genevieve to the abbess's chamber.

At once.

Chapter Eleven

England 1990

Anne

Anne shivered with apprehension, her gaze fixed on the heavy, cold rain falling for hours without any sign of subduing.

The storm brought an awful tumult. Violent thunderbolts crashed down from the sky in fierce whips of fire. Most struck close to where she and Neil took shelter.

They could do nothing except unfold one of their sleeping bags and sit side by side on it. She gazed at the curtain of rain and the vicious lightning, counting between the moments the light flashed over the mountain and when the deafening crack banged near them, to try to work out if the electric front drew nearer or went away from them.

Under no circumstances could they leave the shelter and follow the way back down stream. The small stream had swelled with the terrible downpour, and turned into a roaring, raging river carrying down rocks, mud, and logs.

"What happens to the trout?' Anne expressed her wonder.

"I really don't know. Maybe they hide at the bottom, or they're crushed by the water's force," Neil whispered. They sat side by side. Arm in arm.

At peace. Reconciled. Lovers once more.

"I'm sure this rainfall will stop by tomorrow morning," Neil said, squeezing her shoulder. "It can't keep up like this for too long, or the valley would be flooded. If it keeps on there could be mudslides. Let's hope it's only a summer shower, even if a little bit too loud and too violent. We'll have to sleep here. It's sheer luck we reached this place. A blessing in disguise to me. I don't think our tents would have resisted these heavy pails of rain, no matter how waterproof the manufacturer says they are."

Anne leaned into Neil's firm body and hooked her gaze on the rain hitting the stones outside with hate and fury. She couldn't get the woman who called her to the hollow oak, as well as her face in the stream, out of her mind. All of it surely had some meaning.

"Nothing happens around us without a reason," Anne said and shook her head. "I'm very sure of it. The fact we found not only the oak, but also the bones inside it, proves this all wasn't a simple dream, or a figment of my imagination. Very likely the skeleton belongs to the woman. She wants revenge."

Anne's brows shot up in wonder. "Why me? What should I do for the poor soul to find its eternal rest? Did someone kill her in a war of some kind? Did a jealous husband or lover kill her? Was the woman kidnapped and trying to flee when the attackers caught and killed her? Was she an ordinary woman or someone of high rank?"

"Too many question that we can't find any answers to right now. I'm confident the forensic people will find out the explanation for some. Above all, whether the bones belong to a woman or to a man. You only assume it's a woman's skeleton because you were visited by the apparition. We don't know for sure," Neil argued.

"You're right. The apparition's face, as much as I can recollect, showed fine, delicate features. And the young woman's eyes.... Yes, the meaningful look of those large, sad, green eyes, asking for help, asking for forgiveness. They haunt me."

Anne sighed and promised herself she'd do whatever it took to solve the mystery. For a split second, the echo of her name, uttered like a plea, calling in a wailing, lamenting voice reached her through the powerful drumming of the rain. "Anne, Anne." Startled, she opened her eyes and strained her ears to catch the voice coming on the howling wind.

"Have you heard anything?" she asked Neil in an alarmed tone.

"No, my dear. There's nothing, except the wind and the rain. Nobody could survive outside in such weather for too long," he reassured her.

Anne shivered under a nagging sensation of unease. "It's becoming a bit too creepy," she whispered, shaking away the feeling of déjà vu she couldn't explain.

Not at all.

And the night was new.

***

Anne sat cuddled in her sleeping bag. The rain continued to fall as hard as it had the whole afternoon. Only the lightning and thunderbolts died out. She envied Neil's ability to fall asleep in any circumstances, never bothered by noise or light.

She'd have liked to fall asleep, exhausted after the previous night's events, and the long walk through the wood, as well as the macabre discovery by the stream. Even if she could have slept, something warned her not to; something horrible would happen if she wasn't alert

The cold, furious, relentless rain exasperated her. She strained herself to remain awake, though she'd been on the verge of dozing a couple of times. Anne didn't fear the forest's beasts, owing to the fact they had found no sign of any wild animals in the forest. And even wild animals didn't venture out of their burrows in such a downpour.

She didn't fear any living being. She feared the other world's treacherous, evasive shadows, in which she'd always believed. The anxiety, almost suffocating her, came from the awareness her premonitions always came true. What had happen here? Danger. Her skin prickled with a shiver.

She recalled her premonitions before her parents' death and before Megan's death.

Dolls, sweets, cinema, opera, Zoo, circus, the first high-heeled shoes, the first make-up, the first confession about a boy friend... everything was linked to Megan, her childless aunt. And what beautiful stories Aunt Megan had told her.

"Dragons, wizards, and beautiful fairies made Anne pester her parents to take her to stay with Megan during all her school vacations. Megan passed on to Anne her passion for mountaineering.Sometimes her mother would become a little jealous of her sister.

Although just a teenager, Anne experienced a deep spiritual bond with Megan,.who always remained a bright icon in Anne's soul.

Megan, who lived two hundred miles from them, became ill with terminal cancer.Called to her dying sister's bed, Anne's mother and father left home to stay by Megan's side, without telling Anne the cruel truth.

Anne wrote a few lines to her aunt.

Her mother told her later, that Megan had been conscious to the last moment. She'd left the world of suffering, keeping Anne's postcard close to her heart. Megan's last thoughts flew to her beloved niece whom she'd never be able to hold in her arms again.

During the night, at the exact moment Aunt Megan passed away, Anne woke up with a start from her deep sleep. Her aunt's voice calling her name rang in her ears. Something bad had happened to Megan, no doubt. It was the first time she'd experienced a premonition. The next morning she had its confirmation.

Anne suffered a lot over Megan's death and often experienced a slight uneasiness at the thought that her aunt's death hurt her more than the tragic perishing of both her parents, eight years later.

Though a lot of time had passed since Megan's death, the memory of her bubbly, spirited, and generous aunt brought tears to Anne's eyes. She lowered her eyelids and she fell asleep, her hand tight on the flashlight....

Again, dream and reality mingled in a new apparition of the young woman who had visited her sleep the previous night. The woman's sad eyes stared at Anne on the brink of tears, full of a tragedy and loss known only to her.

"What is it you want from me? Why do you follow me?" Anne whispered. "If you don't tell me, I can't help you. Are the bones we found in the hollowed oak tree by the river yours? What's your name? Did you suffer a violent death? Did someone kill you? Tell me."

Anne's heart sank as the sole answer the apparition offered came as hollow deep sobs. The young woman wore the same long clerical robe from the previous night. A kind of shawl, or large kerchief, hung loose over her shoulders. Anne couldn't tell whether the woman was barefoot. Again, she walked as if not touching the ground.

The apparition headed to the window where the tiny wood anemone rested its slender body on the moss covered stones. She gently touched the flower and a tear slid down her ashen face.

Something only the woman-ghost sensed caused her to turn, then fear flittered across her face, and she vanished, as silently as she'd come.

Anne strained her eyes and ears to catch the sound or movement that had frightened the young woman away. The only sound echoing over the mountain came from the rain splashing on the decayed building's stones with the same unrelenting force. On the point of turning her attention elsewhere, a figure formed in front of her.

Anne focused, trying to see better in the dark. The woman was back, maybe. Maybe she'll manage to persuade the sad ghost to reveal some details and find out what she wants."

It became clear, to Anne's surprise, that the apparition belonged to another woman. This one was tall and dark-haired, older than the previous but dressed similarly, with only the color of their dresses differing. A long, dark-green robe, obviously made of the best brocade, swathed her voluptuous body. Anne recognized in her the woman she'd seen, in the short flash, when she touched the golden cross they found in the hollow.

The apparition drew nearer to Anne. Unveiled hate burned in her menacing dark blue eyes and she spluttered in a hoarse voice, "You shan't have him back. He shall not be yours. You harlot. You tool of evil! You devious witch!" She lunged for Anne's throat with her outstretched hands, her hair turned into hissing snakes.

Chapter Twelve

1478

Genevieve

Sister Camilla rushed into the room, almost bumping into Genevieve, who was on the verge of going out to do her chores. Sister Camilla wrung her hands as her words tumbled from her mouth in an avalanche.

"Come, Genevieve. Come quickly! I'm sure our Abbess needs your assistance. Oh God, oh God. Hurry, Genevieve."

Genevieve's eyebrows shot up. "What's wrong, Sister?"

"Sister Dominica hasn't appeared for the first benedictions in the kitchen, the way she usually does, so Sister Benedicta summoned me to check if the Abbess overslept, although such a thing never happened before. I dashed to her room and...."

"And?"

Camilla's lips quivered and her eyes swam in large tears. "The Abbess is breathing, but she can neither move nor speak".

"Oh, goodness."

With Camilla in tow, Genevieve hurried to Sister Dominica's chamber.

They could do nothing for her.

Genevieve helplessly held the limp hand of the elderly Abbess, who'd suffered a severe stroke. The Abbess died two days later in her sleep.

Genevieve, like all the nuns, mourned. A great lady, a kind soul and a fervent believer, Sister Dominica was an example of piety and kindness to all of them.

***

The very first day the new abbess, Sister Clementa, came to be installed by the bishop, Genevieve's grief intensified even more for the loss of Sister Dominica; she yearned for the nun superior's calm voice and unsophisticated behavior, more motherly than that of a superior.

The moment the cold waves emanating from the new Mother Superior hit her, Genevieve's eyes widened at the shock of realizing that she had an enemy in the woman in front of her. Genevieve turned her head toward the abbess and the waves from Sister Clementa became visible for a slight second, spreading through the hall, engulfing the nuns in their evil net.

Thick, dark grey, ill-omened.

None of the other nuns appeared to be aware of the menacing flow. Although not a word was exchanged between her and the Abbess, only Genevieve's low curtsy while being introduced by Sister Benedicta, Genevieve's heart contracted.

The mean gaze appraising her from head to feet felt almost like a physical blow. The moment their glances met, she flinched inside, a slight shudder passing through her body. My peaceful life here at the abbey has come to an end, she thought.

Genevieve sensed her superior disliked her, but the reason for the enmity remained an enigma. She had said or done nothing improper to attract the new Abbess' unwelcome attention.

A look of total arrogance and disapproval was plastered on Sister Clementa's face the very first and only time she inspected the nuns' rooms, one week later. The Abbess's gaze moved around Genevieve's small chamber, checking thoroughly, and then she stopped, catching sight of the books on the table.

"What's this, if I may ask of you?" she demanded at once, and a greedy look twinkled in her eyes the moment Genevieve let her know how valuable the Latin version of St. Mark's Gospel was.

After listening to the explanations about the other two books, The Leech Book and The Bestiary, the Abbess said they would be destroyed without delay. They represented the works of the devil. The Leech Book, before all else, was 'a book used only in witchcraft,' she stressed in a haughty voice.

"Oh, not at all," Genevieve exclaimed, amazed at the Abbess' determination to criticize something so useful and label it as devilish. "It's a very useful book."

" Yes, indeed. Useful for the followers of the devil."

Genevieve stiffened as though her superior had struck her. She shook her head. "It brings no harm. On the contrary, I prepare many healing potions for the sick nuns here at the abbey using the wise suggestions and recipes in it. Sister Dominica, God rest her soul, knew I had these books and agreed I would keep and use them."

An ugly glare, followed by a torrent of shouted, offended reproaches from her superior poured over Genevieve.

"Are you daft? How dare you contradict me! Who are you to disobey my orders?" The Abbess's words sliced through the room like the crack of a whip. "You are in no position to tell me what's right or wrong. I don't care if your Sister Dominica agreed to this heresy or not. She's dead. Dead! I'm your mistress now, whether you like it or not," the Abbess spoke with open hatred. "Furthermore, your tongue's too ready for your own good."

She glared at Genevieve, her face consumed by a purple red rage. Reaching out, she grabbed The Leech Book and the Bestiary from the table.

"I'll see to their destruction myself. The Gospel has a better place in my chamber," she added, and snatched the last one of Genevieve's treasures, too. Sister Clementa's accusing gaze riveted Genevieve. "I forbid you to prepare any potion under the roof of the abbey. And don't you imagine, for one second, that you'll be able to boil such sickening things behind my back. I'll be watching you.

Once, just once, break my order and I'll hand you to the bishop on charges of witchcraft. Don't say you've not been warned."

All the time nun spoke, sharp prickles of dislike crawled over Genevieve. She bit her tongue hard, trying to control herself for fear she might say the wrong thing.

Before leaving the room, the Abbess caught sight of 'good, old Hans.' She poked her finger at the skull grinning with its obscene, toothless gap."What's that... that... object here?" she asked, whipping around to stare at Genevieve in wide-eyed outrage. "Is it the pot where you prepare your poison? Or is it your dear friend Sister Dominica giving precious advice to you from the dead?"

Her lips were set in a hard line, and she shook her head. "How dare you keep something like this in a room dedicated to prayer and piety? See that this object of devilish work disappears at once from our abbey." The enraged Abbess left the room, slamming the door behind her on a speechless Genevieve.

She sat in numbed silence, not able to comprehend the conversation that had just taken place.

Witchcraft. Dear. Dear. What next? How could she say the books and the things I use to prepare from them represent something connected to the devil? They bring comfort to the ailing people, Genevieve said to herself. In the end it'll be my word against hers and yes, indeed, Mother Superior has the power to push me to the stake if she puts her mind to it.

As Genevieve sat next to Sister Francesca in the embroidery room, she expressed her sadness. "I regret the loss of the books she took from me," What a pity to destroy such exquisite works of art and wisdom. The Abbess called them 'devilish work.' Either she can't read, or she herself is a devil. A bitter irony," Genevieve stared down at the floor and shook her head. "An evil woman ruling in the house of God. I must be careful and watch my back. The woman wants my blood, although I don't know why."

"I don't feel comfortable in the new Mother Prioress's presence either," Francesca admitted to Genevieve, sewing busily. "She has no interest in the opinion of the nuns around her at all. Her decision is the best and the most appropriate in any circumstance. She treats us all as if we're her personal servants; her cold, vulture eyes watching us, her mean stare piercing our souls."

***

"A harridan," Sister Benedicta stated a couple of months later. "Sister Dominica's replacement proves to be an altogether different type of woman -- arrogant, hypocritical, always looking for reasons to scold us, young and old alike, with a tongue ready to chastise everyone for the smallest mistake. And her inclination to gossip and intrigue makes me sick."

"There's indeed a great difference between her and Sister Dominica. May her soul rest in heaven's sunny garden," Francesca added. "You remember Sister Dominica's meal, a plain one consisting of oats, dairy and a little bread. Only on very rare occasions did she eat meat.

Sister Clementa won't hear about such things. She leads such an extravagant life at our expense. Only the most expensive spices and foods are good for her highness."

Sister Benedicta added, "Sister Camilla tells me the Abbess asked her the other day, while she worked in the kitchen, to prepare for her a special elaborate dish that she would eat in her own room. She'll no longer take her meals in the communal dining room with us."

Genevieve nodded. "Yes, I imagine she wants to be far from the others' criticizing looks. What did 'her highness' order?"

"Highly spiced roast mutton, short crust pie and cheese." "Now? During the fasting time?" Genevieve asked, herbrow wrinkling.

"Indeed." Francesca shook her head.

"Poor old Ryan received a tongue lashing from her, too." Sister Benedicta nodded. "I wasn't far from him, in the garden, when the Abbess asked for two plump chickens to be chosen from the poultry for her meal.

Ryan protested, imagining she might have forgotten about the fasting week.

'Your Holiness, this is a period of fasting, no meat allowed. Sister Dominica always obeyed the rules,' he told her, after clearing his throat and throwing me a questioning glance. I wanted to give him a warning wink. Too late. Startled by his comment, the Abbess's eyes widened in surprise. She measured the old man in a disdainful gaze.

'Who are you talking to? In the future, you must learn to keep your thoughts to yourself, old man. I haven't asked for your opinion. I ordered you what to do! Mind your chores, you idiot. If not, the road's yours."

Sister Benedicta continued, "And that isn't all. "I overheard her two days ago ordering Sister Cecile and Sister Theresa to cover the stone floor in her chamber with thick carpets; likewise the walls. She also sent the two sisters to ask the gardener for fragrant herbs."

"What for?" Francesca inquired.

"To be strewn in the corners of her chamber to waft a pleasant fragrance all day long," Benedicta replied. "A vain woman. Anyway, I don't care about her. My concern is that she's a bad example for our abbey's community. I fear God will punish all of us for the Abbess's lax morals."

"Have you noticed she seldom, if ever, wears the wimples?" Genevieve asked. "She does it only when she's informed about official inspections by the bishops."

"I don't imagine she cares a bit about the bishops' control," Benedicta replied picking a lint from her sleeve."

"Why not?" Genevieve asked, "They can scold her, or remove her from her present position and appoint somebody else to lead St. Mary's."

"Well, I haven't told you all," Benedicta went on. "I hadn't intended to spread the word around. Let me tell you what Lady Violet, the wife of the town's mayor, told me during my last trip to sell embroidery. You won't believe it, just like I didn't want to, when she told it to me."

"What? What did she tell you?" Francesca's face brightened with curiosity.

"Well, come closer. I don't want anyone else to overhear," Benedicta whispered throwing furtive glances around. "We all wondered why, unlike the usual rule, the clerical superiors didn't select the new Abbess from among us after Sister Dominica's death."

"Yes, you're right. You or Sister Camilla were the elder nuns and should have been the new leader of St. Mary's." Genevieve nodded.

"According to the mayor's wife, our Abbess had become the bishop's mistress some years before coming to the abbey." Benedicta shook her head.

Genevieve's hand flew to her mouth in total shock. "Oh, no. How can this be possible?"

"Have patience and hear what Lady Violet also told me. Our Abbess was, in her lay life, the second wife of a nobleman in York, yet not at all against a little bit of amusement in the bishop's arms while her husband traveled away from home. Gossiping servants at the manor spoke about a strong, awful argument between her husband and the bishop the day the former, coming back from a hunting trip, found his wife and the bishop making love in one of the manor's rooms.

"The cheated husband threatened he would divulge the bishop's immorality. During their verbal fight, the husband suffered a heart attack and died. To avoid a further scandal and accusations from her stepchildren, Lady Marion, by her lay name, abandoned any claims as a part of the inheritance. " Benedicta's lips puckered with derision. "She said she wanted to become a nun. Not a simple, ordinary one. She aimed high. She demanded to be assigned the highest rank, Abbess. She became at once St. Mary's head, thanks to a lot of the bishop's maneuvering."

Genevieve shook her head, appalled, and sighed.

"What will become of the abbey? What will happen to us? I fear harsh times are ahead."

***

Soon, Genevieve had her instinct confirmed.

The new Abbess seemed determined to make her life a miserable, pure hell at the abbey. Genevieve didn't need anyone to tell her that Mother Superior watched her like a hawk, ready to start the attack if the prey wasn't on guard.

No words needed.

Nothing Genevieve did was to the Abbess's liking -- the way she spoke, the way she walked, the way her rebellious hair escaped from under her wimple. Even the fact that Sister Dominica had allowed Genevieve to use her lay name after joining the order became a matter of deep annoyance for Sister Clementa.

All going wrong at the abbey was, without doubt, Genevieve's fault.

Chapter Thirteen

England 1990

Anne

"You shan't take him back. He shall not be yours!" The enraged woman continued to hiss venomously as she dashed to Anne's throat. Her out stretched hands turned into hissing snakes coiled around Anne's neck.

Anne backed away from her attacker's path. The hissing of the snakes, wiggling and contorting round her, turned louder and louder. She opened her mouth to cry for Neil's help and woke up bathed in cold sweat.

Blinking several times, she sighed with relief it had only been another nightmare intruding on her dreams. Her senses told her something was wrong. She sensed, she almost smelt, imminent danger. She cocked her head and listened as if she caught the soft slithering sound of snake scales on the chamber's stones. Fear-induced sweat trickled down her spine. Anne felt for the flashlight she'd dropped while sleeping.

She turned it on. A cry of terror stuck in her throat at the sight meeting her widened eyes: a snake, sliding in a silent, smooth motion.

It advanced sinuously, without haste. Along her sleeping bag, towards Neil. On the verge of attacking him.

Tiny, nasty eyes captivated Anne, for a second, in the glare of the flashlight. The snake opened its mouth and hissed. Its tongue danced. And then, ignoring her, the attacker continued its determined slide towards Neil.

Anne couldn't believe her eyes. The snake was an asp, a viper of moderate size, with a broad, triangular head.

She knew its venom contained a strong hemotoxin able to affect the blood vessels and cause death by stopping the heart.

Megan had taught her about the snakes one could encounter while mountaineering, and how to avoid the venomous ones during their trips on the mountain slopes.

The presence of the viper here seemed unusual, but Anne stopped wondering about anything. Her breath caught in her throat, she groped with her free hand for the stick Neil carved for her in the forest. She stood up, her heart ready to break her ribs, and pinned the snake's head to the ground, shouting at Neil to wake up.

Neil woke, at once, and turned his flashlight on too.

The trembling light moved over Anne who held down the snake that writhed and twisted around the stick.

Using his flashlight he crushed the reptile's head. He threw both the body and his splintered flashlight outside into the now drizzling rain.

Neil turned to Anne and took her in his arms. An uncontrolled shivering shook her body. "You saved my life. My brave, bold warrior. My beautiful wood anemone," he whispered.

His words let Anne's tears break free. Once she started crying, she couldn't stop. Her tears released the dull ache, her permanent companion during the separation from Neil. And she cried for a lost love and a lost friendship.

She cried for the two wasted years, and she cried for the helpless woman, looking like her, in her dream. After she managed, at last, to calm down, she told Neil about the latest vision and about the other woman and her threatening words.

"Thank God your bad dream woke you up; otherwise the snake would have hurt one of us. Me, I think. We should be grateful to the bad lady for frightening you," he laughed.

"No, Neil. Don't laugh. She's evil, I can feel it. I think there must be a connection between the two women. What exactly, I can't figure out yet." Anne trembled hard. From fear? From cold? She couldn't tell. Neil gave her his sweater, warmer than hers, and she put it on.

"My dearest, first thing tomorrow, rain or no rain, we have to leave this cursed place. We head down the stream and we'll reach a village, a town, a human settlement. No doubt. Or, if not, at least we arrive at the foot of this spooky mountain."

"It seems like someone wants us out of the way," Anne whispered, shivering.

He tilted her chin. "We'll manage to find our way back to civilization, safe and sound."

"Sure," she said, the sound of doubt unmistakable in her voice.

"Don't be so pessimistic. I always had the feeling you were the kind of gal who'd never admit defeat."

She raised her gaze to his face. His hand's tender touch on her skin spread waves of heat through her whole body. Her lips quivered as his mouth covered hers and she succumbed to his embrace.

Using Anne's flashlight they checked their watches. It was midnight.

"In the daylight things will look less scary. Let's try to regain our strength. Go to sleep. I'll watch over you," Neil said.

Anne closed her eyes. She breathed deep and thought about all the sweet moments they'd shared together. A smile stretched the corners of her mouth. Her eyelids became heavy and she fell in a deep sleep, while the rain drummed on, less furious.

***

A whisper close to Anne's ear pulled her out through a tumble of dreams to focus on a dark silhouette waving to her. Calling her out. She turned her gaze to Neil.

He'd fallen asleep, the flashlight tight in his hand. Judging by the cold silence enveloping the mountain, she assumed it wasn't raining any more. The yellowish light of the pale moon threw odd shadows on the walls of the stone room. She hugged herself to ward off the cold and, tightening Neil's sweater around herself, slipped out of the small room. The silhouette had vanished.

Anne couldn't say if it belonged to the same evil apparition pestering her dreams for the last hours. A stirring of unease tickled the back of her neck. Restless souls haunted the mountain, no doubt. Fearless, she ventured to the end of the ruins. Nothing was beyond them, as Neil told her the previous day. Only a deep void.

"Anne, Anne," the whisper came again. Farther away this time.

It sounded like Aunt Megan's voice. "Anne, Anne."

And the chime of a church bell. Low and dark. The toll reverberated in an eerie voice, half wind, half demon. Echoing over the mountain, numbing her soul. Calling her from the void's depth. Luring her closer and closer the edge.

Anne edged cautiously closer to the rim of the bare cliff. Her foot tapped the edge. It seemed solid. An unusual curiosity took hold of her. Should she step ahead? What was down there? Other human bones? Another mystery? Why Megan's voice? She leaned forward a little to get a better view. A thin mist rose slowly from the abyss.

Aunt Megan's face turned up from it. Affable. Smiling.

The same as Anne had always known her.

"Come, Anne. I knew you'd look for me. I waited and missed you, dear child. Come."

Anne took another small step on the uneven, gritty ground and reached her hands to embrace her beloved aunt. The possibility of the ground giving way under her weight never occurred to her. She stopped and glanced down the abyss, experiencing the most malevolent sensation. The presence of evil, creeping up and enveloping her, became almost palpable.

Long arms of fog swirled about her legs. They came alive, real and menacing. The vines of fog folded around her, dragging her to the depth. Sharp, poisonous teeth sank into her flesh. Icy perspiration formed on her forehead.

Megan's face contorted, the voice no longer pleasant. A hoarse gurgle, spluttering distorted words, "Yes, come... I'm waiting... I've been waiting for you for such a long time..."

When the rock gave way, it caught Anne unprepared and the cracking sound of the dislodged stone pulled her back into reality. She lost her foothold and slipped down. Her feet scrambled frantically against the crumbling footing of the steep slope, dropping to the void below, her hands clutching desperately at a small scrub. She opened her mouth to scream, fear widening her eyes.

No sound came through her dry throat.

The tremor of terror, starting low in her stomach and traveling up through her body, climaxed in a defeated whimper that escaped her lips the moment the rock slipped under her.

Chapter Fourteen

1479

Genevieve

Genevieve witnessed, with her mood raging from astonishment to revolt, how Sister Clementa continued skipping many of the abbey's religious services, under the pretext of having something more important to do. Indulging in gluttony became a common attitude with the Abbess. At first she offered some excuses for her behavior, and then she simply ignored the nuns' accusing glances.

To all the nuns' amazement, soon after her arrival at the abbey, the new Abbess, who no longer took part in the morning Mass, made an odd announcement.

"You shall not disturb me before midday," she let the nuns gathered at the breakfast table know. "Under no circumstance. I want it to be very clear to you all. I spend my nights, when there's complete silence, studying the Old and the New Testament and other holy writings. I fall asleep only in the wee hours."

Genevieve threw a bewildered glance to Francesca. She curbed her curiosity. None of the other nuns made any comment on their leader's words.

They weren't supposed to.

The very next day, Genevieve received proof that things were very different from what the Abbess told them.

Sister Letitia approached Genevieve, who was sewing next to Francesca and Sister Benedicta.

"I know I can trust you and I feel I'll burst if I don't take it from my soul," Letitia said in a low voice, casting furtive glances over her shoulder.

"What's wrong?" Benedicta inquired.

"Well, during the night, while I was heading to the bath, I passed by Sister Clementa's room. The door stood slightly ajar, a ray of light coming through the opening. More than simple curiosity made me sneak to the door and steal a glance." Visibly embarrassed, the nun shifted her weight from one leg to the other.

"I saw the Abbess drink from the silver decanter containing the communion wine. She didn't wear the usual, rough nightdress all of us do, but a red, silky, transparent one. Her dark hair hung loose around her shoulders and a strange look, a look full of mean satisfaction, transformed her face," Letitia reported to the astonished nuns listening.

Genevieve shook her head, unbelieving.

"Yes, I know. I myself couldn't believe my eyes," Sister Letitia whispered, in a trembling voice, shaken at the sheer memory of the previous night. She blessed herself several times.

"Grinning like a she-devil our Abbess was, and she kept touching an ugly looking statuette. Whenever she touched the hideous head of...of... that thing, her hair turned into coiling snakes. This woman is the devil. Oh, Lord, have mercy on us!" Sister Letitia blessed herself again. "The very look of her repels me."

Sister Benedicta frowned and patted the poor woman's shoulder. "Don't tell anybody else what you've just told us. It's dangerous." She shook her head, aggrieved, and addressed Genevieve and Francesca. "We'll have to be careful around our Abbess. I don't like what's happening here."

Benedicta turned and checked to see who the nuns working in the embroidery room were. Satisfied, perhaps, that the nuns present were trustworthy, she cleared her throat and addressed them. "Sisters, lend me your ears. You've known me for many years and surely you can't say I am inclined to gossip. Still, things are going wrong in our formerly peaceful establishment. What do you think of the way our new Abbess behaves? Do you agree with her?"

Her questions were met by long faces and disapproving sounds.

Genevieve frowned and touched Benedicta's hand, throwing her a warning look.

Sister Benedicta nodded to her and continued. "I assume that all of you here will continue to lead the same pious and sinless life as you did during Sister Dominica's time. The only thing I fear is the day some of our sisters, those with a feeble character, will start imitating Sister Clementa. I'm aware that the bad influences grow by the hour, and spread like the plague over our former tranquil existence."

"Oh, Sister Benedicta," replied another nun. "Your fears are justified. There are already two of us who follow her example."

"Who?" Benedicta asked, her brow wrinkling.

"Sister Cecile and Sister Theresa," the nun replied. "They are the most fervent followers of the abbess' conduct. They no longer join the others' line to attend the morning Mass; they sleep until noon."

"Yes, I forgot about the two dim-witted ones," Benedicta said. "They no longer perform their daily chores until rebuked."

"You failed to notice, the day you scolded Sister Theresa, how she pulled faces at your back," the nun added. "She and Cecile show an overall servile attitude towards the Abbess in the hope she will notice their flattery and bestow on them her protection."

"Of course the Abbess won't fail to do it," Genevieve shared her thoughts with Francesca and Benedicta.

"We must be cautious and take a stand against those nuns who want to change our abbey into a place of perdition," Sister Benedicta advised the young nuns listening attentively to her words. "We must be united in Our Lord's glory."

***

Genevieve could not repress a bitter smile at the thought of the hard year passed in an atmosphere of distrust, enmity and division among the nuns at the St. Mary's under the leadership of Sister Clementa.

Gone was the atmosphere of calm, piety and unity that reigned during Sister Dominica's time.

Suspicion, intrigue, mistrust and, above all, the gluttony and self-indulgent luxury became more important to the Abbess and her two supporters than celebrating Mass.

Genevieve didn't fail to notice Sister Cecile and Sister Theresa accompanying the Abbess wherever she went, and repeating to her every word or deed of the others. They also made insistent attempts to win most of the other sisters to their side, but they didn't manage it.

At first.

One day while working side by side in the embroidery room, Benedicta, casting cautious glances around, whispered to Genevieve her decision.

"It's high time for such improper conduct to cease. Oh God, the heathen are come into Thine inheritance," she quoted from the Psalms. "I can stand this no longer. There must be something we can do to bring an end to the Abbess's shameful conduct and teach a lesson to the slow-witted imitating her. Come to my room in the evening. I have a plan."

A few hours later, talking in detail in Benedicta's room, Genevieve, Francesca and three other trustworthy nuns concluded it would be better to inform the Archbishop or the president of the synod about the state of things at the abbey.

"We can take advantage of next week's trip down the mountain to buy provisions. The problem suffers no delay," Genevieve suggested.

"Yes, I'll try to inform the Archbishop." Benedicta nodded. "He'll trust me, as I am one of the oldest nuns here. He knows me from the several times he came on inspection here, and I assisted Sister Dominica.

"We can no longer allow things to carry on like this. I've lived all my life here. I was only six when my family brought me to St. Mary's. I grew old within its walls and don't want to end my life surrounded by sin and improper conduct. I believe it's time to protect our faith and morals. I don't care if this stirs the Abbess's rage. Either she changes her behavior, or she is removed from her high position."

"Yes, Sister Benedicta. Do it. And if our superiors don't believe you, we can back your words," added Sister Letitia. "We fully agree."

"That's what I wanted to know. We'll continue to act as if nothing happened," Benedicta concluded, nodding. "Please leave the room, one at a time. We don't want the Abbess to become suspicious."

Genevieve, the first to leave the room, nearly ran into Theresa, who moved quickly along the hall. Genevieve's brow wrinkled. She doubted Theresa heard them talking behind the closed door. And yet, she was standing not far from Benedicta's chamber.

Genevieve stood, undecided. Should she tell the others or not? She chewed her bottom lip and then walked away. It wouldn't change a thing. No use to frighten her friends. She only prayed to God that Sister Theresa hadn't listened to their conversation.

At first, Genevieve dismissed her fears of their 'plot' having been discovered, since the Abbess's behavior didn't change.

One day before the planned departure of the group to town, Clementa summoned all the nuns to make an announcement.

"A lot of thoughts have troubled me lately, regarding the health problems some of the elderly nuns seem to have. I'm very concerned. My decision is for Sister Benedicta to stay at the abbey and tend her tired bones and joints. Starting today, Sister Theresa will be in charge of those going into town."

Benedicta flung her hands out in despair. "Mother Superior, I can do it. I've never complained about this journey. I know how things are done and everybody knows me in town."

"No. My decision is final. Sister Theresa can learn how things are done. You'll stay at the Abbey. We must take care of our elders, mustn't we?" she insisted in a voice all sweetness and benevolence. "Or, are there other reasons I should know about that make you insist on going to town?" the Abbess inquired innocently, silencing Sister Benedicta.

Genevieve and Francesca exchanged knowing looks. It was a clever move on the sly Abbess's part, since only Benedicta would have been able to talk to the superiors. The other nuns, being novices or young and considered inexperienced, weren't usually granted a meeting with the Archbishop or the president of the synod. The chance to talk to the superiors vanished into thin air.

Little by little, the Abbess assigned the most unpleasant chores to the nuns who had 'schemed' at her back. And only these Sisters would do them, according to a new distribution of tasks. It meant cleaning the lavatory, making sure the wood heap was always high, doing the laundry, and helping old Ryan look after the poultry and sheep.

Disappointed, Genevieve read the relief on the faces of many of the other nuns who no longer had to deal with such disagreeable chores.

Closing their eyes on the Abbess' misconduct, they changed sides, to Sister Clementa's unsuppressed delight.

It wasn't difficult for Genevieve to guess that the Abbess's attitude towards her and the other nuns involved was the outcome of their plan having been exposed by Sister Theresa. Genevieve had no power to change a thing. She ground her teeth and carried out everything imposed upon her by the Abbess. Day after day, month after month.

"What's wrong? You've gone pale and your face shows the strain of something bothering you," Francesca inquired, visibly concerned for Genevieve's state.

"I'm so upset by the things happening around us. It became obvious to me," Genevieve told Francesca while working in the embroidery room, "the Abbess accomplished what she intended from the very first day she set her foot at the abbey. Divide et impera. Though I doubt she has any idea of the Latin Wisdom."

"Do you think the new Abbess is able to recite at least the Creed by heart, from the very first line to the last?" Francesca asked.

"I sometimes wonder if she can read at all. I think back to the days we used to be like family here. Sister Dominica, a mother, not a superior. What has become of it all? My friends here are you, Francesca, and Sister Benedicta. It breaks my heart that Sister Benedicta went blind and depends a lot on our help in doing her allotted chores."

"Yes, I'll always do my best to help our old friend. Can't the Abbess absolve her of some of her duties?"

"She can, yet she won't." Genevieve replied, a deep frown shadowing her face. "She will never forget Benedicta's intention of telling on her."

Francesca smiled sadly with a tense nod. "I remember what Sister Benedicta was like when I first arrived here. A stout, healthy, pleasant woman. And she's turned into a shadow of that former, lively nun. Stooped, limping after the accident on the ice that broke her leg, weakened knees from her hours knelt in prayer, deaf and almost blind. Her 'fault' is her too direct, unhindered tongue. She should be allowed in her room and divide her days between praying and the ghosts of the past haunting her empty hours."

Genevieve stopped for a moment. "No. Under no circumstance will the arrogant Abbess allow such 'luxuries' to the old woman. Torture. That's what she's doing to Benedicta. And we can't do a thing to stop her. What kind of a woman, of a human being, is our Abbess to demand so much from Sister Benedicta?"

"You know the answer very well. Mean, cruel and faithless," Francesca replied.

Indeed. The Abbess often made mean remarks about those 'insensible weaklings who consider food comes here for free without having the good sense to work for it.' Remarks aimed at Sister Benedicta.

The nasty words troubled the old nun, making her cry. The Abbess's behavior made Genevieve's throat tighten.

"I've started giving serious thought to the idea of leaving St. Mary's Abbey and finding another religious establishment willing to accept me," Genevieve confessed.

"Yes, I don't blame you for wanting it. You forget such a thing requires a lot of explaining and is very seldom, if ever, allowed," Francesca replied. "In fact, I've never learned heard about a nun being granted a transfer. It means an inquiry on the general activity of the abbey, to justify your leaving it, and a word of recommendation from the Abbess. And, what will it be?"

Francesca shook her head. "If you stand up to her, she'll crush you beneath her feet. No need for me to tell you she knows no mercy, no kindness. She doesn't fear God's retribution for all the misery and immorality she's brought about."

"I know. I'm aware I can't rely on her recommendation. This is out of the question. Sister Clementa would rather see me dead than let me leave this place and tell other people what's happening under St. Mary's roof."

"I fear she might hold a lot of influence over the bishop, her former lover, and thus over the Archbishop," Francesca also warned Genevieve, her voice edged by bitterness. "And, she also won most of the nuns to her side. They'll support her against you. What a shame."

Genevieve took a deep breath, lowering her head to study her hands. Raising her glance to Francesca, she admitted, "To avoid her, I busy myself with all kind of things, which require my presence where ever that dreadful woman isn't.

"And yet, I feel her 'eyes' watching me, spying on my every step. I no longer trust the other sisters. I'd have gone mad if it hadn't been for your support, my dear friend."

"Leave the Abbess be," insisted Francesca, "pretend you don't notice or you don't mind her behavior. You know you are above her. Hide your disapproval and your real feelings. I hope you've not forgotten what happened to Sister Letitia after trying to send that secret letter to the bishop last month. What the devilish woman did to her."

A voice from the doorstep froze Genevieve's blood and made Francesca drop the rosary from her hand.

"Who's the devilish woman you are speaking about?"

Chapter Fifteen

England 1990

Anne

With a piercing creak, a chunk of rock dislodged and Anne's feet lost their fragile hold.

A sudden grip, tightening over her raised hand, saved her from certain death.

"I've got you. Hold on." Neil's voice, heaven's music to her ears, boomed from above.

The mist enveloping her legs vanished at once. She couldn't see Neil's face, because she faced the void; yet she sensed concern and strain in his voice. Instinctively, Anne glanced down and dizziness swayed her unstable world. The light of the moon was enough to display the danger below her feet. The abyss grinned with its black mouth, waiting for her to fall. She bit her lip to try to stop the clattering of her teeth. A wrong move and she'd be history.

Neil grasped her forearm tighter.

"Hang on. I'm not letting you fall. Hang on. Don't look down. Try to raise your other hand too, so I can get a better grip on you. Yes, easy, easy. I'll haul you up," Neil said through clenched teeth. He made an obvious effort to encourage her and keep his balance too. She wasn't heavy, but the position over the precipice didn't make things easy.

Anne closed her eyes and prayed to God.

With a last effort, Neil pulled her up and settled her on safe ground.

Deep sobs sent an uncontrolled shiver through her body. He hugged her to him.

"Shh. You're safe now. Shh. Luckily I woke in time to realize you were no longer by my side. I don't trust this place, so I came looking for you. Half a second later and I would have lost you. My beautiful anemone. I love you so. I've always loved you. I can't imagine my life without you. Please, forgive my foolishness. This trip, the two years of separation from you, opened my eyes. To what I really want from life.

"And I want you. Nobody else."

He wrapped his arms around her shivering body and bent his head close to hers. The warmth of his body around her calmed her.

At last her shivering subsided.

Neil tightened his embrace. "I thought at any moment I might drop you into the void and lose you forever. I'd have thrown myself after you. My life means nothing without you by my side."

While he hugged her closer to him, something pricked her skin from the pocket of Neil's sweater she still wore. She looked in the pocket and took out the bejeweled cross they'd found in the forest. The touch of the cross triggered another vision.

The dark haired woman she'd seen in her dream during the night pinned her in a glance full of hatred. Her brows knit, her lips a thin line. "We'll meet again. Have no fear," the woman spat at Anne and the vision disappeared as swiftly as it came. Anne shook her head to clear her mind.

"What's wrong?" Neil uttered his concern.

"Nothing," she answered. "Visions. Shadows of the past, I think. Did you put the cross in this pocket?"

Neil frowned and shook his head. "No. I remember placing it in the rucksack. Yours or mine, I can't remember. I can't imagine how it ended in my pocket. Strange. Anyway, thank God you're all right. You gave me a fright. I thought for a second I lost you."

Anne gazed deep into his eyes.

His breath caressed her face while he whispered, "Do you still love me?"

She didn't answer at first and then, in a sudden movement, she fell against him and his mouth came on hers, locked together, until she gasped for breath.

"Yes, Neil. I love you. I'm grateful for your concern. If it hadn't been for your worry, I'd have perished in the abyss... Thank you for saving my life"

"Don't be silly. I'll always be by your side and catch you whenever you're in danger. You're my destiny. I can feel it in my heart. I love you, Anne."

"I love you too. Let's go back inside the ruins. As soon as there's enough light, we'll leave."

***

In the morning, Anne and Neil left the abbey's ruins. They started back the same way they'd come the day before. This time, they went downstream. Many jagged trees smoked from the previous night's lightning hits and broken branches covered the damp ground.

Anne walked ahead in silence, lost in troubling thoughts.

The clear blue sky, the fir trees' fresh scent, the sun sending its rays from behind a distant, gray-colored peak would have been the perfect incentive for any mountain lover for a trip along the narrow paths. The stream had gone back between its banks and was running as clear, calm and inoffensive as always.

Frantic ideas raced through Anne's mind. She looked for answers regarding the mysterious events, the eerie way things that had occurred ever since they lost their way. Why isn't this large forest mapped? Whose are the bones in the hollowed oak? Why are the ruins haunted by troubled souls? There must be a connection between the ruins and the skeleton we discovered the day before. Is it a crime, an accident or what? So many unanswered questions for the moment, she thought.

Again reaching the oak tree where they'd found the bones, Neil checked if the skull and bones were still there.

"We'd better not have a rest by the water," he said, his voice betraying the same concern as hers. "Let's continue our descent. I don't want another surprise from this forest."

Anne turned her gaze to the stream. The water became a muddy color and shook violently, as if an underground earthquake had unleashed its power. The next moment, the waters cleared again, mirroring, in turn, two women's faces.

One of them, sad and troubled, her pale face framed by auburn, sparkling tendrils. The other woman, haughty, frowned, with black tresses of hair coiling like snakes over the white shoulders.

Three big black ravens, unmoving on the branches of the tree, pinned Anne with mean eyes. Shock caught in her throat, freezing her breath.

"This isn't only strange. It's starting to become unnerving," she told Neil what she'd witnessed.

He shrugged. "I believe you, though I don't see anything unusual in the water. It's probably meant for only you to see. The sooner we leave the better."

While walking away from the oak tree, Anne confessed to Neil what bothered her. "I'm sure the oak tree has a close connection to the apparitions in my dreams."

"What makes you think so? Maybe the skeleton's presence and the cross have another explanation."

"Like what?"

"After having lost their way, just like us, someone died of exhaustion or was killed while passing through the forest. Later, one of those large birds dragged and hid some parts of the body for provisions for winter in the hollow, and that's why we found the bones there."

"You might be right. I don't want to contradict you, but still, I have a strange feeling whenever I stop under the oak tree. I experienced it, both during the first night while I followed the red-haired woman up, and again these two times we arrived at the same spot. Not to mention the sight of the bones and the touch of the gold chain and cross. It sent shivers all over my body."

Anne chewed her bottom lip, her brow wrinkled for a couple of seconds, before she resumed walking.

"It isn't pure coincidence, I'm absolutely certain of it. Whenever we reach the stream, and especially the hollowed oak, a slight dizziness engulfs me. My soul seems torn apart by a deep sense of loss, by grief. Something terrible occurred by the tree. I don't know when, why or how, but I'm sure the tree played a part in the death of the person whose skeleton we found in its hollow."

Neil turned to look at Anne. His gaze held a mixture of tenderness and concern. "I don't know, hon. The only thing I'm sure about, right now, is that I want us to be out of this place and somewhere safe and cozy. Our lives are in peril here."

Anne nodded and walked on, following Neil down the path.

The descent continued without any rest until, exhausted, they came out of the forest. Tired and footsore from their long trek through the odd, unfriendly forest, Anne's spirit soared the second her eyes met, a large group of houses in the valley below them. It meant they'd reach a village soon.

She was on the verge of tears.

Tears of relief, this time, at what she thought as being the end of the nightmarish trip.

Chapter Sixteen

1480 June

Genevieve

"Who's the devilish woman? What happened to Sister Letitia?" The question came again, startling both Genevieve and Francesca.

"Oh, goodness. You gave us such a fright." Francesca sighed with relief and shook her head, annoyed. They obviously hadn't heard Sister Agnes approach.

Genevieve and Francesca exchanged knowing looks.

"The day I arrived at the abbey Sister Cecile told me my room belonged to a nun who died from a bad stomach and that her name was Letitia," Agnes added, and raised her eyebrows. "From what I've just overheard, things seem quite different."

Genevieve liked Agnes. The young nun reminded of herself when she first came to the abbey. So far, Agnes kept away from the bad lot.

"We'll tell you, but please don't reveal to anyone you learned it from us. We're already on the Abbess's black list," Francesca insisted.

"No, of course. You have my word."

"It's one of the crimes the Abbess has on her conscience. If she has one." Genevieve nodded, dispirited. "Poor, innocent Letitia didn't want to believe in the strong, sinful link between the bishop and the Abbess, or what had happened to the other nuns who disapproved of the disgusting things happening at St. Mary's."

"You mean our Abbess and the bishop…are…." Sister Agnes's eyes widened in shock.

"Yes, they were, and we assume she still has power over him," Genevieve replied, and then she continued, "In a letter to the bishop Letitia described, to the last detail, the scene she'd witnessed within the walls of the abbey one afternoon. She also said she possessed indisputable evidence of the Abbess' immoral conduct.

"Her words still echo in my head. She wrote, 'You'll no doubt think my mind has left my head, but you've known me for so many years, please bear with me and listen to what my eyes saw yesterday.' Genevieve made a pause. Her eyes gazed in the void. She clenched her fists and went on,

"Realizing Sister Theresa and Sister Cecile were absent from their duties in the kitchen, not that this was unusual, she searched for them. All the nuns were busy, some praying, others performing their daily chores, except the two.

"She couldn't find them in their rooms either. She gave up the search and, returning to the kitchen, some muffled giggles coming from the Abbess's room attracted her attention."

Genevieve sighed and shook her head. After a slight pause, she continued.

"Letitia drew closer and through a crack in the wooden door she stared, unbelieving, at the appalling scene unfolding in front of her eyes: the two nuns she was looking for were naked, fondling each other and touching each other in their private places.

"A silver decanter for wine and two silver cups on the table led her to believe that before such shocking, disgusting behavior, the two nuns had drunk the wine. The look in the Abbess's eyes frightened the poor nun further.

She didn't appear as if she had drunk the wine, yet her eyes were red, 'like Hell's fire,' Letitia told us..

"An inhuman grin spread across the Abbess's demonic face, while her red, cruel eyes twinkled in a menacing way.

Sister Agnes cried out and crossed herself quickly. Then she covered her mouth with her hands. Her eyes were filled with dread.

Genevieve cast her a warning gaze and spoke on, "A large book with black bindings lay open on the table. All this time, Cecile and Theresa, oblivious of her presence, were involved in whatever they were doing, while the Abess kept looking in the book and whispering unintelligible words. Strange words, sounding to Letitia like some kind of an incantation.

"Beside the book, among the cups of wine and burning candles, stood a strange looking statuette that Sister Clementa touched from time to time. Sister Letitia swore to me and Francesca that, whenever the Abbess placed her fingers on it, her face distorted, changing into a horrible hideous mask."

Sister Agnes's hand flew again to her mouth to repress a cry; her face mirrored her disbelief and, little by little disgust and fear overcame her features. "Oh, Sisters, are you sure? You're frightening me."

Francesca patted her shoulder. "We don't want to frighten you. We want to warn you. We were as shocked as you are now hearing Letitia's story. There's more to come."

Then, she turned to Genevieve who shrugged. "Yes, it's hard to believe, but trust me, poor Letitia was right.

"Letitia confessed to us, trembling , she needed more than human effort to prevent her from screaming when the shock of what she had witnessed came upon her.

'She couldn't help it and uttered a sound between a choke and a gasp. Feeling faint and nauseated at the same time, watching the two shameless nuns, she leaned on the door and it creaked under her weight,' she said.

'Her heart stopped in her chest when she realized the noise revealed her presence.

The Abbess' face changed back to normal, the noise bringing her head round quickly. Her hand remained poised above the open, strange looking book that she then closed with a swift movement. She threw the bed coverlet over the two women, too drunk and too busy in themselves to notice anything around them, and she dashed to the door. She'd not been swift enough to catch the intruder.

Letitia ran as fast as her feet could take her and hoped the Abbess didn't recognize her."

Francesca patted her clerical dress and added. "We hoped the Abbess couldn't have recognized Letitia's robe. We're all dressed in the same way, after all. We told her to stop worrying. Letitia did it and tried to put on a brave face."

"How wrong we all were," Genevieve recalled. "Give the devil its due, the Abbess has a sharp mind and started making connections. She also very likely ordered Sister Cecile, in charge of any received or sent message at that time, and to bring them to her at once. No letter, not even a small note can leave the abbey without her checking it first. That's how she laid her hands on Sister Letitia's letter."

A slight noise in the corridor interrupted Genevieve's story.

Francesca hurried to the door and checked to see if someone was listening to them. She turned and nodded to Genevieve and Agnes.

"Nobody. The wind must have slammed a window."

"I couldn't find an explanation to the Abbess' change in behavior at the time," Genevieve spoke on. "She acted faultless for a week after the incident. She attended all the services in church, spoke in a kind voice to everyone, especially to Sister Letitia, who began to express doubt what she'd seen. She feared what would happen if the bishop came to the abbey to start an inquiry after receiving her letter, and all the sisters would say the Abbess wasn't guilty of any of the accusations against her.

"On the following Sunday, I met Sister Letitia on her way to the kitchen. She'd received the Abbess' orders to prepare a baked apple pie for her, claiming she wanted to celebrate something personal. Sister Letitia was famous among the nuns for her cooking. And her fruit pies always tasted delicious. Though she couldn't even stand looking at the Abbess, Letitia had no choice. She headed to the kitchen. By obeying the order, she was the last one to come and receive the communion.

"I'd received mine and was leaving when Clementa told Letitia there wasn't any wine left in the cup for the ceremony.

"My curiosity was aroused, since something like that had never happened before, I turned my head and watched.

"The Abbess, false smiles and kindness plastered on her hypocritical face, took another cup she no doubt had prepared in advance, and offered the wine to the poor nun.

"Sister Letitia drank it and two hours later, she died in agonizing pain. Poisoned."

"If Sister Letitia hadn't told us what she'd seen that day in the Abbess' chamber, we'd have had no idea why the poor woman was swept away. Why the horrible Abbess killed her," Francesca added. "And if Genevieve hadn't read so many things in the Leech Book about herbs, potions, useful and harmful plants, we'd have not realized the Abbess poisoned Sister Letitia. Murdered her. All the other nuns believed the Abbess's words that Letitia died of convulsions, or stomach problems."

"How did you find out about the letter?" Sister Agnes asked.

"Two days after Letitia's death," Francesca replied, "I overheard Sister Cecile and Sister Theresa talking about 'the old hag who deserved her death for trying to defile the Abbess's name in front of the bishop.' It became clear why poor Letitia had to be removed from the Abbess' path. You should avoid antagonizing the Abbess. She's dangerous, too dangerous for us." Francesca concluded.

Genevieve addressed Sister Agnes in a stern voice, "I think you understand why you mustn't tell anyone what we told you. It endangers not only Francesca's and my life. Yours may come to harm. And, beware of Sister Cecile and Theresa. They are not what they pretend to be. Their presence is always bad news."

"Yes, Sisters. I fully understand. I'll be careful. And, don't worry. No word about what you've just told me will leave my lips." Sister Agnes swallowed hard and hurried out of the room looking frightened and dismayed.

"So many sins, so many terrible things happened in the last year under the roof of the abbey; it makes me wonder why the walls haven't already crumbled down over the evildoers. I realized the very day she came here that she was after my blood and she's waiting for the slightest reason to punish me. I do my best not to step on her toes, and ... I fear it's not enough. Have no worry. I won't provoke her in any way," Genevieve promised her friend and left to her chores.

***

A couple of hours later, the sound of hurried footsteps along the abbey's stone hall interrupted Genevieve's tranquility

Sister Francesca pushed Genevieve's door open and rushed in. "Sister Genevieve, Sister Genevieve, come quickly. Your help is needed outside. Come, at once."

"Slow down, Francesca, I can't understand you." Genevieve eyed, intrigued, her friend fluttering her hands.

"What's wrong? I've never seen you like this. Look at you. Your face is like Ryan's musk roses," Genevieve remarked.

"Oh, yes, I can feel the heat. I've run all the way to your room, and the sun's burning hot today. Come, hurry."

"Calm down and tell me why you're so agitated."

"Hurry Genevieve. I thought the noise unusual in the garden. I had no idea what I would find there but I checked to see what was it. Poor old Ryan sprained his ankle. I found him lying and moaning behind the bush of white roses. I imagine the poor man's in great pain. I've never seen him cry.

"I'll need my ointment and a piece of cloth, so we can bandage his leg should the need arise. It can't be so bad." Genevieve gathered the things she needed from a small wooden chest next to her bed, and briskly walked out the room.

Advancing along the path of gray stones separating the flowerbeds, Genevieve inhaled the strong, almost palpable smell of musk roses. Closing her eyes for a second, she turned her face up to the scorching summer sun and let the warmth envelop her. She wasn't used to such heat this high into the mountains.

Francesca followed right at her heels.

"Have the other sisters noticed you talking to him? If Mother Superior finds out about us helping the gardener, we'll all be in for great trouble," Genevieve said and shook her head.

"I know. I heard her promising to throw him out if she found him talking to one of us again. She's afraid he might tell the villagers the things that are going on around here. As if he ever leaves the abbey."

Francesca followed close, tripping on Genevieve's long dark gray robe. They reached the place where the gardener uselessly struggled to haul himself to his feet. Genevieve considered him the grandfather she'd never had. Such a hardworking, decent man. He always had a good word or piece of advice for everyone around him, except for their present day Abbess. Never for her.

Genevieve gently touched the old man's arm.

He gazed up at her, deep affection warming his gaze, and renewed his effort to stand on the injured leg. The attempt tore a muffled cry from between his clenched teeth.

Genevieve shook her head alarmed. Her voice was shakier than she would have liked, "No! Don't try. It'll strain you more. It's not good for your ankle. Let me see your leg. I've brought my... what do you call it? Yes, my Miracle Ointment. Lean on our shoulders and we'll get you out of the sun. It is too hot for you. Here we are," she said when they reached the cool, fragrant shadow of the trees.

Genevieve and Francesca helped the old man sit in the shade. "Sit down. Easy. Yes. Let me see your leg. Hold tight to Francesca's hand if the pain's too sharp."

Genevieve knelt by the old gardener. "What do we have here? I think you've hidden one of the abbey's potatoes under your skin. Some provisions for the coming winter, Uncle Ryan?" She tried to joke to distract Ryan's attention from his pain while gingerly fingering his swollen ankle. "Nothing seems to be broken. I'll rub some of my ointment on your ankle and tomorrow you'll be on your feet again."

"Dear child, God bless thy gentle soul," old Ryan answered. "Pray, beware not to be seen by the Abbess. She is not like Sister Dominica who would have been the one asking you to tend my leg."

"How much I miss her." Francesca wiped away her tears, nodding regretfully.

"We all miss her," Genevieve agreed.

Ryan passed a calloused hand over his half-blind eyes and continued in an embittered voice, "Yes, things were different during Sister Dominica's time. It's not for me to complain, anyway. You suffer more.

"If someone hears my talking to you and tells Sister Clementa, she'll throw me out, back to the village. She promised it to me the day she became the new head of the abbey. There are times I reckon keeping her word may be a blessing in disguise for me, not a misfortune like she imagines."

"Don't worry, Uncle Ryan. She doesn't venture outside in such heat, so she cannot see us. And her minions stay close to her. They fear the heat might melt their piety masks. Don't trouble your mind. We'll be careful," Genevieve promised.

A stranger's voice from behind Genevieve startled her into attention.

"Oh, good day, Sisters. And good day to you, too, old man. I am Father Andrew, and I want to speak to your Mother Superior. I'm your new priest, the new confessor. Can you show me the way to her?"

Genevieve and Francesca helped Uncle Ryan stand up, before offering the priest a graceful bow.

Straightening, Genevieve raised her face to Father Andrew's. She gasped in surprise. Her heart stopped for a second and then it beat so loud she imagined even the stranger heard it.

Waves of heat washed over her. Good, warm waves, rooting her in place. She couldn't move her lips. She didn't as much as blink.

For a split second, the waves turned into a powerful whirlpool which caught the priest and brought him closer to her.

The closer he got, the hotter the waves became. A consuming heat, devouring them both. The burning breath singed their hair and their faces, delving deep into their hearts and their souls.

Genevieve couldn't explain her feelings regarding the priest. Glancing at him, she experienced a profound, inner pain. Not a physical one. Something inside her heart.

As if her whole being sensed she would be linked to this man, somehow, some day, and it would mean a great loss for them both.

The new confessor stood taller than most men, and was about twenty-five years old. His face, a pleasant one, like that of a chiseled Roman statue. The kindest, warmest, brown eyes Genevieve had ever seen and a true Roman nose enhanced his face.

The priest turned an intrigued, bemused expression on Genevieve. His deep, sensual voice filtered through Genevieve's haze. It brought her back to the awareness of having, very likely, offended the man with her uncontrolled stare.

"Is something wrong, Sister? You're watching me as if you want to unveil some dark secret I might bear. Do I fit your general idea of a confessor, of a nuns' priest, or not?"

Genevieve blinked several times, while a hot, guilty blush crept into her cheeks.

"I'm sorry, Father. I didn't mean to be rude. I feel you are a good man and that's what really matters."

Genevieve examined his gray coat and tall black riding boots adorning his figure. Although it was the middle of the day, with a hot sun above, he didn't seem tired or too dusty. He must have come a long way. The nearest village at the foot of the mountain, Glennridge, was at least a three hour ride on horseback. She glanced about. No horse in sight. Judging by Ryan and Francesca's amazed looks, Genevieve surmised they hadn't heard him arriving, or his horse, either.

The young priest nodded and flashed a bright smile. "I rode my mare up to the abbey gate and left her to graze. She seems very content with such a delicacy after the long journey through this dark, unusually quiet, forest.

"To tell you the truth, riding through it gave me an uneasy feeling. Being my first visit might explain it.

Anyway, I don't want to keep you from your tasks. Please, tell me the way and I'll follow my duty."

Francesca smiled at the priest. "Our Abbess wondered the other day whom our new confessor might be. She'll be glad to meet you. Follow me, Father."

After Francesca turned to lead him to the abbey, Father Andrew held Genevieve's gaze for a lingering moment. The reflection of her own anguish in his eyes sent an unexplained shiver through her body.

The young priest frowned and shook his head, as though trying to clear his thoughts. Abruptly, he turned to follow Sister Francesca, who already approached the end of the path leading to the main entrance of St. Mary's Abbey, where Mother Superior ruled with an iron fist.

"Father, beg pardon," old Ryan called after the priest. "Please, don't tell Mother Superior the nuns were taking care of me. She won't like it. I don't want to cause the young ones any trouble. They've already enough on their hands as it is."

"Don't worry, kind man. I always mind my own affairs." Father Andrew turned on his heels and continued his way to the abbey's heavy doors.

Genevieve led the gardener to his cottage, still shaken, and troubled by the turmoil of emotions the priest's presence unleashed.

Neither of them spoke.

Ryan's muffled cries of pain, while he attempted to support his weight on his injured foot, disturbed Genevieve's storm of thoughts.

Once inside the cottage, Genevieve helped Ryan lie down. She checked he had everything he might need close at hand. The slight tremor shaking her body subsided a little.

"A nice fellow, this new priest. Don't you think so?" Ryan's voice echoed in Genevieve's ears as though he spoke from far away.

"Yes, I hope so." She managed to suppress the tremble in her voice.

"You yourself should tend to your body, my child. I felt you trembling all the way coming here. Your voice sounds weak. With all the sun we have now, it would be a shame for you to come down with a cold. Or was my old body a heavy burden for your frail arms, perhaps?"

"Not at all, Uncle Ryan. Not at all. I'm not so frail. Don't forget I'm a simple girl, used to work since I was a child. I'm strong enough. Have no worry about me."

"When I think of what I was once and what I've become...How fate changed things in my life. If it hadn't been for my youthful foolishness, I'd have lived in my own house. I wouldn't have lost my sweet Eloise and our children," Ryan whispered and shook his head. "I feel so guilty, my child, for being such a nuisance to you. "

"No, Uncle Ryan. Don't blame yourself for anything. You're not a nuisance to me, and what happened to you years ago was God's will."

"I don't know, my child. I don't know. You might be right. Well, much as I'd like to bless my ears with your soft voice and my eyes with the sight of your kind face, I think you'd better leave. I don't want you to come to harm for helping me. Go to your duty, child, and God bless you."

"I'll return to check on your leg after the evening Mass. Have some rest, please. Good-bye."

The moment Genevieve closed the cottage door, the priest's warm, kind eyes caught life in her mind. He was a good man, no doubt. The waves of warmth she felt from him were a sure sign of it.

This gift she'd been born with, her ability to tell if the people close to her were good or bad, had improved during her stay with old Bertha. Genevieve no longer told anyone about her abilities, fearing people would consider her a witch. Especially the Abbess. The only one aware of her ability was Sister Francesca, whom she trusted with her life.

The intensity of her reaction to the priest left Genevieve distraught. The uncontrolled force of her response to him frightened her. What could it mean?

On the steps of Ryan's cottage, Genevieve turned her face to the sun again. It would be time for lunch soon.

Well, it was all fate. For Ryan and for her, too.

God's will. He wanted her to live here. He planned her to be one of the thirty nuns living at the abbey.

Like her, all the nuns had come to this abbey for various reasons. Each one of them had a story of their own. Some, like sister Benedicta or Sister Francesca, were brought here by their families when they were children. In exchange, the families received a sack of potatoes and one gold coin, according to the custom of the time. From that moment on, their relatives were never allowed to come and visit them again.

Others, like Sister Letitia, suffered bitter deceptions in their lay lives. They came to the Abbey, in the middle of nowhere, far from any temptation and away from the worldly sins to live an existence of penitence and prayer.

Others willingly offered their whole existence to worshipping God, their one and sole bridegroom. Like the much regretted, and loved by all, their former abbess, Sister Dominica.

Deep in her reflection, Genevieve had hardly left the cottage when a well-known voice broke into her thoughts. Jumping, she almost dropped the ointment box.

Sister Theresa, one of the last nuns Genevieve expected or wished to meet right now, displayed a fake smile.

"Here you are, Sister Genevieve. I've been looking for you. Coming from the gardener's? Well, I imagine it's true what a sister said, you were together earlier. About what do you have to confer with the old drunkard, after all?

"The Abbess wants to have a word with you. You missed all the fun today. You should've seen our new confessor. What a handsome man. I'll be more than glad to tell him all my sins. In detail. Thank God for this gift. I'm glad Ignatius went to meet our creator, be it in heaven or hell. Such a bore and a prude."

"Sister Theresa, how can you speak like this?" Genevieve rebuked her.

"How can I what? I speak my mind. That's all. Don't give me such a long face. Are you such a hypocrite to tell me you wouldn't like to be held in young, strong arms and feel the beat of a man's heart and taste the sweetness of his mouth? Eh, after all it's not a sin to dream." Theresa sighed. She asked, narrowing her shrewd eyes, "What's in your hand?"

"Oh, my ointments box."

"I imagined so. Assisting the old scum. I thought you're not allowed to use that poisonous stuff anymore. I think, my dear, you're looking for trouble. Yet, it's not my concern. I did my duty to summon you. Go to the Abbess," Theresa added and spun on her heels, leaving Genevieve rooted to the ground.

An iron claw gripped Genevieve's heart. Theresa would tell on her, no doubt. Another reason for the Abbess to throw Genevieve dirty looks and spit all kinds of preposterous accusations against 'the laziest, most disobedient nun.'

"Let's face the meanest woman in this country," she said to herself and, her legs like lead, headed to the abbey, gathering all her strength for the inevitable confrontation.

Chapter Seventeen

England 1990

Anne

It took Anne and Neil another half an hour to reach the village. The clock in the market tower struck five in the afternoon when they arrived at the first gray stone houses. They'd been walking for almost nine hours.

Neil asked the first person who came their way about a hotel or inn, a place to stay overnight.

The man, after studying him with open curiosity, told them the way to the Rampart Inn, two streets away.

In front of the inn, Anne frowned as the image of an old woman, clad in a long, dark green dress, with her head covered by a lace-trimmed bonnet like those worn in the Middle Ages, flashed in her mind. The woman was smiling, friendly, inviting. Anne shook her head to clear her view and the image vanished. She sighed but didn't tell Neil anything and entered the inn.

The inn's coquette dining room buzzed with activity. Anne took in the place after she sat with relief in one of the comfortable armchairs not far from the reception desk. There was a group of tables where the guests enjoyed a glass of beer or cider and enjoyed the house specialty – roast wild boar -- while listening to the soft music oozing from a CD player.

Neil walked to reception to book a room for the night and asked the receptionist about the village's location.

Fragments of animated conversation reached Anne's ears. Her eyes stole a glance in the direction the voices were coming from.

"You say you're a witch, Jennifer. Snap you fingers, please, or wriggle your nose or do whatever you do and find the word I need for my crosswords, so I can send it to the competition." An elderly woman grumbled and shook her head. She addressed a tall, slender woman, around forty years old and elegantly dressed, who stood beside the table.

The two men seated next to the elderly lady burst into laughter. "Or, at least, only this once, ask your Goddess. She might give you a hint for me," the woman continued.

"Oh, Mrs. Dunbar. That's cheating if Jennifer tells you the solution. When we were your pupils you always taught us to be honest and never cheat," one of the two young men addressed the old lady, shaking his head with a twinkle of gratitude and warmth in his eyes for his former teacher.

"Yes, it serves me right," replied the woman. "I should have made you stay in school for twenty years, you naughty lad," she said with the same warm voice. "What's the use of us having a witch if she can't solve my puzzle here?"

"Yes, Mrs. Dunbar. A modern witch, who doesn't dance naked in the field at midnight around a sacrificed animal. Or doesn't travel from one part of the village to the other flying on a broomstick. Nevertheless, a witch. A gorgeous one, according to most men in our village," the man added and winked to his companion.

"That's what you say," his table companion intervened. "I understand your wife and other women in the community imply she's a sly, dangerous one. You know what people say when a woman has beauty men admire and wives envy. It is wise to tread carefully."

"Young man, I'm ashamed of you," the elderly teacher said. "How can you say something like that? It's not Jennifer's fault if you or other young men linger around her inn, even if everyone can see she's immune to all of your advances. Wives shouldn't hate her. They should put the brooms on your backs and shut your blabbering mouths. You all know she deals only with white magic. Don't you, dear?" Mrs. Dunbar said in closing.

"I don't mind." Jennifer waved her hand. "Sooner or later they'll understand, if they keep their minds and hearts open." "By the way, Ms. Jen," the young man rebuked by the teacher asked. "Would you be tempted to sell your small treasure of old books?

"I mean, especially the skillfully illuminated Latin version of St Mark's Gospel. and the book with the first English fables, the Bestiary? I've an American friend, an avid collector of rare books. He told me he'd offer you $1,000,000 just for the Leech Book."

The woman standing in front of the table shook her head. "No, thank you. That book isn't for sale. It's belonged to my family for generations, though at times it was lost. It fell into evil hands before finally coming back to my kin. I wouldn't sell it for the whole world. Well, enjoy your food. I have to see to my other tasks," she said. She left their table and turned to look in Anne's direction.

As soon as Anne's gaze met the gaze of the woman the others called Jennifer, a slight dizziness engulfed her. The same sensation that had bothered her since the previous morning. The feeling of déjà vu, the eerie warmth spreading in her soul the moment the woman looked her directly in her eyes, were signs Anne couldn't mistake.

It was as if she and the strange woman called Jennifer had been close friends, sometime before, and Anne harbored no doubt Jennifer would be involved, in one way or another, in something of importance which would happen soon.

The woman held Anne's gaze for a couple of seconds and then she turned and left the room in a hurry.

"Are you all right?" Neil asked.

"Yes, I'm all right," Anne replied, though feeling right was far from her at the moment.

"The girl at the reception desk showed me on the map what our present location is. We are in Glennridge. I checked and it's on the other side of the mountain from where we should have been."

"Nothing makes me wonder any more," Anne said.

"The receptionist also says that the owner of the inn is Jennifer Archer, the lady who just passed by you."

Anne didn't reply, her mind's eye was troubled by a mix of visions.

Blurred.

Hazy.

Ominous.

***

Hungry and exhausted, after a long, fragrant bath, Anne only took a bite from the dinner Neil ordered from room service.

"I'll phone the Alpine Chalet regarding our reservation. I'll let them know an unforeseen situation occurred and we have to cancel it," Neil said. "You go to sleep. Nothing wrong can happen here. As soon as I get that done, I'll be back to join you in bed. Nothing's so urgent it can't wait until tomorrow."

Anne smiled and waved to him.

The moment he closed the door, a shadow clouded her eyes. The persistent gaze of the owner of the inn came to her mind. It had been a thoughtful and worried look.

Piercing her soul in an unnerving way.

Chapter Eighteen

1480 September

Genevieve

Genevieve headed inside the abbey to find out what the Abbess wanted from her, though she could guess the reason. She was in for great trouble; she'd disobeyed the order of not even talking to old Ryan. Sister Clementa considered her offence even greater, since she had also taken care of old Ryan's leg.

Luckily for her, due to Father Andrew's presence, the Abbess limited her usual firestorm of rage to killing looks and the postponement of their talk for another time.

"You can very well see that I've a guest now and I'm showing him the abbey, Sister," Clementa hissed between clenched teeth and waving her hand, she dismissed Genevieve.

Genevieve had no doubt the Abbess wouldn't forget her 'misconduct' and sooner or later she would pay for it.

***

The unusual heat of the summer slipped into the colorful palette of autumn. The morning wind was blowing over the abbey, rustling the tree leaves and bringing with it fresher air. One day, Sister Francesca summoned Genevieve at once to the room of old Sister Benedicta, who could no longer climb out of her bed.

Genevieve hurried to her old suffering friend and found Benedicta shivering and delirious.

Feverish, her eyes and nose red and teary, she could hardly speak because of a sore throat. A dry cough shook her frail body from time to time. She didn't recognize Genevieve or Francesca, her gaze lost and lacking its usual glint of life.

After covering Sister Benedicta with the thin blankets they brought from their own rooms, Francesca shook her head. "I don't think she'll make it until tomorrow. Unless you prepare one of your healing potions or teas for her."

Genevieve gave no thought to the interdiction against preparing healing potions that the Abbess had imposed on her. The life of the old nun was too dear to her.

"I'll try to persuade the Sister who's in charge of the kitchens today to help me prepare a healing tea for Sister Benedicta, as quickly as possible. Hopefully it works," Genevieve said in a determined voice. She took the required dried herbs from her wooden chest and hurried to the kitchen to brew them.

The smell of cooking potatoes and beans filled Genevieve's nostrils as she entered the hot room.

One of the Sisters was busy at the stove. The moment she saw Genevieve and the herbs, she raised her eyebrows. "You're forgetting something, aren't you, Sister Genevieve?"

"No," Genevieve replied in a firm voice she hardly recognized as her own. "I haven't forgotten anything."

For a moment, heavy silence enveloped the room. Genevieve continued, "No doubt you've been informed that Sister Benedicta's not well. I want to prepare a brew for her, though I fear it might be too late. I want to try. I don't want to regret for the rest of my life not having tried. Help me. Please."

The cook shook her head slowly. "No, Sister Genevieve. No. I don't think I should help you. I'm sorry for our Sister, but we are under strict orders not to allow you in the kitchen. I mean...you know...."

"You're not helping me," replied Genevieve in an embittered voice. "You're helping Sister Benedicta, for the sake of your spending so many years beside her and for her having always been like a mother to all of us."

"Oh, please, Sister Genevieve..." The cook continued to reluctantly shake her head. She cast frightened glances over Genevieve's shoulder to see if there was someone else in sight. "This is no place for you. Leave. You've always been a reasonable person. I don't think it would be right for me to disobey the Abbess's orders. If she ever found out, you know what she'd say, or worse, do."

"You disappoint me, Sister," Genevieve said and stabbed the cook in a hard gaze.

The cook lowered her head. "I'm sorry. And it isn't as you say that I don't want to help poor Benedicta. Not at all. It's that I don't want to drag all of us into hot water. You very well know that allowing you here to prepare what you need for Benedicta would only lead to trouble."

"Let me face the trouble and whatever it may lead to, when it happens. I can't believe you are so unmerciful. I want nothing else from you except to pretend I'm not here. I only need a large mug and some of the boiling water from the stove. That's all. I won't involve you in preparing anything, though a helping hand would speed things along."

"Speed things for what, Sister Genevieve?"

Genevieve's blood ran cold at hearing Sister Theresa's shrill voice. She turned and found Theresa leaning against the doorframe.

The cook's face turned as white as her headdress and then a deep red. She mumbled something and turned to her pots on the stove.

Sister Theresa, who'd come to the kitchen to bring the Abbess's order for lunch, brightened and seemed delighted to have witnessed part of their conversation. Learning about Sister Benedicta's illness, Sister Theresa expressed her concern for the old woman's state. She even insisted Genevieve prepare a large quantity of the healing tea. After telling the cook what the Abbess wanted for her meal, Theresa left the kitchen in a hurry.

Genevieve didn't doubt where the hateful nun was heading. She didn't care anymore. She hoped it was in her power to save Benedicta's life. She boiled the needed tea.

As she prepared to leave the kitchen, another nun entered. It came as no surprise she let Genevieve know that the Abbess summoned her right away to her room, and asked her to bring along the healing drink as well.

Genevieve gathered her things and, without any word to the cook, she hurried to the Abbess with a worried heart. Nothing good would come out of a confrontation she couldn't avoid. She kept a calm face, although her heart raced. She knocked on the door and, squaring her shoulders, pushed through it.

"I'm informed that Benedicta's been taken ill." The Abbess beckoned Genevieve to sit and, in an unusual mellifluous voice, she asked a lot of questions about Sister Benedicta's health.

"Yes, your Holiness. Very ill. She can hardly breathe. I fear it might be fatal."

"And you've made for her some herbal brew, right?" Genevieve swallowed hard and nodded. "Yes. I have."

"Well. Do you think it will help her?"

"I hope so."

"Do you still have such herbs? In case another one of the nuns has need."

"No. It was the last bunch. No more."

"Pity. Well, let me add a few drops of honey into the brew. It eases the cough. Hand me the mug."

Unsuspecting, Genevieve held out the steaming mug.

The Abbess took it and in the following second, she let it drop to the ground. The entire mug of precious tea spilled on the floor.

A shocked moment of silence fell upon the room. Genevieve stood, staring at the lost liquid.

The Abbess's horrible deceit came to her too late.

She glanced up at the abominable woman to meet the unveiled mirth in her eyes.

At once, the Abbess's voice, her face, her whole body became menacing. Her hands, clenched tight into fists, came in a fierce bang down the table separating her from Genevieve. She jabbed her finger towards the young nun,

"You stupid, disobedient witch," she yelled. "What did I tell you? It seems it was to no purpose. You deliberately disobeyed my orders. You took yourself to the kitchens with your filthy weeds to poison us all. I'll punish the cook who allowed you there to boil this demonic..."

"Your Holiness, Sister Benedicta might die if she doesn't drink it. I made it only to save the old woman's life," Genevieve defended herself.

The Abbess dashed from behind the table and slapped her hard over her mouth.

"Shut up, shut up, witch. What makes you think I care if the old hag, may her soul rot in Hell, lives or dies this very second?" the woman shouted at her and raised her hand to hit Genevieve again in her rage.

Meeting the dark threat of the Abbess's fury, Genevieve gripped Clementa's hand and in a calm, quiet voice, though anger made her cheeks flush hotly, she addressed the maddened woman, "May God forgive you." She released the Abbess's hand and stood up, turning to the door with her cheek and mouth a burning flame where Sister Clementa had hit her.

"How dare you turn your back on me? Be careful how you behave. One more word of disobedience and I'll turn you to the flames of justice. Do you hear? I'm not finished with you," the Abbess yelled and tried to grab Genevieve.

The unexpected entrance of Father Andrew stopped her harsh words.

After looking from the nun to the Abbess, he nodded, and said in a bright tone, "I knocked, but nobody answered. Hearing loud voices, I took the liberty of entering the room at once." He, no doubt, realized by the look of both women that he'd done the best thing in coming in.

Genevieve blinked to stop the tears threatening to burst down her burning face and curtsied low without looking at him. "Father."

The Abbess arranged her disheveled look and displaying a fake, warm smile, she welcomed the priest, while a hidden threat gleamed in her look. "Please, Father Andrew, have a seat. What an unexpected pleasure. I was just scolding the naughty girl for being so clumsy. We've a sick, old nun and Sister Genevieve here wasted the only remedy that could have saved the poor woman. Eh, so's life. Young people tend to be so careless."

Genevieve's blood ran cold, draining from her burning face down to the soles of her feet at the Abbess's shameless lie.

"I'm sorry to hear about the ill Sister. Let me see the poor woman. I've arrived here sooner than planned. You haven't forgotten, I hope, this afternoon is your confession time for the nuns, have you?" the priest said addressing the Abbess, his glance fixed on Genevieve.

The Abbess's slightly irritated voice startled Genevieve. "Shall we leave, Father, or is it something else you wanted to tell me?"

Shaking his head, Andrew followed the Abbess and Sister Genevieve to Sister Benedicta's room.

The Abbess invited him to enter.

"Here we are. Let's step in slowly so we don't disturb the poor, old soul."

The blatant difference between the opulence of the Abbess's chamber and the dire simplicity of the nun's room was nothing new to Genevieve. The wooden bed, a small table and a wooden stool, a water basin chipped and faded by so much use and a small wooden chest under the table. The crucifix and a burning candle were the only things indicating it was not a cell.

Nothing could be done for the old nun who didn't recognize any of them anymore.

Father Andrew gave her the last rites and, after blessing the dying woman, left the room followed by the Abbess, while Sister Genevieve remained by Sister Benedicta's bed.

"I'm not done with you," the Abbess couldn't help herself from saying to Genevieve before she walked out to catch up with the priest. She was unable to master the tone of her voice and her words must have been heard by Andrew as well.

Genevieve pretended she hadn't seen the mask of geniality fall from the Abbess's face. She no longer cared about her mean words and simply chose to ignore the Abbess and her vicious threat. She stood like a statue, her hands clasped in front of her to stop them from shaking until the door had shut and the hateful Abbess disappeared from sight.

She knelt down by Sister Benedicta's bed and held one weak, frail hand in her own, as if wishing she might instill some of her youthful energy and vitality into the kind woman whose life's candle was slowly quenching.

Large tears dropped on the nun's inert hand. Genevieve wiped away the tears of grief and regret running down her face and forced a whisper out of her mouth. "Tell Mum, and my sisters and brothers, and Bertha I haven't forgotten them. Go in peace, Sister Benedicta. I'll always pray for your soul."

The old hand's feeble twitch, as if in response, came as the nun's last movement in the imperfect human world she left behind.

Genevieve kissed Benedicta's hand, while tears knit on her chin and she prayed.

***

The nuns buried Sister Benedicta after the Liturgy of the Hours the following day.

Father Andrew came back to the abbey to perform the funeral service.

After Benedicta's burial, Genevieve told Sister Francesca what happened in the Abbess's chamber.

"I have a strong feeling that more than ever the Abbess wants me out of the way. In a frightening manner. Dead. The woman is looking for a pretext, the smallest reason, to send me to death. A spark to start the fire on a stake she'll order me tied to, accusing me of witchcraft."

"Dear Genevieve, please be careful. This woman is evil personified. Why don't you ask Father Andrew if he might know of another abbey or nunnery willing to accept you? He might, perhaps, even write you a recommendation so you won't need the Abbess's.

"Try and talk to him. He travels more than we do and he might ask other priests about an abbey to welcome you. I'm sure the priest can help you out of here." Francesca stopped and eyed Genevieve, with an amazed look.

"What? Why are you looking at me this way?" Genevieve asked.

Francesca shook her head, her forehead wrinkled. "You should see your face. Burning like a fire."

Automatically, Genevieve raised her hands to her cheeks. Hot blood flooded her face as soon as Francesca mentioned Andrew's name. Whenever his name came into someone's conversation, she experienced the same sensation.

Something about Andrew left her breathless. She found him stunningly good looking and his eyes most compelling. Deep, hazel ones holding the kindest look she'd ever seen in a man. Hard as she tried, she couldn't dispel from her mind how she'd warmed to his gaze the day she first met him in the garden.

On his first visit to the abbey, she'd blamed her wish to hear Andrew's voice again on sheer womanly curiosity. The following week, and the next one, and the next, Genevieve found herself outside in the yard about the time Andrew might arrive. Even months later, after she first talked to him, her heart always jumped at the sound of his husky, low voice. A voice you could trust, Francesca once told her, full of understanding and encouragement filtering through the wooden lace separating the confessional booths.

She never let herself be seen by him. If the weather turned rainy, she waited for his arrival standing at her window overlooking the main path. Little by little, it became a habit and she restlessly counted the days until he came to the abbey.

With startling suddenness, there came into her heart a strange feeling; for a moment, she was afraid, and at the same time amazed, by its intensity. She pushed to the back of her mind the thought catching shape and nagging at her, but at last, she was forced to admit the truth to her own conscience. She'd become interested in the priest in a way she shouldn't have.

She wanted desperately to open her heart and tell Francesca her feelings for Andrew. It strained her to keep quiet about it. Despite the fact she and Francesca had been friends and confidantes for years, her feelings towards Andrew were too intimate to share. It was a burden she alone had to carry.

Her own sigh brought her back to reality. She saw Francesca, silent, watching her intently. Nervously, Genevieve moistened her lips and said, "It's nothing. I'm just upset remembering the Abbess' threat. Francesca, you're such a loyal friend. You're in fact my only friend left here, now that Sister Benedicta's no longer among us.

"I'll try and open the subject with the priest, as you suggest, but I fear he might tell something to the Abbess. I don't know about him, yet watch her whenever he's around. Haven't you seen her gaze and how her speech changes as soon as Father Andrew enters the room?

"I'm sure she has her sly eyes on the poor man. She always takes him to her room to have dinner, a thing she'd never done for old Father Ignatius. I wonder how long it lasts until he becomes her powerless prey."

Francesca replied, "Don't be a child. Father Andrew's a priest. A decent, honest one, I might add without being mistaken,"

"I heard Cecile talking about him some days ago. She said that the death of Father Andrew's father, a rich nobleman, left his mother and his sister Joan well provided for and he himself inherited a huge part of the estate and enough money to not need to work his whole life.

He felt he was called to the clerical life. Lady Margaret, his mother, tried in vain, to make him change his mind. She'd have liked him to become a doctor, get married and have children."

"This doesn't mean he can't believe the abbess's lies. She is a very cunning woman."

"I'm sure he heartily dislikes Sister Clementa, yet veils his feelings under his usual civil, urbane behavior. He'll never go against his vows. I saw him backing away while she tried to envelop him with her false, wicked smiles. He's not like the bishop we've heard about. Or, at least, I hope so.

"During the confession try to tell him about everything happening around here. How the very person who is supposed to be an epitome of faith, kindness and honesty turned our abbey into a place of sin. Tell him that prayer, fasting, and purity are words long forgotten here. Tell him our life has become a vile one."

Francesca sat down on Genevieve's bed and lowered her face into her hands. She shook her head as if trying to clear her thoughts and continued, "Tell him the few nuns who try to live in piety are scorned and threatened by Sister Clementa's followers.

"Even faith has become dangerous. The Abbess, this harbinger of evil, might kill us one by one, and nobody will find it out. Tell all this to him during the confession, and he'll be forced by his duty as a priest to keep your secret."

"You might be right. I'll try. The sooner, the better," Genevieve replied and heaved a large sigh. "I don't know if I can tell him everything during confession. The other nuns might become suspicious if I stay too long in the booth."

"Ask him to meet you at Uncle Ryan's cottage. Nobody can hear you talking to him."

"I'm not sure that's such a good idea. Uncle Ryan's own stay here's already under great peril. Imagine Sister Clementa catching wind of it. Not to mention the latest argument between him and the Abbess."

"What argument? I've no idea about it."

"It happened a week ago. Don't you remember the day of the last inspection?"

"Yes, I do, but what happened? Nobody told me anything."

"I heard about it only yesterday from Uncle Ryan. I found him watching the white roses with distress, talking to the beautiful flowers like mothers talk to their small children. I asked him what was wrong and he told me what happened. While the Abbess was seeing out the high official, they passed along the flowerbeds. She said she intended to increase the number of animals at the abbey.

"'Your Holiness, there's not enough room for more animals here,' Uncle Ryan interrupted her.

"'Who says so? Why not?' The Abbess threw him an ugly look. 'We'll get rid of the flowerbeds and place the pigs here. We need pork, not flowers,' she continued in her habitual haughty manner. It's obvious Ryan's intervention angered her.

"The high official who'd known Ryan since Sister Dominica's time took his side.

"The Abbess said she'd think about it. A few minutes later, coming back from the gate after the official left Uncle Ryan told me she let loose. Poor Uncle Ryan told me how she called him a lazy drunkard and that he should be sent to jail for murdering his family. Choking on her fury she yelled at him. She said he was a criminal and didn't deserve to live an idle life at the abbey.

"No matter how hard he tried to calm her down she was unstoppable. She said she'd throw him out if he dared open your his mouth to contradict her again. Then she added he wouldn't be the first obstacle she removed from her path. I tried to put his mind at ease," Genevieve continued, "telling him she did it to annoy him. Ryan told me he was not a murderer. He didn't kill his family. Then he told me what happened back in his youth."

"Indeed? He never told anyone else what really happened to him. Maybe only Sister Dominica."

"Before coming to work here, he had a family. He and his wife Eloise and their two small children lived in South Dalestride. He earned his living as a 'reeve,' a kind of high ranking supervisor, very appreciated by the lord. To his and his family's misfortune, his fondness of too much ale carried him away."

"Oh, I'd have never imagined Uncle Ryan being a man fond of drinking," Francesca exclaimed, amazed.

"Neither have I. It's something that happened a long time ago," Genevieve resumed her story. "He said his drinking lead to the sudden, tragic death of his wife and two children, a boy and a girl. He blames himself for his foolishness, though an accident caused their deaths.

"He's not a murderer as the Abbess implied. One day, while a storm was brewing over the forest, he'd come home dead drunk and had fallen asleep, completely forgetting to gather the kindling for the fire, as he promised Eloise.

"Having no other choice, it seems Eloise took the children into the forest during the terrible storm. The following day, Eloise was found by some villager's not far from their home, next to the lifeless bodies of her beloved children. Eloise didn't recognize any of her neighbors. She was cradling the rigid, half burnt bodies of her children at her bosom.

"The fir tree Eloise and the frightened children stood under to take shelter from the heavy rain was split in two by a tremendous lightning bolt, half of the tree burnt down and the other half stood bending in a grotesque angle over the dead children. Eloise escaped alive, thrown to the ground by the force of the blow."

"What a tragedy," Francesca murmured.

"That's not all," Genevieve continued, "When the neighbors took the tragic news of the children's death to

Ryan, he woke from his stupor, amazed and upset it was so cold in the cottage and Eloise nowhere in sight. On hearing the terrible misfortune that fell on his family, he howled like a wounded beast and tore out his hair. Too late for regrets.

"The next week, after the funeral, Eloise died too. She'd sat soaked, outside, in the cold forest until the villagers found her.

"The old people in the village said the 'cursed forest' took another toll.

"You know, dear Francesca, it broke my heart to see Uncle Ryan so shattered by the tragedy's bitter memories." Genevieve shook her head. "He'd tried to take his own life, yet his hand trembled hard and he cut his cheek deep, not mortally though."

"I always wondered where he'd gotten the scar on his face," Francesca said.

Genevieve nodded and continued with Ryan's story. "He said that people avoided him and shook their heads in great disbelief.

"The nuns at the abbey who likely considered him to be a decent, honest, hard working man, hearing about his tragic loss, took pity on him. They informed Sister Dominica of his story and she hired him. They needed a gardener, someone they could trust. This is how he came to live here."

"Clementa's inconsiderate words opened old wounds. What a base creature she can be," Francesca added, disgusted. "She knows no mercy for anyone. She's cruel in her very soul. I don't even want to think that she might keep her word regarding sending you to the stake on a claim of witchery.

"Talk to Father Andrew. Don't delay asking him any longer. I'll miss you, but it's the only thing for you to do. You must leave this no longer holy abbey. Get away."

Sister Theresa burst in, making no effort to mask her radiant face. "Sister Genevieve, the Abbess wants a word with you. At once. No delay," Theresa addressed her in a voice both commanding and scornful.

"Oh, not again," muttered Genevieve under her breath and, turning to Sister Theresa, she answered in a bright voice, hiding her apprehension, "I'll come right away. Thankyou, Sister."

"Be careful, dear Genevieve," Francesca warned her friend again in a worried voice. "Try to suppress your disapproval and contempt for her. Don't offer her any reason to suspect anything, above all that you're trying to leave this place and be free of her. She might try to provoke you. Keep quiet and do whatever she wants you to. At least, for the time being."

Genevieve braced herself for the vile reproaches she had no doubt would welcome her in the superior's chamber. She realized her suspicion regarding Sister Clementa's threats towards her were right. The feelings grew with every passing minute.

The cold waves were stronger than ever, arousing in her soul the darkest fears. The longer she remained here at the abbey, the greater the danger to her life. She knocked on the door and entered the room, her heart thudding fast against her ribcage, her mouth dry.

The unveiled menace felt thick in the 'dragon's lair,' as she and Francesca had come to call the Abbess's private room,

The two women stood staring at each other across the room.

The Abbess favored Genevieve with one of her measuring, haughty glances. Genevieve's look didn't waver in front of the Abbess's triumphant one. Sister Clementa waited a moment.

She narrowed her eyes and shouted at Genevieve, each word cutting the air like an ice shard. "I can't ignore your disobedience any more. For constantly ignoring my orders, until I decide otherwise, your only duty starting now is to clean the lavatory. You're the only nun who'll do it. All the others will be excused. And you shall not set foot again in the embroidery room. I don't want your filthy hands and stench to spoil the work of my nuns. I can make the other nuns shun you. None of the other nuns will touch you, address a word to you, or look at you.

She paused, as though waiting for Genevieve to protest, to offer a word of refusal or to beg her not to do it.

Genevieve's eyes brimmed instantly and she opened them wide, tipping her head back to keep the tears inside. She bit down hard on her rising anger, restraining herself from any visible display, and forced her mouth closed to keep the protest from bursting out.

The Abbess leaned across the table, her manner more aggressive than ever, and in a spurt of rage she spat, "Listen to me. Listen hard. I'm not sure what your game might be, but I warn you it's the last time I will forgive your misbehavior. There's a limit to my patience. The next mistake takes you to the stake.

"One word, just one word from me, and you'll burn like a pig. And don't imagine I'll ever allow you to leave the abbey and go somewhere else. I know you can hardly wait to spread tall stories about me and about life here. No, I'll never let you leave. You are too precious here.

"Who else is better skilled in cleaning the lavatories than you are? I don't want to deprive you of an activity you're so fond of. Now, leave. I don't want to see your hypocrite's face in my room any longer." The Abbess turned her back on Genevieve who had listened to her spiteful orders, not even blinking.

Genevieve frowned. She headed to the door and left the room without uttering a word. It was no use to defend herself. The cold waves coming from the Abbess were stronger than on other occasions, and antagonizing her any further would have been complete foolishness.

"I must do something about this. I can't wait any longer. I have to find a way to leave," she said to herself.

The very same day, at the end of her confession, she fearfully revealed her identity to Father Andrew and told him she wanted to talk to him.

In private. Since she needed a piece of advice from him. He agreed, and sounded intrigued by her request. Genevieve suggested they should talk in old Ryan'cottage, away from the Abbess's prying ears, before the priest left the abbey in the evening. Genevieve came out of the confession booth in a more relieved state of mind. He hadn't refused her, or insisted to know on the spot what she wanted from him.

The nuns' dinner took place in an unusual silence. Genevieve cast a quick glance at the other nuns and read a glimmer of pity in their eyes. It became clear to her they all were informed of what the Abbess had ordered her to do. It was obvious Sister Theresa and Sister Cecile hadn't failed to spread the word. She'd reached a point where she didn't care anymore. She'd deal with her chores and try to move from this abbey as soon as possible.

At all costs.

The moment the meal was over, she sneaked to Uncle Ryan's and asked his permission to meet the priest there.

The old gardener didn't raise any objections to Genevieve talking with Father Andrew in his little cottage. On the contrary, he also agreed with her idea to find another abbey and free herself from the Abbess's persecution.

Chapter Nineteen

England 1990

Anne

The following morning, Anne woke up refreshed from her long sleep.

No red-haired, blonde, brunette or God knows whatever other woman visited her in her dreams.

She regarded the last couple of days as nothing but a series of constant revelations about herself and Neil. Despite his past betrayal, it became clear to her she still loved Neil and, in her heart, she'd forgiven him long before their trip. Neil stood for everything she'd ever wanted.

She'd also discovered an aspect of her former self: the delicate, vulnerable, sad-eyed, red-haired young woman of her dreams. Though she had no explanation for this feeling of certainty, the red-haired woman of her last days' dreams was herself in another life. The woman from the past and Anne of the present, what else could they be if not another reincarnation of the same spirit? She couldn't explain why she'd come to this conclusion, or when the idea flourished in her mind; she had no clue as to why all of it had happened.

The blinds were drawn, yet sunrays managed to sneak between the slats, drawing islands of light on the walls. She glanced towards the other bed where Neil should have been to see it empty and already made. She smiled, recalling what a tidy person Neil always was.

Then Anne frowned, troubled by remorse for being such a nuisance. She'd been the one to drag him through the forest to follow her visions. On the other hand, she was grateful to him for respecting her troubled state of mind, and for not making any attempt to lure her into a night of lovemaking. She got up from the bed, washed and dressed, intrigued about where Neil had wandered to so early in the morning. While she finished combing her hair, the door opened and a radiant Neil entered the room.

"Good morning, sunshine. How gorgeous you look today. I think I might eat you for breakfast, instead of what I brought."

Neil's words warmed her heart. He presented her with a small bag full of her favorite croissants, the only thing she liked to eat in the morning, before sipping her tea.

"The owner of the inn told me she wanted to have a word with us before we went out or we phoned anyone. She's waiting for us in her office downstairs."

"Is she? Well. Then we'll go talk to her. Oh, Neil. It's such a glorious day. Everything that happened in the forest seems like merely a bad dream," Anne felt her face flush, self-conscious of her own desire for him and his loving glance. "I think the croissants can wait a little. Come," she said with a playful smile and patted the bed next to her.

Neil eyed her with his disarming smile and he answered in the same playful voice, "Shall I hope I'm at last forgiven?"

He gathered her to his chest.

She wrapped her arms around him and their mouths met. She raised her glance to him and Neil's gaze softened.

"I'm glad we brought down the fence of misunderstanding and mistrust separating us," he whispered.

"I'm glad that I decided to grant my old love a new chance. It's the best thing to do." She melted under his hot mouth. "I love you with body and heart," she murmured. He slowly eased the dress off her shoulder and stroked her skin with sizzling kisses along her neck, along her shoulders, and along her silken breasts.

Anne closed her eyes and sighed.

"My beautiful wood anemone," Neil whispered into her ear. His urgent kisses unleashed the throbbing hunger of her desire.

"My beautiful wood anemone" he repeated, triggering odd flashes of memory in her mind. Neil captured her lips again and the flames of passion soared high blocking out the face in her mind.

A kiss, which started out tender, quickly grew heated and urgent, his tongue possessing her mouth. He lowered his head to her firm breasts.

She let out a little cry.

He raised his face and whispered, "I love you. I'll always love you."

She held his face in her hands and called his name in a breathless whisper as their entwined bodies traveled through a universe of blissful infinity.

***

Anne and Neil entered Jennifer's office.

The clean glow of whitewashed walls gave the large room a luminous radiance. A comfortable leather couch and two matching armchairs faced away from them. The pale yellow of the upholstery added a bright splash of color to the threadbare beige carpet, and offset the prim beige curtains covering the windows.

A mahogany bookcase, stacked with leather bound books and a desk in a similar mahogany finish with black metal accents completed the office area. A monitor and a keyboard sat on the surface of the desk. A matching coffee table and natural flower arrangements, as well as several watercolors, mostly landscapes, added splashes of color to the cozy room.

A trickle of smoke wafted from an incense burner on the desk. The faint scent of lavender enveloped Anne and stirred in her a pleasant feeling of tranquility and well-being.

"I hope you're not bothered by the smell. Lavender, due to its balancing and harmonizing nature, has a restorative effect on your state of mind and stress level.

She reached out with her hand. "I'm Jennifer Archer, the owner of this little place. Your friend told me you were supposed to arrive at the Alpine Chalet. I feel we need to talk a little, as he also implied you've encountered some problems before reaching our village."

"Yes, he's right, Ms. Archer."

"Jennifer, please. Or better Jen."

"Yes, Jen. I'm Anne."

"Please have a seat and relax until your tea arrives. You know, I prefer a large cup of coffee to the endless cups of tea people around here are so crazy about. Though I like very much the saying that our past and our future are tea leaves in the cup of our present," she said and stared straight into Anne's eyes.

The words made Anne gasp. Time blinked.

Her blood ran cold; a time warp sucked her in. For a second, she found herself in a small, cozy room filled with the aroma of lavender and lime. She was facing the elderly woman she'd seen in a flash before entering the Rampart Inn.

The woman offered her a cup of steamy, fragrant tea. "Here, my child, drink this. And never forget these words, 'Our past and our future are tea leaves in the cup of our present.'"

Anne reached out. As she grasped the cup, shock swept through her body, and she found herself again in front of Jennifer, pinned beneath her penetrating gaze. Anne's throat was tight, but she forced her voice to sound nonchalant. "Interesting and wise thoughts, indeed."

"Drinking coffee, for me, is perhaps something that comes from my ancestry," continued Jennifer. "Way back, hundreds of years ago, it seems an ancestor of mine came from the continent, where they enjoyed the black, bitter drink, and settled in England. I have no idea where. It could have been Glennridge, for all I know.

"I came here from Swindon, after the unfortunate death of my husband. A simple surgery for appendicitis, supposed to be as easy as a tooth extraction, turned into a sudden infection and fever; in less than five hours he passed away."

"I'm sorry," Anne whispered.

"Thank you," Jennifer murmured, her eyes covered by a haze of tears. "He passed away about ten years ago. The pain has diminished over the years, but I miss him so much sometimes. We lived a nice life together, though we weren't blessed with kids. After his death, I sold our small property left town without any definite destination. While passing through Glennridge, I stopped to fill up and somehow I felt my trip had come to an end. This house, in an advanced state of ruin, was for sale. I bought it and I turned it into the nice inn you see today."

Jennifer glanced around her, obvious tenderness twinkling in her eyes. "Well, here I am. The business is good, although not so many tourists come visiting this part of the country. They don't know what they're missing.

The mountain's wilderness, the fresh air and the peace are unique. At first, open suspicion glinted in people's eyes when I told them I was a witch, and they considered me weird and avoided the place. In time, little by little, they began to like the food and the atmosphere and things changed."

"A witch," Neil said. "Why did you tell them such a thing? Even nowadays, people have an ancestral fear of what they cannot explain by the standards of their knowledge. On the other hand, many consider whatever can't be seen, touched or heard nonexistent." Neil expressed his astonishment.

"Well, I always tell the truth, no matter what. If people want to believe me or not, if they want to talk to me or not, is their own problem and choice. I'm what many people call nowadays a 'Wiccan,' a Sylvan Wicca."

"Does it mean a witch?" Anne raised her eyebrows. "To be honest, I don't know a lot about Wiccan History. I've heard about Wicca, but really, I wasn't interested in details. I've no idea there are several types of Wiccans."

"Well," Jennifer replied, "if the concept isn't familiar to you, let me offer you a few hints, without sounding too scholarly. The term Wicca is supposed to have been an early

Anglo-Saxon word for witchcraft. Many say at that time, Wicca represented the nature and fertility religion of pre-Christian Europe.

"Nowadays, Wiccans emphasize and worship the sacred meaning of nature and its cycles. We find of utmost importance modern themes like equality of male and female. We also carry a sense of wonder and belief in magic, -- the white, helpful one, of course -- and above all, a profound respect and love of nature, which many people seem to ignore these days.

"We've nothing in common with the old paganism forms, or animal sacrifice. Nothing at all. And we are way different from Satanism. We practice magic as an integral part of our religion. Some like to derisively call it witchcraft. I don't care."

Anne raised her eyebrows again. "Interesting. And it doesn't sound harmful. On the contrary. Aren't you disapproved of by the Christians in the village?"

"No. At least, not openly. And you know what? It really matters little whether we associate with the Divine as Father, Son and Holy Spirit, or The One, Goddess and God."

"I agree," Anne said. "Do you have an altar or something of the type? I remember I saw something similar in a documentary on Discovery .A lady who practiced a kind of witchcraft, was surrounded by altars and candles and so on."

"Many set up an altar before talking to the Divine, but similar to a real friend who comes to visit without expecting to be offered refreshments, so will the Divine. The Divine is there for you, no rituals needed."

Anne nodded, interested.

Jennifer shrugged. "Well, anyway I haven't invited you here to talk about myself. I understand you encountered some serious and odd events on your trip. Your friend told me a few things, before talking to the Alpine Chalet. Can you tell me what happened exactly? I think I might be of help."

Jennifer listened with great attention to Anne's story, and then she explained to the astonished couple about her forebodings in connection with Anne and something tarred by evil in their possession. Anne took out the crucifix.

Jennifer looked up sharply and frowned, her eyes suddenly dark. She took it in her hands and the very next moment her body was shaken by a sudden tremor, as if a searing pain passed through her. She didn't say a word and performed a brief ritual of 'cleansing,' as she explained to the questioning looks of Anne and Neil.

"I can be of assistance to you in another respect, too. The police."

"Great," Neil said, brightening. "Our intention was to go to the police and report our discovery, after talking to you."

"Mr. Randall, the police constable in our village, is a good acquaintance of mine. A friend, I might say. He would be the best person to deal with your gruesome find. As a rule, he has his morning coffee here at the inn. I'll check to find out if he's still here or not," Jennifer said and called the bar. She listened for a moment, nodded, and replaced the receiver.

"He's no longer here. The girl says he's not at his usual table. No problem. His office is two doors away from here. I'll accompany you."

Anne smiled. "Thank you, Jen. You're a great help."

"Don't mention it. I feel I'm already involved," Jennifer replied and taking the crucifix, she led the way to the police station.

Chapter Twenty

1480 September

Genevieve

Late in the afternoon Father Andrew finally arrived at old Ryan's cottage.

Genevieve was waiting anxiously in Ryan's cottage, only half listening to the old gardener's monotonous voice.

At last, a sharp knock at the door interrupted Ryan's monologue.

"Who is it?" Ryan asked before carefully opening the door.

"It's me, Andrew," the reply came in a low voice. Ryan invited Andrew to enter his lodge.

"Does anyone know you are here?" Genevieve apprehensively asked the priest.

"No, have no fear." Andrew replied shaking his head. Andrew wore a deep frown with his forehead glossed by alight sweat.

"Is anything wrong with you? Maybe something you've eaten in the dragon's lair?" the gardener tried a joke.

"Nothing's wrong. Don't worry," Andrew replied.

The gardener shook his head and replied, "I've never seen you so livid. What did the harridan do? I think she is the devil on earth. Take the burden off your soul. Don't let it poison your heart."

Andrew nodded and addressed Ryan, as if embarrassed to speak directly to Genevieve. "I don't think you will believe what she did during the dinner served in her chamber. The atmosphere had grown very tense during the meal and I regretted not having made some excuse to leave St. Mary's as soon as Mass was over. I even contemplated how, on my next visit at the abbey, I'd ask to have my meal in the communal dining room. I'll have to think of some plausible pretext for my request."

Andrew went to the door. He cracked it a bit open and checked the path leading to the abbey. Then he turned and said, "I thought I heard someone near the door. But there's nobody. My imagination, maybe." He sighed and continued his story.

"I grew more and more impatient during the dinner. I toyed with the food on my plate, unable to swallow a bite. Sister Benedicta's burial, the Abbess's shouted insults to Sister Genevieve before I entered the room, Sister Genevieve's request to talk to me, the state of disorder the abbey has come to, contributed to my strained mood. Above all, I became aware of how the Abbess threw herself at me without any restraint or shame. It was the first time she left aside the innuendoes, double meanings and glances I have grown accustomed to from her."

Genevieve shook her head. "Nothing this woman does makes me wonder."

"At the end of the meal," Andrew spoke on, "while I was preparing to leave the table, relieved the ordeal had come to an end, Sister Clementa came closer to me. Looking me straight in my eyes, she unbuttoned the front of her bodice, revealing her voluptuous breasts. Unflinching, she finished unbuttoning her dress and she took one of my hands and put it over her breast."

Genevieve's breath caught in her throat. She pressed a hand over her mouth to stop the cry ready to escape.

Ryan's eyes widened in utter shock.

"Yes." Andrew nodded. "I was appalled by the naked lust in the woman's glance. She'd drunk less than usual, so I couldn't blame her conduct on the wine. The words my father used to say about women came to my mind: 'a woman without modesty is like a flower without fragrance.'

"'Tell me you don't want to do it,' she said in a strange, coarse voice. 'Show me you are a real man, not just a wimp, under that coat of yours.' She bent over me. Her hot breath scorched my cheek. She licked her lips and closed her eyes, moaning. Electrified into awareness, I pulled my hand away from her naked breast and pushed back my chair, standing up. I mastered my real feelings towards the depraved woman: not disgust, but pity."

Ryan shook his head but kept quiet, perhaps at a loss of words.

"Yes, a deep pity and compassion," Andrew continued. "And in an attempt to bring her to her senses, I reminded her, hiding my real thoughts,that we were not ordinary people; I was a man of God. That she was in His service as well. That we were in God's house and our vows were sacred. That it would be a great sin to break them. We were aware, the day we joined the creed that all the worldly things and desires were forbidden to us.

"The Abbess still stood beside the table. Her eyes wide open. Wild. Staring at a point on the wall opposite her. Her exposed nakedness stirred in me not the lust, not the man, as intended, but the priest and his compassion for the woman in front of me. For the 'lost sheep,' who had come to the abbey not because she had any calling for it. Not at all. She'd come because it proved more convenient for the bishop to remove her, to push aside the 'walking sin' from his path.

"I learned, a few days ago, about the bishop's latest affair, involving one of his other parishioners. A widow younger than the Abbess. Another passionate brunette willing to share with him the pleasures of her bed.

"How shameful," Ryan exclaimed. "You'd expect the Bishops to give a good example to the other people. Not behave like shameless womanizers."

The priest continued, "I promised her I would forget everything that happened there and that I would tell no one. Still no answer or reaction came from her. I also suggested it would be better to join the other nuns for dinner after confession rather than having it in her chamber. I said I was sure she would judge things better by the next day."

"And what did she reply?" Genevieve asked. "Knowing her, I'm sure she rebuked you."

"Not exactly," Andrew nodded. "But she told me not to bore her talking about righteousness and faith. That I had no idea how she felt, what she thought in this God forgotten place, among a bunch of idiotic females whose sole concern is to pray from early morning until dawn, as if it would ever change their gray, dull, nauseating life."

"As if someone forced her to come here," Ryan exclaimed.

"She spoke in a faint voice," Andrew went on, "a tormented one, hoarse and strangled at the same time. In spite of that, her eyes sparkled, bringing shivers down my spine. Hatred, contempt, arrogance and, above all, an unquenched thirst for revenge, scrolled through them in a fraction of a second.

"I bade her goodnight adding I hoped God would bring her the most needed peace. And I left. Aware, nevertheless, what huge enmity I'd unleashed in this scorned woman.

"An unpleasant situation, anyway," Ryan sighed heavily and passed his hand over his brow.

"I wish I could say that I am surprised, but I am not," Genevieve said. "Nothing this woman does amazes me anymore."

Ryan nodded thoughtfully. "It's a sad story. I believe every word you've just told us. This woman is capable of anything. Be sure she'll harbor ill feelings towards you. The same as she does towards me and Sister Genevieve. Towards anyone who doesn't humor her."

"Well, you are right. I feel a little better having told it to someone, though it's not why I'm here now. Please, forgive me for being selfish," he said. "What did you want to tell me, Sister?"

Ryan's cabin was too small for three people, so Genevieve and Andrew sat side by side on the cot, while Ryan sat on the window sill with his hands folded over his chest. There was no place for a stool or other furniture, except a small, round table.

Leaving aside introductory explanations, Genevieve started telling the priest her life from the moment she'd become an orphan until that very day. She didn't look him in the eyes. She kept her gaze on her hands, clasped on the table in front of her. Andrew listened through the whole story without saying a single word.

The old gardener confirmed her words by adding his own opinion of the new Abbess. "Faith and compassion are two words strange to our Abbess, as if she'd never heard of such things," the old man said, shaking his head. "She's a dreadful woman."

Heaving a heavy sigh, he continued, "I thought I'd end my life here at the abbey. It's been my home for such a long time. I imagined I'd be buried in the graveyard in the back, alongside many of the nuns I've known, like Sister Dominica and Sister Benedicta, God rest their great, kind souls in His sunny garden.

"If things continue like this, I'll go back down to the village and find some work at the manor house. The only thing to bring pleasure to our Abbess is to see the people around her suffer and her greatest satisfaction is to be the one to do it. Help the young lass here, if it's in your powers, please," the gardener insisted.

"Genevieve will come to harm if she remains here. God knows what this wicked creature might be up to. You perhaps wonder why I worry so much about the well-being of this nun. All I can tell you is that I consider Genevieve the daughter I lost many years ago. Lost because of my foolishness."

Ryan paused, regret and sorrow filling his eyes. "And another thing making her special to me," the old gardener confessed, "is the connection we both have to the cursed forest. Yes, the forest destroyed both our families. God knows what else it has against us.

"You understand, I hope, why I care for Genevieve it breaks my heart to see the way our Abbess treats her. I'm not wrong if I say she hates the bonny lass. She hates her bright mind, her pretty face. And, above all, the fact Genevieve stubbornly opposes the Abbess's attempts to 'tame' her, the same way she did with most of the others. She can't stand someone who speaks her mind.

"Much as she'd have liked to, she couldn't turn Genevieve into one of her minions. To show Genevieve who's the master here, Clementa forced her to take on the most distasteful task that could befall a nun at St. Mary's: cleaning the lavatories."

Andrew turned his glance to Genevieve, who nodded.

"Yes, Uncle Ryan's right. The Abbess wants to provoke me, to push me to revolt against her. Like a spider watching and waiting for the fly to fall in its web, she awaits a reason to catch me and devour me. She wants me out of her way, but not alive. She wishes me dead. She keeps threatening that she'll send me to the stake. I believe she's up to doing it. If she hadn't won most of our Sisters on her part, she wouldn't have dared behave in such an outrageous way. I fear even the few friends I have here might come to harm."

Father Andrew listened to everything Ryan and Genevieve related.

"I must admit what you are telling me doesn't come as such a big surprise. And after today, it's all the more clear just how bad things have gotten. Yet, I never imagined they'd gone so far. Despite that, my duty being no more than to receive the nuns' confession, I have no power to change a thing.

"I can feel nothing but bitterness and revolt. Not only does the Abbess lack the minimum decency required in her position, but she also spoils the whole atmosphere at the abbey. I believe you," he added, patting Genevieve's hand.

A pleasant warmth, like the one she always experienced whenever in his presence, enveloped her. She willed her hands to remain still, and gritted her teeth until her jaw ached.

"You understand I don't have a choice," Genevieve said in a voice little above a whisper. "No other choice. If you bring the Abbess's disapproval and displeasure, the way she considers I did, sooner or later she sweeps you out of her way. We were enemies from the very beginning. I must leave the abbey without delay."

It was a second or two before she spoke again. "I thought...maybe...." Genevieve hesitated, thrown off balance by the intense heat coming from him. "Can you help me?" she asked the priest in a tremulous voice, lifting her gaze to look him straight in the eye for the first time since she'd seen him five months ago.

And the moment their looks met, it was as if a thick veil fell to the ground to reveal what they'd not been aware of, what they didn't want to admit even to themselves, until that very second.

Against their reason, against their beliefs, against their mission, against their will, they'd fallen in love. It happened, no doubt, the day he arrived at the abbey while she attended the old gardener's injured foot. The events of the last hours offered her logical explanation to the odd reaction she experienced there in the garden. She'd blamed the warmth draining her body on the unusually scorching sun. It had been love at first sight.

The intensity of her feelings towards the young priest in front of her shattered Genevieve. And the irony of the situation hit her hard, like a thunderbolt. Andrew, who'd refused Sister Clementa's wanton abandonment half an hour ago, who'd spoken about vows to God, who'd harbored feelings of pity for her sinful behavior, who'd crushed the Abbess under the heel of his firm beliefs, who'd been a devoted church pillar so far, he, of all people, shared Genevieve's feelings.

Andrew raised his hand and his fingers caressed the shape of her lips and lowered her wimple to release her rebellious auburn hair, flaring against his palm, all along his gaze holding hers. His face was within a couple of inches of hers and the warmth of his breath fanned her cheek.

"My beautiful wood anemone," he whispered, and he bent his head and brushed her full, moistened lips with a swift kiss.

A very gentle kiss. A mere chaste brush of the lips, as gentle as the soft brush of a night breeze wing on the moon's eyelids.

Gentle, but powerful enough to unleash the turmoil of emotions and desires lying dormant in her heart and soul. Genevieve's shudder was so strong it passed like an electric charge through her body. She drew in her breath but didn't move away from him. She lowered her eyelids and, sighing softly, she found herself in Andrew's strong, protective arms. She glanced up again and met her own love and guilt reflected in his eyes.

For a brief moment, coming from a deep corner of her soul, flickered the awareness that their love was doomed. There would be no future for them in this part of the world. They'd be condemned, despised and driven away for having broken their sacred vows.

Still, all the future misery was worth the endless love mirrored in his face and felt in the beating of his heart. Aware that she shouldn't be in his arms, she couldn't find the power to let go. Any word would have been useless. She read it clearly on his face. His pounding heart next to hers said it all. She wanted this entrancing moment never to end.

A soft movement made her conscious of the old gardener's presence. Embarrassed, still in each other's arms, she turned her head towards him to see large tears running down his wrinkled, sun-burnt face.

The old man wiped his tears with the back of his hand and walked out of the cottage, dragging his rheumy legs with painful effort.

For a long moment, neither of them spoke.

Through the crack of the closing door, Genevieve caught sight of a shadow sneaking out from the cover of the white rose bushes under the window, hurrying back to the abbey's main building. She thought, though not very sure of it, the figure to belong to Sister Cecilie.

An icy claw gripped Genevieve's heart. Sister Cecile's presence meant bad news to all three people who'd been inside the cottage. She frowned, yet didn't tell Andrew anything. It was no use anyway. If they'd been overheard, all hell would break loose. Hopefully the shadow belonged to some other nun, and she hadn't heard what was said in the cottage.

Chapter Twenty-One

England 1990

Anne

Randall's office was located in a small stone building, quite close to the Rampart Inn. The room looked large; there was a counter partitioning off one section for the public.

Jennifer introduced Anne and Neil to Constable Randall. Anne frowned and blinked several times. Half remembered faces and words flooded her mind for a second, and then vanished. The man's face seemed familiar to her.

Constable Randall raised his eyebrows, not taking his gaze from Anne. His look was not insolent or indecent, but simply half questioning, half intrigued. As if he couldn't remember where he'd seen her before. A glint of vague recognition followed but he asked nothing.

He was a tall, middle-aged man with wavy salt-and-pepper hair and a penetrating stare, which scrutinized and didn't miss a thing. The way he carried himself spoke of authority and power. His strong, broad, clean-shaven face brightened into a large smile at the sight of Jennifer.

"Well, well, good morning, Jennifer. A real surprise. What brings you here to my office? Are these two young people some burglars? Have they eaten all your cherry-pies? Let me guess, they've come to confess stealing your broomstick." He chuckled.

"You know," he addressed Anne and Neil, "the only 'violent deed' around here happened several years ago, when a couple of strangers, teenagers on a motorbike, tried to leave the gas station without paying the owner for the petrol."

"My friends here are no criminals," Jennifer said, smiling. "They've come to you with a problem requiring your advice and involvement. They discovered some human bones up in the forest."

"Indeed!"

"Yes," said Neil. "They are human bones and judging by their aspect I'd say they are quite old. Belonging to an adult. We came upon them in the hollow of a tree."

"Quite so? Odd. Are you sure the bones are old?"

"There's no doubt," Neil replied nodding. "I've written a couple of articles on forensic work and I learned a few things myself. Of course, this does not qualify me as an expert; however I'm not ignorant, either."

"Right. I believe you. Did you take them down?"

"No. We thought it better to leave them in the hollow, for fear animals might carry them away. Though we met no such things in this strange forest. The skull's split open. This person didn't die of natural causes, clearly."

"You did a good thing leaving the bones where you found them. We don't have any reports on missing persons around here. Might have been a tourist. We must inform the forensic anthropology department in London. Science has advanced to unthinkable heights these days. They should be able to narrow down the age of the bones and even what age the person was."

"Yes, we thought about DNA analysis too," Anne replied.

"They'll tell us the year the person died, if male or female," Constable Randall continued. "My nephew, Allan, is one of the best analysts in the office. I'm so proud of him. He's my only family."

"No children of your own?" Neil asked, out of politeness.

"No. I'm nothing but a childless widower. After my wife died, I didn't try to find another woman willing to put up with my 'follies.'"

"Can't Jennifer help you with her spells?" Neil inquired, laughing.

"Oh, no," Jennifer said, laughing too. "The Constable here is an adult. He doesn't need my spells to find his sweetheart if he really wants it. I'm not a matchmaker. I told you what Sylvan Wiccans do. All we can offer is protection against evil. We never use magic to harm others and there's no point doing it, since it returns three fold. The Wiccan creed says, 'an it harm none, do what thou will'."

"Yes, she's right," Randall admitted. "The odd thing is, some years ago, an old gypsy woman told me a few things about my past lives. She spread a pack of strange cards and after some mumbo-jumbo over them she turned one. She told me I was a widower, yet she might have found it out from village people.

"She added I had to suffer a punishment to be childless and alone in this life, since in the previous one my family died because of my carelessness. She said I lived, not far from those places and I'd paid part of my guilt through hardships in my former life and the rest of the punishment was for this life. I thought it gibberish. Later, when Jennifer settled here and I told her about the woman's words, she said the old gypsy was right."

"Don't forget my advice," added Jennifer, "the three bad things in life are fear, confusion and doubt."

"Yes, I know, and I promised I wouldn't have doubts on why certain things happened like they did. There's a reason behind everything."

"I agree with you," Anne said. "Can you tell us if you're aware of a convent, monastery, something of the kind up there on the mountain in the forest?"

"Monastery..." Constable Randall shook his head. His gaze became alert at once.

"Well, not a monastery proper. We found some ruined walls, they don't look like the ruins of a castle or manor. We assumed it might have been a clerical establishment."

"Oh, those ruins...." The policeman nodded again. "You reached the part of the forest that once housed an abbey a long, long time ago. Several hundred years. Six, I think."

"Was the abbey a place for nuns or monks?"

"Nuns," Constable Randall replied.

"What happened?" Anne inquired. "Why is this one so badly ruined when others are so well preserved?"

"People say," Constable Randall replied," the immorality and scandalous behavior of the last Mother Prioress contaminated most of the nuns and led to the destruction of the monastery. Many consider it was God's punishment. The proud St. Mary's Abbey was brought down by hard sins."

"You speak about an Abbess's doubtful behavior," Neil said and raised his eyebrows, amazed. "I wonder about such lack of morality in the head of a clerical establishment. Especially, in an age when the English Church gave edicts allowing sex only for procreation. It considered pleasure, as the motive for intimate relations, to be sinful. Wednesdays, Fridays, Saturdays and Sundays were banned days even for marital relations."

"Well," Constable Randall replied, "I read once, that during the fifteenth century, Henry V imposed a broad program of reform, meant to answer growing criticism regarding the state of morals in England's monasteries.

"The king himself called for more prayer and less interest in worldly goods. Clerics were advised to devote more time to God than to hoarding, feasting and entertaining female guests."

"Amazing. Disappointing in many ways," Anne replied. "The words abbey and convent are always associated in my mind with self-denial, piety, prayer."

"We made a connection between the ruins to another discovery, in the hollow among the bones," added Neil.

"What do you mean?"

"There's an object," Jennifer intervened, "which might offer a clue to the identity of the person whose bones they found."

"We discovered a bejeweled cross on a thick gold chain in with the bones. A valuable piece of jewelry. This led us to believe the victim might be a monk or a nun."

"Here it is." Jennifer held the cross out in front of her by the chain. "I advise you not to touch it. It has an evil imprint."

"Hmm. I trust your sense," Constable Randall replied and studied the cross without taking it from Jennifer's hand.

"And there's more, the young lady here can tell you," Jennifer said, encouraging Anne to tell Constable Randall about her strange visions in the forest. "She's reluctant to speak about it for fear you'll think her crazy."

"I'm all ears. Let me hear your story first. I'm not one to issue judgments beforehand, believe me."

Anne told him, to the last detail, about the events and the visions or dreams in the forest, although shy at first, imagining his derisive laugh at the end of such a story.

Constable Randall didn't laugh. On the contrary. He listened to them in quiet bewilderment.

"I find it strange," he said when she finished relating their adventure of the previous day. He shook his head several times. "I find it strange, you know, what you've just told me confirms a legend, better said a story, linked to the eerie forest and the ruins in it."

"What legend?" Anne and Neil asked at the same time.

"Oh, I heard it when I was a boy. My grandfather told it to me the day I wanted to know why I couldn't venture into the forest with some friends to camp." Constable Randall said. "The story came down from generation to generation, though I can't tell how much was left out or how much people embellished it along the way. I also have here the rhymed legend about two young people who followed their hearts, and I think there's a connection to your visions."

The policeman turned to look for a book on a shelf behind him. The moment he turned his head, a long pale line along his left cheek, like an old badly healed scar, caught Anne's gaze. Her breath caught in her throat. In a sudden flash she saw the image of an old man, older than Constable Randall, shabbily dressed, with a similar scar. She didn't say a thing, no longer surprised by the odd visions.

"I've always been impressed by the lines of the poem, and in a way, I feel as if I've witnessed the events myself. To tell you the truth, the moment you entered my office," he said, turning to Anne, "before stating the reason for your visit, I said to myself, this is how Genevieve, the nun in the legend, looked."

"Was she called Genevieve?" asked Neil.

"Yes, quite an unusual name for a nun. It seems she was allowed to keep her lay name, a favor granted to her by the first Abbess, who had welcomed her at the Abbey."

"What did your grandfather tell you about the events?" Anne asked. She made herself more comfortable as Constable Randall started a startling story about the young nun and the nuns' priest.

Anne almost guessed what he intended to say before Constable Randall even began. Unable to explain why, a blanket of deja vu spread over her.

"Well, my grandfather said it all began the day the old Abbess at St. Mary's Abbey, Sister Dominica, died and was replaced by a younger woman who had nothing in common with religion, faith or sacred vows. As with the saying that a bad apple spoils the whole cart, the wicked Abbess managed to attract and corrupt a group of nuns who imitated her, forgetting why they joined the abbey. The new Abbess's presence at the abbey brought only misfortune, misery and death to the nuns who dared to oppose her immoral behavior."

"That's why you spoke of murder earlier," Jennifer said.

"Yes, indeed." Constable Randall nodded. "Life for Genevieve became unbearable and she decided to find another nunnery and leave St. Mary's forever," Constable Randall continued, "The nuns' priest was Father Andrew, a young man known to everyone as being dedicated to his calling. He belonged to a rich, noble family of the county. Nothing's known about his family anymore. It's as if they disappeared after the tragic death of their son and brother.

"Genevieve had asked Father Andrew for his assistance in finding her a place in another monastery. The deep feeling of love between the two young people -- love lying deep down in their hearts from the very day their glances met -- surfaced and endangered not only their lives, but also the lives of the people who protected and helped them." Constable Randall looked Anne straight in the eyes and his gaze held a sad glint.

"And, for the Abbess, this came as the final straw. Genevieve had captured the attention of a man she wanted for herself. His cold politeness to her had been an ongoing disappointment, yet the Abbess might have been able to accept it, if no one else achieved what she hadn't. Finding out that the nun she hated most wanted to secretly leave the Abbey, helped by the man who rejected her advances, made her rage boundless."

"Interesting," Anne whispered.

"Yes, this is what my grandfather told me. How much is truth and how much is story I can't tell. Please, listen to the ballad, and afterwards tell me what you think," he said. Opening a leather bound book, he read the lines in a deep, throaty voice.

Chapter Twenty-Two

1480 October

Genevieve

"God, please forgive me," Andrew muttered under his breath and bowed his head to kiss Genevieve fully on her trembling, moist mouth.

Their lips met in their first, deep, passionate kiss. Genevieve's fear of the forest, her determination to give Andrew up vanished into the night. She became vibrantly aware of Andrew's warm hands holding her. A quiver raced through her.

"Oh, Genevieve, sweet Genevieve," Andrew murmured. He touched the soft skin of her neck with his lips. "I love you so." His kisses turned more urgent. His hold grew tighter, pressing her soft body against his taut one. As his lips touched the base of her throat, liquid fire raced through Genevieve's veins. Her whole body throbbed with a fierce desire, matching his.

"I love you too, Andrew," Genevieve whispered and she sagged against him, her body limp with the warm delight enveloping her. She succumbed to his passionate embrace, responding to his kiss.

Genevieve's spirits fell and her heart skipped a beat when, a couple of seconds later, she opened her eyes and her gaze fell on a knot of strangers.

They wore dark cloaks covering their shoulders. Their faces were hidden by large, dark hoods.

"Oh, no," Genevieve stifled a cry.

"This must be our little witch accompanied by our wicked little priest," one of the strangers said in a hoarse voice. The others laughed aloud.

Andrew pushed Genevieve behind him. She glanced around for an escape like a hunted animal. They were trapped. Behind her and Andrew ran the stream, and the strangers closed off any other escape.

"Who are you? What is it you want from us?" Andrew did his best to stall for time, although maybe he was already aware who the men were and what they were doing.

Another person stood away from the rest, careful to keep his or her face covered by a black cloak. Several others advanced on Genevieve with brutish, grinning faces in the moonlight. She hadn't seen them before.

"It matters not who we are, Father. There's somethin' yer can do. Tell us if yer know what happens to witches and to the scum who betray God? Let me freshen up yer memory a bit, in case yer have no idea. They are taken to the stake for the first and they are hanged for the last."

He laughed, the sound sharp and menacing. "And methinks we've both cases here," the hideous man croaked, nudging the ribs of the cronies next to him. "Tell us, Father, like man to man, is she as good a harlot as she's a witch?" They all laughed, slapping their thighs.

Her heart beating fast, Genevieve lowered her gaze to the men's hands. They were fingering thick clubs half hidden under their cloaks. Nothing in the world might save her or Andrew from them.

The hands of these brutes would finish them both here. Who was their leader? Whose orders did they obey? She had no need to wonder. The Abbess must have hired the men to deal with the dirty job of killing them and disposing of their bodies afterwards.

"Leave the nun alone! I'm the guilty one. I'm the one who forced her to leave the abbey and follow me," Andrew said in a desperate, useless attempt to save Genevieve.

"No, Father. We've heard something else. Yer don't fool us and yer know it pretty well. And by the way she's responding to yer kiss, yer forced her real hard. Yer trip is ended. Yer shall both be punished. She's a harlot, a wicked witch who made yer sin. Yer're both sinners and sinners mus' get their retribution," the one who seemed to be the group leader addressed Andrew.

"Grab him," the man yelled. His companions dashed for the priest and tied his hands together, fastening him to the hollowed oak tree trunk. "Prepare the rope to hang him. We mus' hurry. Meanwhile, I'll have a word with the naughty, little nun. Let's see if her spells are of any good to her now.

"Come to yer uncle, little witch. He has something for yer. Something special. A broomstick yer can ride to hot hell," the man said and he laughed while he towered over Genevieve.

"Please, have mercy," Genevieve begged in a feeble voice. The man's intentions became more than obvious, judging by his leering look and gestures. "Please, let the priest go. I won't run. Do whatever you want with me. I'm to blame for everything that happened. It's my fault. Only mine. Leave him alone, please." Genevieve's eyes swam in tears.

"Yes, I'm glad yer agree, my little, wicked witch. I'll do whatever I please with yer, but the man can't go. I've me orders," the man replied and he indicated with his head the stranger who stood to the side. "The one here paid a fortune for both o' yer. Yer upset the person very much. Now, let's not waste our time," he said and he pushed her to the ground, ripping her clothes off.

Genevieve forced her mind to fly away from her earthly body. She forced her spirit to reach the sky above and not let her human body feel anything. There, high up, she caught sight of Mother, and her sisters and brothers.

They waved to her and smiled, calling her to them. "Come, Gen. At last we're together. We've been waiting for you. Come. You'll meet Bertha here too. And a lady who says her name is Dominica. She told us nice things about you. Come to us."

"Hey, Bull, I think she likes it. She doesn't even fight," one of the men said, pulling up his pants.

Genevieve, with a huge effort, turned her gaze to Andrew who, chained to the tree, witnessed her torment, unable to do a thing. She had no more tears left to cry.

He was as white as chalk, large tears raining down his face. He lowered his head and prayed, for the last time in his life. "Blessed Virgin, Almighty God, I've sinned along my life. In my words and in my thoughts, and in what I did. Not in loving Genevieve. Lord, have mercy on her. Help her," he whispered. "Spare her life. Take only mine. She has suffered enough."

A shrill voice and a bitter laugh which, to Genevieve's horror, she recognized as being the Abbess's, brought Andrew back, making him open his eyes.

"Well, dear Father, I suppose it's time you confessed. Pray, listen to my words. Do they sound familiar? Do you remember? 'I think you don't know what you're doing, my child. Man is weak, but he must find strength in faith.'"

The stranger, who had come closer, was indeed no other than the Abbess, dressed in man's clothes. Her mouth twitched in a derisive twist, her glance, her voice, her posture betraying her hostility and blistering rage.

"I almost thought you to be above any human desires. Cecile heard you and the two despicable liars, telling a lot of lies about me, and scheming behind my back. You're a pathetic disgrace, Father Andrew. Aren't your vows to God sacred anymore? Have you become an ordinary man, no longer in the service of God?" The woman continued in a cruel, scathing voice, her rage turning her eyes into two burning points, as if the fiendish gates of hell were waiting there to be opened.

Andrew raised his glance up to the small patch of sky, seen through the tree's thick branches, and uttered his bitter reproach to his creator, in a voice deep with mourning. "Why have You allowed them to harm her? I'm the one who offended You. Not her." His head fell back onto his chest.

He and Genevieve were in the hideous woman's power. The Abbess grinned viciously and hissed between clenched teeth, savoring her triumph. "Save your breath and don't waste the precious time left to pray to your God. He's deaf. Deaf and blind to us mortals' suffering. He doesn't care one bit of you, or her or them," she said and pointed to the dastardly group of rascals who retreated beside the stream, keeping their eyes on the scene.

"What do you say, Father?" the woman mocked him again. "I might spare your life. Do you repent for having hurt my feelings, for having favored this fallen woman, this peasant? Think of what could have been, think of what we still might have together. One word from you and I'll order the men to set you free."

Andrew didn't answer or look at her, and the Abbess stepped away from the tree trunk.

The evil woman's barked order to the men who were standing a few feet away reached Genevieve's ears.

"Enough talk. Wake the witch up. Take water from the stream and make sure she's wide awake. Don't let her faint or look away. I want her to watch him suffering and dying. And then you can finish her too." She grinned again, devilish and cruel. "Nobody treats me like dirt and gets away with it."

She turned and backed away from the tree. Passing by Genevieve's half naked, tainted body, she spat on her but suddenly stopped. The Abbess's eyes widened as her gaze fell on the golden cross around Genevieve's neck.

The sight of the cross unleashed her laughter in a roaring, hysterical sound. Its' horrible shrills echoed all along the mountain slopes, coming back in continuous, frightening waves as if swarms of devils laughed with her.

Genevieve could only watch dimly as the Abbess returned to Andrew with a hateful, triumphant look plastered over her face. She stared at him. Her voice sounded like the hiss of a venomous snake.

"So, my handsome. How stupid of you. You gave the cross to her. The present I offered you, the token of my feelings for you. You'd no idea I put a protective spell on my gift, only for you. The moment it goes to someone else, the jewel cross becomes a damaging thing for the person wearing it. I understand now why we've had no difficulty in finding you, although I thought everything was lost. The posse proved worthwhile." She spat towards Genevieve again.

Genevieve said nothing, She looked at Andrew's tormented face, where he stood tied to the tree. The men threw a thick rope over the tree branch that pointed ahead, as if showing the way to the monastery.

Genevieve's mouth bled as she cried to him, her voice tinged by bitter sadness, while the men untied Andrew from the tree and pushed the noose over his head.

"Dear Andrew, we're not destined for each other. Not in this life, not in this world. I knew it from the very beginning. I forgive God for the bad things He let these people do to us. I love you, Andrew. I love you to the end of the world. Wait for me, in Heaven. I'll join you soon, my love...."

With a cry of rage, Sister Clementa sprang at Genevieve. The Abbess' face drained to a sickly gray, losing any trace of humanity, her breath came like hisses.

"Shut up. Shut up, you witch. Shut your filthy mouth. Witch! Witch! Witch," With a daggar the Abbess had concealed in her robe, she struck Genevieve's over and over until blood gushed from the split in Genevieve's head.

The sickening crunch of her skull as the Abbess' knife carved through her head was the last sound Genevieve's heard. A searing bolt of pain shot through her. Her blood sprang from the gaping head wound, splashing the hideous woman all over her demented face.

Through the thick flow of blood gushing freely over her half closed eyes, while life ebbed away from her, Genevieve's gaze touched Andrew's dear face before death dragged her into oblivion.

Chapter Twenty-Three

England 1990

Anne

The soft, pearly gray mist hanging above the mountains,
  Is covering in cool folds two shadows on the run-
  They try to lose their traces, still hope to be forgotten-
    A young priest and the nun.

They've given up all saintly vows and caught in love's
    sweet magic,
  Oblivious of the people considering them scum,
  Will live a new, free life with Passion as their Goddess.
    The young priest and his nun.

But little do they notice, quite close to them, in hiding,
  And ready to chastise them for the shameful thing they've
    done,
  A group of silent figures, who grab the wicked sinners,
    The young priest and the nun.

So, soon, the dangling bodies will feast the black, death
    ravens.
  Avengers deaf to pleadings as mercy there was none
  The creatures of the forest will be the only mourners
    For a young priest and his nun.

Thus, even to this day, the travelers through the forest
  Will hear desperate moans, like none under the sun.

There's no eternal rest; lost souls haunt the mountains
The young priest and the nun!

"Well," Constable Randall said, rubbing his chin, "that is the ballad." He closed the book. The chair creaked as Randall leaned sharply back.

In the silence following the ballad's reading, Randall's words sounded to Anne's ears like a curtain over the final act of a play.

"Please," he addressed Anne, "accept the book. It's a great pleasure for me to know you have it."

"Thank you," Anne answered, reaching out her trembling hand to receive it. "Touching, touching."

"All in all, quite a gruesome episode," Neil said, nodding. "At the risk of stating the obvious, it looks to me that what happened to the two runaways, the young nun and the priest, sounds like the punishment of the hand of God."

He took hold of Anne's trembling hand. Her eyes brimmed with tears. How to account for the dread that had swept through her when Randall had described what Bull and his cronies had done to Genevieve and Andrew.

All through the story, Jennifer had sat unmoved.

Anne met Jennifer's intense gaze as if trying to read the depths of her heart and soul.

"It's very likely the bones they found in the forest belong to this young nun, Genevieve. If we take into account the cross among them, the probability is even higher," Jennifer said, shaking her head.

Anne glanced at the golden chain, her brows furrowed. "We must get rid of the evil thing at once."

"Yes", nodded Jennifer, "we'll see to it, later."

"What happened to the Abbess and the abbey?" Neil asked. "Who or what destroyed St. Mary's?"

"Good question, young man," Constable Randall resumed his story. "The events don't stop with the two unfortunate young people's death. Everything I tell you came by piecing together all the information the villagers got from the rascals who did it and from the nun who escaped alive."

"And another thing," Jennifer intervened. "The ballad implies they were both hanged, though it seems to me a little bit different, since Anne and Neil discovered only one human skeleton. There should have been two."

"For the moment, we don't know if it's Genevieve's or Andrew's body," Constable Randall said, shrugging. "We only assume it's Genevieve's because of the vision that kept haunting Anne and the cross you found. Anyway, I think what I'll tell you next might be an answer to your question."

"After the 'two sinners' found their deaths, the Abbess paid the hired murderers the rest of the promised gold and all left the place."

"Didn't they fear the bodies would be discovered?" Anne wanted to know.

"No. People seldom ventured up to the abbey. Bull, the villains' leader, returned to the oak tree a few hours later, the way he arranged before, with the Abbess. He cut the hanged priest down and dug a large grave at the roots of the tree, placing Father Andrew's inert body inside. He threw earth over it and turned his attention to Genevieve. He chopped off her hands and legs. Her head too. For a moment, Bull seemed undecided what to do with the cut pieces. He'd received strict instructions not to bury the two bodies in the same grave." Chief Randall hesitated, throwing Anne a thoughtful glance.

She shifted in her chair, nervously twisting her hands.

"He felt tempted," Randall went on, "to pocket the cross hanging at the body's neck. It looked worth a lot of money, more than the Abbess had paid him. So he struggled to pull the golden necklace from the severed trunk. All of a sudden, eerie noises, like voices, moans and a dog howling, came from the river and made him stop. He said he glanced around, and was taken aback at the sight of red eyes watching him from behind the tree trunks. An unexplained feeling of fear troubled him and he gave up on the cross. He covered the trunk of the severed body with his own cloak and threw it inside the tree's hollow, although it wasn't as easy a thing to do as it had been with the limbs. He slanted a sideways glance to the trees; he imagined he'd seen red eyes watching him. Nothing. Relieved, he washed the blood off his hands in the stream and checked once again to make sure there were no traces left. Having reckoned the money the Abbess gave him was not enough, he left the forest and instead of returning to the village or to the hiding place of the others, he headed to the abbey. He decided he could do with more gold from Sister Clementa if she wished him to keep his mouth shut about the dirty affair." Randall paused to catch his breath, the silence looming over them like a heavy mist.

He stood up and went to the window overlooking the front garden. Then he turned to the visitors in the office and went on speaking. "Bull arrived at St Mary's after midnight to find the gate standing ajar. He had no difficulty in finding his way to the Abbess's room, because this wasn't his first visit at the abbey. He'd known Clementa for a very long time and better than anyone else. He'd worked as a stable man at the manor house, and used to take messages to and from her lover, the bishop.

"After the scandal that ended in his master's death and in the lady of the house becoming the Abbess at St. Mary's Abbey, Bull also left the manor. Too lazy to earn his living by honest work, and known to everyone as a violent, base man, it came as no wonder he joined a group of villains.

"Whenever Sister Clementa needed him, she sent Sister Theresa and Sister Cecile down into the village to leave him word at the inn. His last job for her was to dispose of Francesca's and the old gardener's bodies. The Abbess didn't want the other nuns to guess the signs of poisoning on the dead bodies." The police Constable paused again and taking in all the people in his office he continued. "The moment Bull reached Sister Clementa's private room...."

Anne's attention was distracted. She had turned her gaze from the police official standing by the window, and her look fell on something that was hidden to her view up to the moment Randall stood up.

There, behind his desk was a small oval table with a pile of books that lay on top. A big leather book. She was sure she'd seen it before, but the memory refused to come. Anne drew in her breath. She stood up, and ignoring the others' questioning looks, she headed to the table. "May I?" she asked Chief Randall.

"Go ahead," he replied. "They are books that I borrowed from Jennifer and intended to return to her later today."

The title of the old leathered book read: Leech Book. For a moment, Anne didn't move or breathe. A slight dizziness engulfed her, blurring her sight. Another vision? Will it ever end? She reached out her hand and touched the cover. Images of plants and descriptions of diseases and the herbal potions recommended as cures flooded her mind.

The days, months and years rolled into each other and she found herself in a dark lit room. There was a strong smell of incense and staleness, unable to cover the stench of evil that seemed to pour out of the walls. There was something familiar about this room; as if she'd been here once, long ago. Everything was gloomy and dark, except the darting tongues of light from the candles in the wall alcoves. Anne narrowed her eyes to adapt her sight to the dark room.

A shelf with books was illuminated by the candles above. Anne recognized The Leech Book cover at once. She also sensed somebody's presence and turned her gaze. The scene unfolding in front of her eyes dismayed her. A man, dressed in shabby clothes and looking like a brute, was leering at a tall woman in front of him.

The dark haired apparition in Anne's visions. She knew it was Sister Clementa, the Abbess. She seemed half drunk and raving madly, her hair loose, spit dribbling from her mouth and an enraged look in her eyes. She didn't seem to notice the man standing in the doorway. Or Anne.

"Hey, lady. Yer recognize me, don't yer? Bull, the handsome an' the handy."

Anne covered her mouth with both her hands but too late. A loud cry escaped her lips. Yet, neither Bull nor Clementa gave her a sign they were aware of her presence. Maybe they couldn't see me, Anne hoped.

"You seem more alive than the nun's not moving body you wanted all of us to rape in front of the priest," Bull addressed the Abbess. "Women, more often than not, flock together. Yer prove different. No warmth, no kindness. Nothing but solid hate for the others."

In a dry voice, he snapped, "Yer hear me, lady? I wan' more gold. I know yer have some gold stacked somewhere around. Yer can't say yer got no money. I brought yer yesterday the nice sum I got for the three old, heavy books yer asked me to find a buyer for in the town. Some books they was if the customer gave me a fat purse with shining, yellow coins. An' what about yer an' me having a little bit of fun together? Yer know what I mean, 'yer holiness,' don' yer, eh? Yer look a bit stale, me thinks," Bull kept on.

He took a few steps towards the Abbess and winked obscenely at her. The grin made his scarred face hideous and disgusting. "I might anytime find some willing ear in which to pour many spicy stories about yer and yer odd rituals.

"There mus' be somethin' special, somethin' fishy about the thing if yer want no one else to see it," Bull said and pointed with his dirty hand to the ebony statuette on the table in front of the Abbess; the figure representing a three headed woman, a stare of horror in her eyes and serpents entwined around each head.

"That thing over which I saw yer, when yer was Lady Marion, mumbling somethin' I didn' understand and sprinklin' a sort of black powder over it and sayin' yer husband's name. After which he died."

The Abbess stopped in her tracks and suddenly turned into her usual arrogant, cold, mean self. She stared at the man with her evil eyes until he backed away from her. She rasped, enraged, "How dare you, tramp... you... a nothing... to come into my room and insult me? Do you want to hang by the priest's side?"

"No, I don' wan' it, woman. Try to be friendlier. I just wan' me gold. I wan' me money now," he said again in a lowered voice. "Me thinks I'm a too tough nut for yer to crack. Yer told me lies. Yer said yer'd discovered the nun an' the priest spurning this holy place, an' making love in her room. Yer lied.

"The nun was a maiden. I was her first man. I can tell yer fo'sure. So if yer deceived me about it, how should I know yer not invented the woman was a witch? Maybe she weren't. Yer jus' wanted her out of yer way for other reasons, I reckon. Perhaps we took the woman's life fo' nothing after all. The priest too."

"So what? What's it to you? Why do you care all of a sudden if she's a maiden or not, if she's a witch or not, if they're guilty or not? I paid you to do the job," raged the Abbess.

"Don't give me the top drawer tongue, lady. No, it's not as simple as this. I may be a thief an' a villain like many says about me, but I've me limits. I don't kill no innocent people. I neva' killed no man, no woman without guilt. Yer said they're sinners an' deserve to die, to spare the abbey of shame.

"Yer repeated they're the devil's servants. So yer made me sin. If yer wan' me trap shut, pay me more gold. Yer have no use for it anyway, here," he replied, unwilling to yield. His gaze darted to the table behind the nun, and then he advanced menacingly towards Clementa.

When she answered, the Abbess's voice rang hard, cold, devoid of emotion. Each word dripped slivers of ice down the Anne's spine.

"You despicable piece of dirt. Get out of my abbey or I'll accuse you of heresy and ask the soldiers to flog you to death. Leave right now. Do you want me to think you're slow-witted and don't understand you've gone too far? I know you too well. You're more cunning and dangerous than a rabid fox.

"You think you know me. How wrong you are. I am worse than you. Don't try me. Leave and never return without being asked."

The Abbess' voice turned little by little into an unearthly shrill; froze Bull on the spot he stood. She advanced to the table, holding the small ebony three-headed woman in her hands. Her eyes alive and venomous, hideous like the eyes of the serpents in the statuette.

Bull, who must have felt cowered by her fierce look and sharp words, retreated and left the abbey, swearing obscenely.

"Anne, Anne!" Someone is calling her name. A familiar man's voice rang in Anne's ears. Then the soft touch of fingers on her arm. Anne feels the real world rushing back. The vision of the Abbess, standing enraged in the room, started to fade. Her eyes flickered and opened.

Neil was standing by her with a worried expression on his face.

"Anne, are you all right?"

She nodded and then turned to Randall and Jennifer who were watching her with concerned faces.

"I'm well. I had a vision that was brought by touching the Leech Book."

They all faced each other in stony silence.

"Please, take no notice. Go on with the story," Anne said and went back to her chair after carefully putting the book back on the small table.

Constable Randall resumed the story, "Bull returned the following night. The entire group of malevolent thugs who'd been in the forest accompanied him. They were all drunk and ready to deal with the arrogant woman who had not paid them enough for the dirty work they'd done. She would be taught some manners.

"The villains sneaked along the abbey's cold stone walls, as noiseless as death, creeping on quiet toes. They blocked all the nuns' rooms and entered the chamber where the Abbess slept.

"Enraged, she refused to pay them more money, and the infamous men gagged her, beat her up and abandoned her, agonizing, in a bath of blood.

"They plundered the room of all the valuable things they found. Equipped with heavy iron bars, they smashed the beautiful stained glass windows. They even managed to dislodge pieces from the surrounding walls. At last, satisfied with the bounty, the attackers left the abbey. Not before starting a great fire to destroy almost everything.

"Only one nun escaped alive. Sister Agnes.

"The next day, the village people came to see what caused the thick smoke billowing from the abbey's direction. They found Agnes almost out of her senses with fear, still hiding in the toilets.

"She'd been in there before the men entered the abbey and, hearing the shouts and crashing noises, she remained hidden, confident her death was near. She told the villagers she saw them leave through a crack in the privy door, yet she couldn't do a thing to stop the fire or help her mates. She also gave a brief description of two of the hoodlums she'd seen in the yard admiring their 'masterpiece' before leaving.

"All that was left of the former magnificent religious establishment was a huge heap of stones and glowing cinders, sticks of furniture and splintered glass. Fragments of ash spiraled up into the sky, scattered by the wind over the forest and the mountain. They found all the nuns dead. Most had been suffocated by smoke, slumped behind the half burnt doors they'd been trying to pry open. The only body never found belonged to the Abbess. No trace left of it. No ashes, no pieces of her clothes. Nothing. As if she'd vanished into the night.

"Sister Agnes soon recovered her sanity and identified the wrong doers several days later. Although they denied their involvement, at first, the village people believed the nun's words, not theirs. Sister Agnes also said that Sister Clementa ordered Genevieve's death and also the nuns' priest. She herself had overheard the Abbess talking with Sister Cecile and Sister Theresa, and she admitted being too afraid to tell anyone the horrible thing at the time. She feared she might have met Sister Francesca's or the gardener's fate. Sister Agnes also had no idea where the two unfortunate young people's bodies were thrown.

"The villains admitted, at last, they had dealt with the priest's killing and of the nun too, and they also confessed who had asked them to do it.

"Shocked and enraged, the villagers handed the thugs to the law. They were sent to prison and then executed. Before dying, Bull told the people he buried the bodies at the roots of a tree, but nobody discovered the bodies' exact location.

"This is how the abbey and the nuns inhabiting it ended," Constable Randall concluded the story.

A heavy, overwhelming silence followed, broken at last by Anne's deep sigh. "This Abbess sounds more like a serial killer than a saintly person," Anne added.

"Is it necessary to start further investigation?" Neil asked. "What if the bones we found belong to a stray tourist or to some vagrant?"

"Of course the police will start an investigation, although I'm pretty sure it's Genevieve up there in the hollow. The DNA analysis will tell us exactly what we want to know. To put things right, I'll phone Allan at once and ask him to come here, if he can, with his team and do what they usually do in such cases. Excuse me for a few moments. I'll be back and tell you what he says."

Constable Randall went out of the room leaving Anne, Neil and Jennifer alone.

"I'd like to ask Allan, or whoever is responsible for this, if the bones do belong to the nun, to allow us to bury them under the tree where we found them. Do you think it may be possible?" Anne wondered.

"I'm not sure, but it's worth a try." Jennifer said. "The police have strict rules to be followed, especially in murder cases. You touch nothing, do nothing until the police have finished with it. But if and only if the DNA proves the bones belong to a person who died centuries ago, I'll have a talk with Allan. He's the expert who can give the okay to allow us to bury the bones here, though it may take months.

"Another element that may help us, though, is that he is a Wiccan and will understand our request, even if it would seem odd to others. I'll have to tell him everything you told me about your visions."

"No problem. You have my permission," Anne said. Constable Randall returned. "My nephew says he'll be here with his team tomorrow morning. He asks that you meet him and take him to the place you discovered the bones."

"Sure, we'll assist him in finding the tree. What do you think happened to the Abbess? Where did she vanish?" Anne inquired frowning.

"Nobody knows. The forces of Evil may have summoned her spirit to their dark, frightening den, the only place willing to have her," Constable Randall replied, shaking his head.

"This is what we'll do," Jennifer said, "we'll all meet in the hotel lobby tomorrow morning. We'll have a strong cup of coffee or tea together and then after Allan comes, we'll head to the forest, find the tree, and the poor woman's skeleton."

"Assuming the skeleton belongs to her," Randall nodded.

"Well, thank you for your time, sir," Anne said and she turned to Jennifer." And you too, Jen, for helping us with this matter. I think it's time for us to leave, now. Good bye,sir."

"Good-bye and we'll keep in touch. I must wait for the forensic team to arrive"

The three left Constable Randall's office and returned to the inn.

***

Jennifer invited Anne and Neil upstairs to her room, a large, airy and cozy place.

"My cove," Jennifer told them, laughing.

Luxuriant flowers in large ceramic pots, matched the room's soft color, lending the place a pleasant, relaxing atmosphere. Comfortable armchairs and a sofa piled with small, decorative pillows indicated this was Jennifer's favorite place after a hard workday.

A huge oil picture hung above the mantelpiece, contrasting with the other pieces of furniture. A landscape dominated by the image of an old, thick oak tree whose large crown had taken hold of the whole canvas. The dark background enhanced the leaves' color. Here and there, tiny sprigs of mistletoe sparkled mysteriously among the thick branches.

"A friend of mine brought the painting to me for a birthday present. He read somewhere that a 'modern witch' should worship the oak tree and its mistletoe. They are sacred and have been present in magic rites, starting back with the Druids, the Celts' high priests," Jennifer explained to her guests.

"Oak trees are considered good for protection and it's considered lucky to have a small piece of an oak branch. Oak is also thought to be linked to the powers of the moon and enhances its energies like a conductor. Pine and fir trees, willows and birch trees are also wise and possess their own specific energies, but I favor the oak tree."

Anne glanced around the room and her gaze fell on a computer in the corner with a shelf of books above it. Nothing in the room indicated the owner was a witch, a modern one anyway. Anne stood up and studied the books behind the glass on the shelf. Among them she discovered some old looking volumes, several Latin books and an English fables one with exquisite cover illustrations.

"You have quite a treasure here, I think. Are you interested in antiques?" Anne questioned Jennifer.

"Not so much, but these books are a kind of family inheritance. It seems they belonged to an ancestor of mine, who was a sorcerer and healer. My roots lead back to the Netherlands. In fact, to a family of traders. I might have inherited the gift from that woman. I don't recall any other woman in my family having this, let's say, special power."

She eyed Anne, sheer amusement glimmering in her eyes. "I hope you didn't think I kept all the paraphernalia of an ancient, traditional witch. There's no large cauldron, boiling and bubbling in the middle of the room. As you can see," Jennifer said and smiled, raising her beautifully shaped eyebrows. "There are no mysterious black cats following your movements with her evil, green eyes, or bats hanging from the ceiling."

Anne smiled as well. After sipping her tea, Anne fidgeted with the cup and cast a timid glance to Jennifer.

"Jennifer, please tell me, do you think there might be a connection between Genevieve and myself? Is it possible for me to be her? Is this why she appeared in my dream and led me to the hollowed oak tree? She's red-haired like I am, and her eyes are green, but this is where all resemblance between us stops."

Jennifer shrugged and after pouring herself some hot coffee brought from the hotel bar, she sat down. Looking straight at Anne, she said, "You wonder if you are Genevieve's reincarnation. I really can't say it for certain. All I can tell you is that even I feel in a way we've known each other, somewhere, sometime. Not in this life, for sure."

Anne admitted she also shared the same feeling.

"Death is not an ending of existence; it's a step in an ongoing process of life. Our physical world has an evolution, a destiny, in my opinion," Jennifer added. "A fixed destiny. This doesn't mean we walk blindfolded along a thread taking us from the entrance to the way out. No, there are always choices to be made, and the temptations throughout all our lives are those that in the end become the landmarks for the route we follow."

Jennifer paused briefly to refill their cups and continued, "We're all sent here with a purpose. To learn our moral lesson and accomplish a communion with our own spirit. Only thus can we evolve to a higher spiritual level." Anne nodded in total approval of Jennifer's words, expressing her own ideas.

"For all I imagine," Neil offered his opinion, "Genevieve didn't learn her lesson during her lifetime. She sinned. She broke her sacred vows. Andrew did it too."

"Was their love such a horrible sin?" Anne asked.

"Well, my dear," Jennifer spoke on, "people changed the meaning of sin and faith according to their interests, and to the part of the world or the epoch they lived in, so it's very difficult to find an answer. One thing's certain. Everything happening to you indicates without doubt you were chosen to discover the remains of what we consider to be the woman in your dream, the young nun in the legend. Shed blood never dies, they say. It cries for the settling of things."

"This is what I think, too," Anne replied thoughtfully.

"When we climb up there with Constable Randall, you'd better be the one to place the wrapped remains under the old oak tree where the legend says the man she loved was buried. If the authorities agree, of course, and if the DNA shows these are old bones belonging to a woman."

"Yes, you're right. I'll do it. Maybe we'll put her tormented spirit to eternal peace, I hope. I also want to ask you, if it's possible for Neil to be Andrew?"

"I'm not sure. He might be. Quite often, groups of interacting souls reincarnate together and take on the role of relations, friends or even rivals they had in previous lives. Have you ever met someone for the first time, yet feel you have known them all your life?"

"Oh, yes, yes, indeed," Anne said and smiling, she turned her gaze to Neil.

"Many say," Jennifer continued, "this happens to balance karma in the world."

"Well, Jennifer," Neil said, frowning. "What has happened to Anne—to us—these last days, and the things you've just told us about spirit communion and our aim in life has made me reconsider an old project. Some time ago I studied the evolution of religion, of faith throughout human history. I'm attracted to the idea of writing a comparative study."

"I had no idea you were interested in such subjects," Anne said and turned a questioning look to Neil.

"No, of course not. During our unfortunate two years' separation, I spent a lot of time reading, studying, and trying to find something more philosophical to write about. The concept of reincarnation, resurrection, afterlife or whatever you want to call it, within different cultures and different ages."

"Quite interesting and intriguing at the same time." Jennifer nodded. "I've been wondering, ever since Constable Randall told us the legend, what your link to Andrew might be. I think I've found out the answer. The connection to Andrew is your involvement or interest in religion, in one form or another."

"Considering everything Constable Randall related to us about the tragic events at St. Mary's, I'm sure this is the subject of my next book. I'll write Genevieve's story."

"Yes, a good idea," Jennifer added. "Well, we'll meet all here when Chief Randall gives us the okay and we'll embark on this odd trip. Don't worry. I'll keep the cross here, if you trust me with it, and if I can persuade Allan to leave it with me for a little while."

"Of course. You can keep it for as long as you need. It'll probably end up in a museum. I wouldn't keep it for the world, now that I know its story," Anne answered at once, happy to be rid of the evil thing.

Anne took Neil by the hand and they went out of the room

***

Constable Randall's phone call came a few weeks later. "The investigation is over sooner than we expected. Everything we told Allan made him hasten things a bit. As a rule, the whole process is likely to last a minimum of three to four months. The DNA analysis proved our assumption right: the bones belong to a young woman and date back to the 15th century. I managed to get Allan's promise he'll send the bones back here to Glennridge.

The normal routine would have them taken to a designated place or buried in consecrated ground or cremated. But, this time, the experts finally agreed. We are allowed to bury her remains here. I also received approval from the County Council. I pointed out to them that the place may be included in the tourist plan. So, she'll have a small grave under the tree where her bones were discovered. That's why I called you."

"Thank you," Anne replied. "I'll settle my things here, talk to Neil and we'll arrive in a couple of days."

***

Anne and Neil arrived in Glennridge in the afternoon and went directly to the Rampart Inn. Jennifer welcomed them warmly. She phoned Constable Randall and he came to the inn as well.

"We received the remains yesterday morning," he said. "We'll do it tomorrow morning. And though unusual for the modern times, I also talked to Father Brown, our old priest, who agreed to accompany us and assist us with this atypical burial."

"The chain and cross are still with me," Jennifer added, concerned. "I'll start a new purifying ritual. I felt, from the very first second I laid my eyes on it, the evil that tainted it. We'll all need some strong protection tomorrow morning.

"When you're confronting the dark forces you must be very determined and show them you're the one in control, not them. I have to be careful and not let my guard down for the slightest second. Tomorrow's a crucial day."

"Jennifer, what do we have to pay you for all these rituals and… whatever…?"

"Dear Anne, we Sylvan Wiccans don't believe in making money from witchcraft. People have a right to earn a living from healing and divination as long as our religion isn't exploited, but I don't want anything from you. I consider you a friend."

***

Anne and Neil had a stroll around the small, coquette mountain village, a visiting tour they hadn't done when they had arrived in Glennridge for the first time. Later, they spent a quiet afternoon revisiting everything that had happened to them and everything they had found out about the abbey and its inhabitants. At last, they went to bed.

"I feel more secure knowing that more people will accompany us. Let's hope the weather stays dry. I wouldn't like another bout of storms in the forest," Anne told Neil.

"I'm sure everything will be fine. Don't worry," he replied. "We've been driven apart by Gillian, a woman who in some ways resembles the evil Abbess. For the first time, I can think about Gillian with indifference and not spite.

"You're the woman for me and I have, in a stupid way, almost lost you because of a moment of folly. I'm confident that while Father Andrew and Genevieve's love was doomed, our love will bloom again in an everlasting relationship. Only after we broke up did I become aware of how much you mean to me."

Neil stopped and chewed at his bottom lip and then he continued. "It hurt so much that you considered me a cheater and thought I didn't love you. I can explain, in fact...."

Anne placed her fingers over his lips. "Don't! Let's not spoil this moment. Some other time."

Neil shook his head. "After the burial of Genevieve's remains is over, we'll finally leave on a real holiday and if you still want me—"

Anne didn't allow him to finish his thoughts and shut his mouth with an ardent kiss.

***

The woman's piercing eyes narrowed before she spoke. She toyed nervously with a richly bejeweled cross attached on a golden chain around her neck. The ghost of a derisive grin touched her lips. Then her expression tightened into a cramp of rage.

She threw Anne a measured, hostile glance and spat her words contemptuously, her voice dark and brooding. "Hear me, well. You shall never have him. I'll not allow you to carry on with your plans."

"Oh, leave me alone," Anne snapped, losing her patience. "I don't know who you are and don't care about your problems. You've mistaken me for someone else."

"Leave you alone? Don't know me? How dare you speak to me like this? You dirt!" the woman yelled and dashed at Anne...

***

Neil's soft nudge woke Anne after what seemed a mere second after she'd fallen asleep.

"Anne, Anne, wake up. Wake up, honey."

Anne sat up, dazed, and glanced around her. When her eyes finally focused on Neil, she threw her arms around his neck. She sobbed with relief.

"I dreamt about her, Neil. She came in my dream again. This time the cross hung around her neck. She threatened me again."

"Calm down, calm down. Let me bring you a glass of water." He went to the bathroom amd returned with a glass. "Here, drink this." Neil held the glass out to Anne and asked her, surprised, "Who threatened you? The red-haired woman? She hasn't acted in an aggressive manner towards you before."

"No, no." Anne shook her head vigorously. "Not that one. Not Genevieve. It was the Abbess, I think. Do you remember what I told you when she appeared in my dream, up on the mountain, while we took shelter among the monastery's ruins?

"She kept repeating the same thing, 'You shall not have him. You shall not have him.' What if this 'him' is not the priest, Andrew, but you?" she whispered and a fresh surge of tears started down her cheeks.

"Dear Anne, nothing can happen to me. No doubt she meant Father Andrew. She doesn't want you to bury Genevieve's remains next to his. Assuming he's buried at the roots of the tree where we found the bones. And you know what? I'm grateful to this harpy who made you cry at the thought of losing me. This means you care for me or, maybe, even love me a bit," Neil said in a playful voice.

"Of course, I love you, silly," Anne replied, smiling to him, tears brimming in her eyes.

"Come. Let me hold you, and I think I'll tell you a story. Which one would you like to hear?"

"It doesn't matter, but let it be one without ghosts or wizards or dragons. Make it, 'The Three Little Pigs,' you being one of them," she joked.

Half way through the story, Neil fell asleep and Anne covered him up and kissed him softly on his brow. She whispered, "Sleep tight, my brave defender. I'll watch over you."

***

Early the next day, Anne and the small party climbed up the steep slope along the narrow paths to the hollowed oak tree. They had everything they needed: spades and a small wooden box with the bones the authorities allowed them to bury in the wood.

Constable Randall and the village's old priest led the way. They walked in line along the stream bank and advanced into the forest.

It took about three hours to reach the spot. At first the silence was heavy over the mountains; then, although the weather forecast indicated a glorious day, thick clouds gathered above while the wind picked up. Thunder growled in the distance.

"This is what I feared most," Neil uttered in a low voice to Anne.

Anne stared at some red points, like a pair of red eyes, glowing from behind the trunk of the tree. She shook her head in amazement, but didn't tell the others about them.

Neil addressed the rest of the group, "We should hurry. I'm in no mood for another weather show."

Anne wrapped Genevieve's remains in a pretty white shawl she'd bought in the village the previous afternoon, and waited for the men to be ready with the digging.

Constable Randall helped Neil and they both dug a small grave under the oak tree. While digging, Neil's spade uncovered another piece of bone. They enlarged the hole and the remains of a whole human skeleton came out from the crumbling soil. The bones were picked clean by time.

"Let's bring them all out with care," the police officer said. "It looks we've found Andrew's bones. If we assume the legend to be based on true events, I mean," Randall said and threw a glance towards Anne.

The sight of the bones, presumably belonging to the priest, triggered a devastating sense of grief, closing around Anne's heart like a tight claw. She closed her eyes and shook her head to get rid of the strong unnerving feeling.

"They are better preserved than those in the hollow of the tree. The skull is larger. It must surely have belonged to Andrew."

"I think the best thing to do is to place, if you allow us, a bone of this skeleton in the same grave as Genevieve. I know you'll have to call your nephew's forensic team again, but this skeleton must surely belong to Andrew. The two will finally be together. As they wanted. At least in death, if not while they were alive," Anne said softly.

"Right," added Jennifer.

While wrapping the two bones, belonging presumably to Genevieve and Andrew, in the shawl, Anne had a short flash.

Genevieve's face. No longer afraid. No longer crying. She nodded to Anne in a grateful gesture before turning and vanishing.

The job finished, Anne lowered the bundle into the wooden box and then into the grave.

Father Brown read the usual prayers, while Neil and Constable Randall covered the grave back over. On the end of the earth mound they placed a small stone slab with Genevieve's name carved on it. Anne laid down a wood anemone.

Jennifer stayed by the stream and supervised their activity, a deep frown on her face, concerned and quiet. From time to time, she glanced to the ceiling of gray black clouds coming down inch by inch over them.

Jennifer came closer and using a long stick, she placed the bejeweled cross around the barren branch on which father Andrew had been supposedly hanged.

The wind picked up and blew with fury. Powerful rumbles shook the sky.

"I think we're in for a powerful storm," Neil said. "Take shelter. There's a group of smaller trees with a wide crown of leaves. Go ahead. I'll follow you," he shouted to Anne who tightened her sweater around her slim body.

All of a sudden, it turned very cold, as if it were January and not mid-July.

They all headed to the group of trees indicated by Neil, Anne last in line. She and Jennifer turned at the same moment to look back at Neil who was cleaning the spade with a tuft of grass and they called for him to hurry.

The storm broke, fierce torrents of rain pelting down. Neil glanced at Anne and nodded. The following second, a thunderbolt struck the old oak tree, deafening and blinding the two women.

All four ran back to the place where Neil lay, his face in the earth of the newly dug grave.

The bolt had hit the oak tree, but only the branch where Jennifer had hung the golden necklace with its bejeweled cross had fallen.

A fierce, tearing pain gripped Anne's heart. Trembling and too shocked to be able to cry, Anne crumbled by Neil's inert body. She grabbed his shoulders and shook him hard, willing with every fiber of her being to make him open his eyes.

"Stay alive, please. Don't give her what she wanted all the time. She wants you dead. She wants you in her world of the dark. She wants revenge."

Neil's head lolled back, like that of a lifeless rag doll. Anne raised her gaze to the once again clear sky. Fury and agony got a hold of her. Bitterness rose in her throat. If she hadn't tried to give him a second chance nothing bad would have happened to Neil.

Anne shouted, grief and regret almost palpable in her words, only Jennifer would understand the meaning of her words. "You damned, wicked creature. Why? Why him?" she cried and fainted next to Neil.

Chapter Twenty-four

One Year Later

Standing on top of the church steps, Neil glanced along the road. A friendly, late summer sun enveloped him and the small group of foreign tourists who'd gathered in front of the village church to take photos of an English wedding.

They held glossy, colorful leaflets recommending the area for its unique landscape, for the eerie forest devoid of wild animals, and recommended seeing its clear stream that ran between green banks with big, tasty trout. Neil smiled to himself. The leaflets had been his idea and design. He helped the Glennridge local community to promote their objectives through national and international tourist agencies.

The photo of an ancient abbey, in the process of being restored, thanks to the generous contribution of an anonymous woman sponsor, occupied the front page. The abbey's walls, shrouded in grey mist, perched perilously at the top of a steep abyss. The text beneath the image spoke about passion, broken vows and past crimes. All the necessary ingredients to advertise the region. The leaflets hinted to unusual happenings in a spooky forest.

The place had become a major point of attraction on the tourists' maps and word traveled fast. The leaflet also presented two legends: the one of the grave under an old oak tree, where wild anemones grow all year round in spite of the shadow of the tree, and the second, the legend of St. Mary's Abbey.

Neil turned his gaze to the beautiful woman beside him and held her hand. She was dressed in a simple but fashionable ivory bride dress. "My beautiful wood anemone," he whispered. "I love you more than the world."

The bride, her eyes shining with unveiled happiness, smiled back at him and then turned her head, to the photographer's despair, and addressed a woman next to her, "I'm so relieved and content, you know. Thank goodness, since we buried Genevieve's remains last year, my dreams haven't been haunted by the poor girl or the horrible Abbess, again."

"It's as it should be, dear Anne. I think you are Genevieve's reincarnation. That's why she appeared only while you were sleeping. She visited your dreams since her soul has a new body. Your present time body. We may say a part of your mission in life was accomplished. You found and buried her remains."

"Oh, Jennifer, if it hadn't been for your powers and your white magic, our wedding would never have happened. We thought Neil was another toll taken by the cursed forest," Anne continued then stopped for a moment and frowned, as if overwhelmed by a feeling of anxiety.

"No," Jennifer replied, "don't thank me. Thank your God and my Goddess. They protected Neil. I did nothing but help them a little. It would have been a pity for such a nice guy to become food for the grave so soon. His women readers and admirers would have been devastated, wouldn't they, Neil?" Jennifer laughed at him.

Neil nodded and flashed a smile to Jennifer; his hand went involuntarily, up to his scarred cheek. The scar was a permanent reminder of the lightning striking him in the wood a year ago. The scar and a slight stiff movement of his right leg. Women used to tell him the scar didn't spoil his good looks. On the contrary, it added a shade of mystery to his appearance. He wasn't too much interested in their opinion. He had by his side the woman he'd always loved.

He glanced sideways at Jennifer who was scrutinizing his face and smiled again. He hoped she couldn't guess his smile to be a guilty one. At the same time, he touched his pocket with the tips of his fingers, the sharp edges of a letter that had arrived in the morning. A short message from Gillian.

The letter brought back memories. Not very happy ones. Too proud to admit to Anne he had no idea how things really happened three years ago, he blamed himself for their unexpected separation. He suspected Gillian had carefully planned her foul play, waiting for the right opportunity to appear.

Of course he couldn't deny having caught, several times, Gillian's long looks and inviting smiles. Yet, he never answered her advances, keeping a polite, distant attitude.

Gillian was a smart woman, a stunner, but not to his liking. Furthermore, Gillian and Anne being business partners and friends would have made it preposterous for him to be the one to come between them and damage the relationship. That's what Anne considered him to have done in the end.

He vividly recalled part of the day the unfortunate event occurred. The other part, how he ended in the same bed with Gillian, remained a mystery, only Gillian knew the real development of the things, to this day.

The only thing he recalled was Anne's angry glare and her distraught, fuming expression as she stood in the doorway and watched Gillian come out of the bathroom wearing nothing at all.

His separation from Anne had hurt like hell. The same foolish pride prevented him from insisting on giving her an explanation. Anne wouldn't have believed a word of it.

Gillian's letter felt as though it was burning his leg through the cloth of his trousers.

Gillian congratulated him and Anne, in her message, for the decision to get married at last. She'd learned the news from a mutual acquaintance visiting New Zealand. She also let Neil know she'd return to England in a few weeks, as soon as she finished all the paperwork needed after the sudden death of her rich husband. She expressed how she could hardly wait to be home again with her little daughter Nellie, and to refresh all the ties with her old friends.

This last statement made Neil reluctant to show Anne the letter. He had no doubt she wouldn't be glad to hear it. He'd tried all morning to bring up the subject; yet something, a hidden anxiety, the budding sensation of threat, prevented him. In the end, he'd given up. He'd pretend he never received the message.

In the back of his mind a small, nagging voice warned him the letter predicted real danger and its author might cause Anne and him great trouble.

"You are the naughtiest people I've ever immortalized in a wedding picture. Why have you sent for me if you don't stay still?" the funny little man taking the pictures protested again, fluttering his chubby hands to the amusement of everybody present.

The pictures finished, Neil and Anne and their guests climbed down the church steps and passed by the tourists who applauded them. They waved to him and the other wedding participants; and then, chatting excitedly, they followed their guide along the path leading to the forest.

***

Far in the forest, the sprightly stream's clear waters sang their ancient song down the moss-covered banks. Reaching an old, crooked oak tree, bearing the seal of recent lightning damage, the waters trembled, turned muddy and the pale, distorted face of a woman emerged.

Her raven black hair floated around her head, the long black tresses writhing and coiling on the waves, like snakes trying to pry free and attack. Her eyes flew open and a hideous grin stretched her lips. She blinked several times and gurgled a hoarse threat to someone known only to her, "You imagine you thwarted my plans even from beyond the grave, but you're wrong. You shall hear from me. You shall all hear from me! Soon."

Little by little, the waters of the river became an ugly shade of green, covered the ghastly face, and continued down to the green pastures in the valley while an ominous silence, harbinger of the woman's spiteful threat, settled over the rugged mountain and its mysterious forest.

The End

About Carmen Stefanescu

Carmen Stefanescu resides in Romania, the native country of the infamous vampire Count Dracula, but where, for about 50 years of communist dictatorship, just speaking about God, faith, reincarnation or paranormal phenomena could have led someone to great trouble—the psychiatric hospital if not to prison.

High-school teacher of English and German in her native country, and mother of two daughters, Carmen Stefanescu survived the grim years of communist oppression, by escaping in a parallel world, that of the books.

She has dreamed all her life to become a writer, but many of the things she wrote during those years remained just drawer projects. The fall of the Ceausescu's regime in 1989, and the opening of the country to the world meant a new beginning for her. She started along the fascinating road of publishing. Her poems were released first, and then her novels. Both in English.

She joined the Marketing For Romance Writers group and is the coordinator of #Tursday13 post on the MFRW Author blog.

Social Media Links

Blog: http://shadowspastmystery.blogspot.ro/

Website: http://carmenstefanescu.simplesite.com/

Twitter: https://twitter.com/Carmen_Books

Pinterest: http://www.pinterest.com/carmens007/

Facebook: http://www.facebook.com/pages/Carmen-Stefanescu-Books/499245716760283

Goodreads: http://www.goodreads.com/author/show/6624397.Carmen_Stefanescu

Google +: https://plus.google.com/117216040843648957646/posts

Amazon Author Page: http://www.amazon.com/Carmen-Stefanescu/e/B00APVDGAA/ref=ntt_athr_dp_pel_pop_1

National Association of Women on the Rise: http://www.nawomenrise.org/author-carmen-stefanescu/

Cold Coffee Café: http://coldcoffeecafe.com/profile/CarmenStefanescu

Note to the Reader:

I want to take this opportunity to thank you, dear reader, for spending your valuable time reading my work. I truly hope you enjoyed Shadows of the Past.

A book review is a great way to let me know if you enjoyed it.

Thanks again,

Carmen

Connect with Carmen Stefanescu Online:
http://shadowspastmystery.blogspot.ro/

If you enjoyed this story, check out these other Solstice Publishing books by Carmen Stefanescu:

Till Life Do Us Part

Barbara Heyer can hear the voices of dead people. They whisper of their deaths, seek comfort for those left behind, and occasionally even warn her about future events. But when Barbara's brother, Colin, is accused of murdering Catherine, his girlfriend, it will take more than her gift to prove his innocence.

Detective Patrick Fischer feels something compelling about the woman who claims she can talk to spirits the moment he meets her. Maybe it explains the instant attraction he feels, a serious complication given he's assigned to her brother's case.

Equally smitten with the handsome investigator, Barbara senses there is something far deeper—and perhaps much older—than surface attraction between them. Could that be why she's visited by a mysterious woman named Emma in her dreams? And is a past life regression the answer to tie all these seemingly unconnected events together?

Barbara and Patrick must overcome heartache to find the truth and save Colin, and perhaps themselves.

Dark and dramatic, the story explores the many twists and turns of true love.

Release date: June 2016

Buy link: https://bookgoodies.com/a/1625263856

Goodreads reviews :
https://www.goodreads.com/book/show/30115839-till-life-do-us-part